## *Leslie listened to Grady's dreams for a family.*

At first with an awkwardness that broke her heart, then with more fervor, Grady talked about how he imagined raising his children, how he'd spend time with them, how he'd love them. How they would have the happy childhood he'd never had.

Every word confirmed the heartache she'd seen coming all along. Backing away from him might cushion some of the inevitable fall, but how could she pull away from him now?

Leslie would love Grady with every bit of her soul, until he could not possibly doubt the value of the heart he had to offer a woman—another woman.

And then she would tell him a future for them was impossible.

\*    \*    \*

*GRADY'S WEDDING—You met Grady Roberts
in Patricia McLinn's WEDDING DUET—
Prelude to a Wedding and Wedding Party.
And now, it's Grady's turn!

Dear Reader,

Welcome to Silhouette **Special Edition** . . . welcome to romance. Each month, Silhouette **Special Edition** publishes six novels with you in mind—stories of love and life, tales that you can identify with—as well as dream about.

And this wonderful month of May has many terrific stories for you. Myrna Temte presents her contribution to THAT SPECIAL WOMAN!—our new promotion that salutes women, and the wonderful men who win them. *The Forever Night* features characters you met in her COWBOY COUNTRY series—as well as a romance for sheriff Andy Johnson, whom many of you have written in about. Ginny Bradford gets her man in this gentle tale of love.

This month also brings *He's the Rich Boy* by Lisa Jackson. This is the concluding tale to her MAVERICKS series that features men that just won't be tamed! Don't miss this tale of love at misty Whitefire Lake!

Rounding out this special month are books from other favorite authors: Barbara Faith, Pat Warren, Kayla Daniels and Patricia McLinn—who is back with *Grady's Wedding* (you remember Grady—he was an usher in *Wedding Party*, #718. Now he has his own tale of love!).

I hope that you enjoy this book, and all the stories to come. Have a wonderful month!

Sincerely,

Tara Gavin
Senior Editor
Silhouette Books

# PATRICIA McLINN

## GRADY'S WEDDING

*Silhouette*®

SPECIAL EDITION®

Published by Silhouette Books New York

America's Publisher of Contemporary Romance

To Mary, Christine, Judy, Sara and Tommye,
for the listening and the laughter

SILHOUETTE BOOKS
300 East 42nd St., New York, N.Y. 10017

GRADY'S WEDDING

Copyright © 1993 by Patricia McLaughlin

ISBN: 0-373-09813-8

First Silhouette Books printing May 1993

Printed in the U.S.A.

**Books by Patricia McLinn**

Silhouette Special Edition

*Hoops* #587
*A New World* #641
*\*Prelude to a Wedding* #712
*\*Wedding Party* #718
*\*Grady's Wedding* #813

*Wedding Series

---

## PATRICIA McLINN

says she has been spinning stories in her head since childhood, when her mother insisted she stop reading at the dinner table. As the time came for her to earn a living, Patricia shifted her stories from fiction to fact—she became a sportswriter and editor for newspapers in Illinois, North Carolina and the District of Columbia. Now living outside Washington, D.C., she enjoys traveling, history and sports, but is happiest indulging her passion for storytelling.

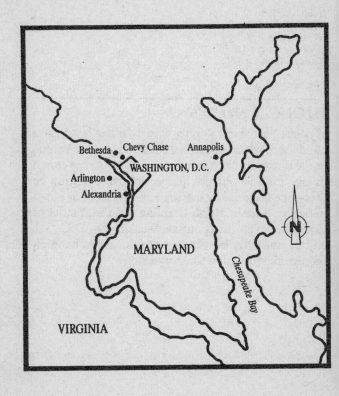

## Prologue

*I now pronounce you husband and wife...*

Grady Roberts felt as if he'd been hearing that phrase more often lately than "Have a nice day."

It still echoed in his head as the reception shifted from the dinner phase to the dancing phase.

He smiled reflexively at the knockout redhead who'd ignored her date to make eyes at him as he'd sat with the others at the head table. She was truly a knockout. He was stupid to let it bother him that she looked at him like a succulent chocolate dessert she wanted to devour.

Then the bride and groom moved into the open expanse of polished wood floor to begin the dancing, and his smile softened.

God, Michael and Tris looked good together. Rightness glowed from them. A rightness that had spurred them to move up the date of their wedding three times, until the caterers, dressmakers and gift givers could only sprint like mad

to keep up with the bride and groom's eagerness. A rightness that left a hole deep inside him. Or maybe the hole had
been there a long time, and the fact of his best friends getting married one after the other had simply brought it out
of hiding.

Paul and Bette joined them on the dance floor. Then more
and more couples. Couples . . .

First Paul and Bette, now Michael and Tris.

How could you be so happy for people and also feel so
left out and so . . . what? He'd say lonely except that was an
odd word for someone who'd never spent an evening—or
night—alone unless he wanted to.

Even odder, he'd recently found himself spending more
and more of his evenings and nights alone.

Maybe he just needed to get out more. Maybe that was all
that was the matter with him.

"Grady? Grady, come back to earth."

He blinked into focus on Bette Wharton Monroe's smile.

"Paul's dancing with the bride. Are you feeling brave
enough to dance with a pregnant lady?"

"For as long as the pregnant lady's husband will let me."
He smiled back. "Which we both know won't be long."

A dance and a half later Paul claimed Bette. Then Grady
danced once with Tris before Michael claimed her. Even his
dance with Judi—Paul's kid sister and practically his own—
ended with her father claiming her.

He looked around for Leslie Craig, the remaining member of the wedding party, Tris's co-worker and her maid of
honor. He wouldn't mind dancing with her. She didn't look
at him like a high-caloric goody. And Leslie more likely
would slip in some pointed remark than gush or stumble
over her words.

But she was still dancing with a man Judi had informed
him was someone's recently widowed uncle. Grady frowned.
The man looked young for an uncle and a widower. Some

might even consider his gray hair and dark mustache distinguished. And from the way Leslie smiled, at least one person found them charming.

Grady turned away and danced on. The redhead. Friends' mothers. Michael's boss, U.S. Sen. Joan Bradon. Leslie moved on to other partners, though the uncle showed up a couple more times, and Grady never could reach her before someone else did. He danced with miscellaneous relatives of Tris or Michael and assorted wedding guests. The redhead again.

She made it clear she was willing and eager. Trouble was, he wasn't either one.

The dance ended, and she stayed at his side.

"All right, everybody, while the band takes a break, my cousin Tris is going to toss the bouquet." Paul had a firm grip on the microphone and the crowd. Dancers wandered off the floor, anticipating his next announcement. "Will all the unmarried ladies please move over there by the doorway."

The redhead gave Grady a look under her lashes, slid her hand down his sleeve until her fingertips brushed the back of his hand, then started across the floor to the designated area with a walk that should have gotten her arrested for attempted arson.

Maybe he just wasn't flammable lately.

To let another bouquet candidate pass, he moved to his right, and bumped squarely into Leslie Craig.

"I don't object when men trample on my affections," she said in that faint drawl of hers, "but I draw the line at my toes."

He grinned. "Sorry, Leslie." He stepped back to open her path to the growing group of would-be flower catchers.

She didn't move.

He stepped farther back, making the opening more obvious, even gesturing that the way was clear.

She arched a brow at him. "What're you doing there, Grady? New dance step?"

"That would be the closest I'd come to dancing with you tonight." Her hazel eyes glinted with humor at his dry response. "But what I was trying to do was politely let you past so you'd have a chance to catch the bouquet."

She shook her head. "Thanks, but I'll stay here."

He saw Tris, already with her back to the growing group of women, glance toward Leslie.

"I think Tris is looking for you."

"She'll understand."

"You object on feminist grounds?"

"Not me. I'm from the feminist school that says a woman can do anything a man can do—including love and marriage. No, I think bouquet tossing is a quaint and archaic tradition, and I'm all for that. You learn to cherish your quaint and archaic traditions when you're from Virginia. It's just that I'm too archaic myself to go in for this one."

Grady had been watching Paul consult with Tris some eight feet away, but now turned to consider the woman by his side. He knew from Tris that Leslie Craig was older than his thirty-three, but it couldn't be by much.

Besides, he'd spent time with enough attractive women to qualify as something of an expert, and her appeal was the kind age didn't diminish. It came from her bones, and her brain. He'd spent many childhood hours with old movies as his only companions, and he could see a lot of the young Katharine Hepburn in Leslie Craig.

But he was too late to make his observations. She'd already continued the conversation without him.

"Believe it or not, Tris and Michael want to get things moving faster. You'd think moving their wedding up from June to late April would be fast enough for anybody."

She smiled at him, a friend sharing their mutual friends' happiness, and he felt the uncharacteristic urge to ask her i she didn't have any of the feelings he'd been experiencing. The left-out feeling. The wondering about when—or if—it would ever be his turn.

Doubly uncharacteristic. To have the feelings, and then to consider confiding them. Why even Paul, who'd been his first friend, would be astounded if Grady Roberts ever said what he'd just been thinking.

He remembered his earlier thought that maybe he just needed to get out more.

Leslie Craig's smile had slipped and she studied him in some puzzlement.

In their encounters since Tris introduced them last fall, he'd realized that Leslie was a perceptive woman. Dangerously so. He turned on his smile. "They do seem in a hurry, don't they?"

In the background, he heard Paul giving final instructions.

All the puzzlement didn't disappear, but her smile returned. "I heard Tris telling Paul that if he wanted her to throw this bouquet he'd better get a move on because she had a honeymoon to start. And Michael flat out said he wasn't going to waste time throwing the garter. He was going to hand—"

A missile struck Grady a glancing blow on the right shoulder, deflected straight at Leslie Craig's chin and shed three petals before dropping into the hands she'd instinctively raised.

A whoop went up from the general direction of Tris, Michael and Paul, quickly picked up by the rest of the crowd.

Leslie's head was bent over the bouquet that had landed in her hands, so Grady had to bend to get a look at her face. She looked stunned.

"You okay, Leslie?"

"Okay?" She still stared at the flowers.

"You took it square on the chin. It wasn't a knockout punch, was it?"

"No. No, I'm okay." She finally looked up, but not at him. "You're a low-down rat, Tris Donlin."

Grady looked around as Tris, Michael, Paul and Bette converged on them. In the background the women who'd waited in vain dispersed, most smiling, a few—including the redhead—looking put out.

"Tris Donlin Dickinson now," the rat corrected with no embarrassment.

"You should have seen that throw, Grady," enthused Paul. "She could have been playing for the Cubs with that pickoff move. She winds up like she's going to throw to the plate, then—whoosh—zips it over to first base."

Leslie's narrowed eyes bored into Tris. "Only she threw to somebody sitting in the stands, *happily* sitting in the stands."

"I wanted you to have it. It's my wedding day. Shouldn't I get to decide who gets this bouquet?"

"That's low-down and sneaky, appealing to my sentiments that way and—"

"I learned it from the best," Tris tossed back at her.

But Grady could see Leslie Craig wasn't one to give up easily. "You could have just handed it to me instead of pelting me with it, not to mention setting up false hopes for all those girls over there."

"Those were exactly my thoughts," said Michael. "That's why I decided to skip the part where the groom throws the garter. Here, Grady."

When a friend extends a hand to give you something, it's automatic to take it. You don't stop to consider whether you really want to accept the item. At least, Grady didn't stop to think.

So he ended up with a circle of flowery lace resting in his wide palm.

"What's this?"

"It's the garter, what do you think it is?" demanded Paul. "You can't tell me you've never seen one before. But this one's special," he added with a wicked grin. "This one means you'll be the next one married."

Feeling as if he'd also taken a blow to the chin, Grady looked around the circle of his friends, then at Leslie.

"But right now what you do," continued Paul, "is go out in the middle so everybody can see, and then you put the garter on the leg of the woman who caught the bouquet. That's what you do."

"Oh, no, he doesn't." Leslie was adamant.

"It's the tradition," Paul persisted.

"No way."

Grady looked from one to the other. Sounded as if Leslie had no intention of cherishing this tradition. Come to think of it, he didn't remember this particular tradition being followed at Paul and Bette's wedding last August.

"But—" Paul started before Bette stepped in quietly.

"How about if we make our own tradition."

"Bless your heart," breathed Leslie.

"What? What did she say?" Paul asked.

"She said, 'Bless your heart,'" Tris told her cousin. "She says it a lot. It's a sort of multipurpose Southern expression Leslie uses for any occasion. Right now I think she's using it to say thank-you to Bette for saving her from the garter-on-the-leg tradition."

On cue, Bette went on, "Why don't we have the man who has the garter dance the next dance with the woman who caught the bouquet. That'll be the new tradition. Okay?"

Grady heard the band start up. He heard Leslie muttering about there being a big difference between catching a bouquet and fending it off out of self-defense.

*Maybe he just needed to get out more. Maybe that was all that was the matter with him.*

And maybe not.

He closed his hand around the scrap of lace and took Leslie Craig in his arms for their dance.

## Chapter One

Grady Roberts opened his top left-side dresser drawer, repository of all the things he didn't know what to do with, and, first thing, he saw the garter.

He thought he'd packed everything he'd need for this trip to Washington, but more business trips than he cared to count had taught him to take one last look.

And there, amid single cuff links, hotel shoe-shine kits, toothpicks, an old pocketknife, matchbooks and spare change—in fact, right on top of them—rested that white band of fabric Michael Dickinson had handed him at the wedding two and a half weeks ago.

He'd shoved it in his tuxedo pocket after that single dance with Leslie Craig. Later he'd seen it on the dresser when Harriet, his housekeeper, sent the tux to the cleaners before last week's museum board benefit. He left it on the dresser because it didn't seem right to throw it out, but what did you do with a bride's garter?

Apparently Harriet had figured the best thing to do was to put it back where she'd found it, because he'd discovered it in his pocket during the benefit. He couldn't blame the garter for his not enjoying the company of his stunningly beautiful and stunningly boring date, but the fact was, when he came home—early—that night, he'd taken the garter out of his pocket and dumped it in this drawer with something close to irritation.

And there it had stayed until now.

He could throw the thing out. He stood there looking at it, making no move toward the wastepaper basket.

Or...

"What the hell."

With that fatalistic mutter, he picked up the bit of material, tossed it in his open suitcase and slammed the drawer closed.


"How about this?"

Leslie Craig looked at the massive Chinese gong Grady Roberts stood next to. It was the largest thing in the Georgetown antique store he'd made their first stop. An antique store in Georgetown and one in a trendy mall, for heaven's sake. The man didn't have a bit of shopping sense.

He'd called out of the blue Thursday, said he'd be in Washington over the weekend and would she be available Saturday to help him select a housewarming gift for the home Paul and Bette had just bought in suburban Chicago. With Tris and Michael still off on their honeymoon, he really could use some help shopping in D.C., he'd said. She'd said yes.

She sighed mentally. Grandma Beatrice had always said men had to be schooled in gift buying just the way they are in world history. Grady Roberts, she feared, would require remedial work.

"I don't think so, Grady."

A tuck appeared between his brows. Lord, even the man's frown was more appealing than most men's widest smiles. "Why not?"

Despite the appeal, she moved closer so she could lower her voice out of hearing range of the supercilious clerk lurking in the vicinity.

"If your heart's set on an antique, there are some towns a little way out we could try. They're much more reasonable."

His frown cleared. "The money doesn't matter."

She'd tried the oblique approach, now it was time for direct. "Maybe not to you, but how about to Paul and Bette? How do you think they'd feel having something sitting in their living room that cost as much as half a year's mortgage payments?"

He looked stubborn.

"Of course, when I say sitting in their living room, that's only a guess. Where exactly *do* you put a genuine Chinese gong? And what on earth would you use it for? I can't imagine Bette calling Paul and their kids-to-be in to dinner with it."

"Not everything has to be useful," he argued, but the stubborn look had disappeared.

"True, but then it should be something the person getting the gift can truly love. You think Paul and Bette would love this?"

The surface didn't ripple, but Leslie thought she saw reactions flicker across the clear blue of his eyes. Poor soul, it was a whole new concept for him. Wouldn't do to throw someone at the remedial level right into a graduate course. Better to ease him into it.

"Why don't we look around a little more," she suggested smoothly. "And you can tell me more about the house Paul and Bette are buying."

He let her ease him out of the antique store and on to other shops that shared at least one theme—outrageous prices. So, she confirmed to herself, he hadn't really had his heart set on the gong or even an antique, because if he had she didn't fool herself into thinking Grady Roberts would have been so easily swayed.

Why on earth had she agreed to accompany him on this shopping expedition?

Because she couldn't resist.

Not because of his looks, though looks he certainly had—a couple inches over six foot, no extraneous inches anywhere else, blond hair, blue eyes, features both regular and manly. Women definitely looked twice.

That was not a recommendation in Leslie's eyes, however. If anything, his handsomeness and easy charm had made her dismiss him when they first met last fall.

But Tris and Michael, Paul and Bette—people Leslie liked and admired—had been friends with Grady Roberts for a long time, so surely there was *something*. And then she'd thought she'd caught glimpses of it herself, especially at the wedding.

Well, there you had it, as Grandma Beatrice would say. A challenge ready-made for Leslie Aurelia Craig. A lost soul—all the more lost because he didn't *know* he was a lost soul—clearly in need of a little gentle guidance.

Besides, she liked Paul and Bette, and for a couple starting off in their first home to be saddled with something like that gong... Especially since Grady would be too near at hand for them to sell the thing at their first garage sale.

This was not going the way Grady had planned.

They'd wandered in and out of Georgetown shops for nearly two hours. He would guide them in, hoping to get this gift bought and shipped, and she would usher them out, not satisfied with any of his proposals. Finally he talked her into a glass of wine and some fruit and cheese in the tree-shaded courtyard of a small restaurant he knew.

This was more like it, he thought as he considered Leslie. Elbows propped on the table, she rested her chin on the backs of her hands, which she'd templed over the wineglass. The position displayed the clean line of her profile beyond a sweep of brown hair glinting with red and gold.

She had beautiful hands. Long, slender fingers and a narrow palm. Soft, but not the least bit fragile. They were hands that accomplished things with a delicate touch.

He'd tell her that, but not right now. Too early. And if there was one thing Grady Roberts knew about dealing with women it was timing.

For now, he remained content to let their interaction fall into the familiar rhythm.

But he'd barely settled back in his chair before she started plying him with questions about the house that Paul and Bette had just bought.

"I don't know. It's just a house. It's in Evanston, just north of the city. It's two stories, kind of big. Not too far from Lake Michigan.

"I don't know," he repeated to inquiries on neighborhood character, construction date and architectural style.

"What's the outside look like?"

"I told you, two stories."

She shot him a look that might have been disgust.

"How about the yard?"

"It has big trees." That was fairly safe. A lot of Evanston had big trees, especially that area. And then he remembered another tidbit. "Paul said something about the previous owner being elderly and very frail, so not much got done to the outside. He said he wouldn't have to worry about getting a lawn mower because there's no grass to mow—just dirt."

But that didn't satisfy her, either.

"Are they planning on renovating? Redecorating?"

"I don't know."

"They must be doing something. At least a room they're going to make into a nursery for the baby."

"I don't know." What was the hurry? The baby wasn't due until August.

"But they must have talked about it. People getting a new house can't help but talk about it."

"Yeah, I guess they did. I just didn't pay much attention."

She took her elbows off the table and sat back, openly studying him. This was not part of the familiar rhythm.

"Well then, how did you expect to buy them a gift?"

What, was she crazy? "I expected to walk into a store, find something and pay for it."

"But how could you know if that *something* was right or not?"

"Right?"

"Appropriate for them. Something Paul and Bette could love. Something that would make them remember you every time they looked at it, and it would make them feel *good.*"

He smiled at her. "Isn't that an awful lot of burden to put on a present?"

She didn't smile back. "Not if the present buyer's truly willing to give."

The trouble with hazel eyes was that they sort of snuck up on you. They seemed just like ordinary eyes one second and then the next they were boring right into you.

He shifted in his chair and slanted his grin. "Hey, you're the one who said that antique gong was too expensive. I was willing to give."

She flipped one hand dismissively. "Money. That's not what I'm talking about."

What *was* she talking about? What was she *doing?*

She removed her red knit jacket from the chair back and slid her purse strap over her shoulder. "Thank you for the wine, Grady. It's nice seeing you. Hope your business goes well Monday, and have a good trip back to Chicago."

"But—but I don't have a present yet."

"You're not ready yet. You've got more thinking to do before you'll know what to get them. And it wouldn't hurt if you paid more attention to what they tell you about the house. Give them my best when you see them."

She stood.

"Wait a minute. Please sit down." She looked at him with polite inquiry, but did sit. This was definitely not going the way he'd planned. "I thought we'd go to dinner."

"Why?"

He'd never been asked that before. Not in the more than half of his life he'd been dating. He'd had women say no before—a few—but he'd never had one ask "why."

Mildly annoyed, he said the first thing that came to mind. "To get something to eat."

"It's only three-thirty in the afternoon and we just had something to eat."

"Well, we wouldn't go now," he said in exasperation, and for some reason that brought the spark of amusement back into her eyes. "I thought we'd go later, take the opportunity to get to know each other.

"After all," he went on quickly in case she had another "why" ready, "we'll run into each other when I'm in D.C., through Tris and Michael, and I know you've gotten to know Paul from his trips for the Smithsonian, and Bette when she comes along. But we don't know each other very well. I'd like to get to know you better."

That was true, he realized with a bit of surprise.

He reached across the glass tabletop and took Leslie's hand in both of his. "I think you're a very interesting woman, Leslie. And very lovely."

She detached her hand.

"Thank you. And I'm sure we will get to know each other over time since, as you've said, we have so many friends in common. But for now…"

She stood again. This time he stood, too.

"But the gift— You said you'd help me."

He started to cover the odd note in his voice with more talk, but stopped when he caught her expression. Something Tris had said about her friend's propensity for mothering people shot to the surface of his memory.

*The one thing Leslie can't resist is someone she thinks is a lost chick.* It wasn't a role he felt any affinity for, but any port in a storm…

"I really could use your help, Leslie."

"But we don't seem to be getting anywhere, Grady, so—"

"But we will. Give it more time." That's what he needed, more time.

"—there's no sense—"

"Wait a minute, wait a minute. I have an idea." An idea? A stroke of genius, and one bound to keep them together for at least a couple more hours. And that would make it late enough that going on to dinner should be no problem. Then…who knows?

"You said I need to think about Paul and Bette, and what they love. I know where to do that—the Smithsonian."

"The Smithsonian? Oh…you mean…?"

"Right, we can't see the exhibit Paul's been working on yet, but he consulted for them off and on even before he started this regular position last year, so there've got to be other displays with artifacts like the antique toys Paul appraises. Americana, that sort of thing."

"National Museum of American History," she murmured. She was weakening.

"Right, we'll go there." He tossed money on the table for their bill plus a generous tip, and took her arm. "That should give me lots of ideas. You can't say no to that."

She couldn't.

They saw the Star-Spangled Banner that Francis Scott Key wrote a country's anthem about. They watched the pendulum that swayed with the earth's rotation knock off a few more increments of time. They studied Dorothy's ruby slipper from *The Wizard of Oz*, Al Jolson's sheet music, Mister Rogers's sweater, Edith's and Archie's chairs from *All in the Family* and Fred Astaire's top hat.

She discovered his love of old movies.

He found out that her grandmother had taught her to play the piano and had a saying for every occasion.

They spent a very agreeable two hours. And when they walked out into the setting May sun and headed across the grassy Mall to where Grady had parked his rental car, he felt they had, in fact, gotten to know each other better.

What he hadn't done was come up with an idea for a present for Paul and Bette.

"I guess you're right," he told her. "I am hopeless when it comes to buying gifts. My personal assistant does a lot of that for me, and the rest of it I usually just get the first thing that hits my eye."

"I never said you were hopeless. You've just never been taught."

Maybe he'd always assumed that if it cost enough no one would notice the lack of thought. Discomfort at that notion was quickly edged away by the pleasure of the moment. To his left the Capitol dome rose, bathed in sunlight. To his right the stark Washington Monument was etched against the blue sky and beyond it the solid serenity of the Lincoln Monument. And by his side walked a woman, a very nice woman.

How often had he stopped to consider the "niceness" of the women he'd spent time with?

"So today was first grade in the Leslie Craig School of Gift Giving?"

She responded to his teasing straight-faced, but with her eyes giving her away. "Make that preschool, Grady."

He laughed and took her hand as they jogged across Jefferson Street ahead of a slow-moving car.

"Oh, look, the roses are blooming."

Leslie started to move away, but he didn't loosen his grip on her hand; instead he followed along where she led.

Most of his experience with roses came in ordering them by the dozen from florists. But here, several beds entirely filled with rosebushes occupied a triangle of space between the original Smithsonian building—"Dubbed 'the Castle,'" Leslie said—and a building with Centennial 1876 Exhibition above double front doors. Colors tumbled over one another. Buds still encased in green nestled next to flowers opened so wide that gravity had drawn some petals to the dark earth below. And perfect blossoms regally posed for their moment of glory against velvet green leaves.

"Aren't they wonderful? Look at that one—Peace. That color..."

Leslie moved from plant to plant. She slipped her hand out of his, but he went with her, observing her reaction more than the flowers. She breathed the scented air in deeply and let it out. Abruptly he remembered what it felt like to hold her while they danced, the feel of her back under his hand, the brush of her arm against his, the soft presence of her hand on his shoulder.

"The first time Grandma Beatrice came to visit me in Washington, we came here and sat on these benches one whole afternoon, watching the people and feeding the squirrels. We come every year when she visits me."

Such a simple thing—some dirt, plants, a few flowers—and she got such pleasure out of it. Year after year, from what she said.

"That's it," he said softly. Then louder, "Hot damn, that's it."

She looked at him, a reminiscent smile still softening her mouth.

"What's it?"

"The idea. The gift. I'll give them this."

He gestured at the flowers around them. She looked around, then back at him, eyebrows raised in question.

"A garden, Leslie. I'll give them a garden," he explained, and her puzzlement started to fade. "I mean, they can choose what they want and everything, but there's a man I know—I helped sell his old business so he could do what he really loved—landscaping. And I know he'd be happy to do it. He can help Paul and Bette figure out what they want, and then he'll landscape it for them." His enthusiasm dipped for an instant. "That's something they'll like, don't you think?"

"Yes, I think that's something they'll like very much. That's a great idea, Grady."

The momentary dip smoothed before a renewed surge of certainty. "And they'll remember it, like you said. And they'll look at it for years and years and think about me giving it to them and they'll smile. Hey, this gift giving can be pretty good stuff, can't it?"

Her smile changed, and he stared at her mouth.

"It sure can."

Pleased with the scent of roses, pleased with the sunshine, pleased with the idea, pleased with himself and pleased with Leslie, it seemed the most natural thing in the world to take her in his arms and kiss her.

## Chapter Two

Grady's mouth shifted on hers, changing the angle of the kiss from that first, exuberant meeting, taking advantage of her stunned stillness to carry this beyond an impulse.

*Move, Leslie. Move away.* Her mind's order faded to a mumble under the roaring in her ears.

It felt so natural, instead, to match her movements to his. To meet his lips, to echo the exploration. To put her hands up to his neck when he slid his arms around her, to settle into his hold when he drew her nearer.

So natural. And nature was a powerful force. A force to be reckoned with, a force to fear.

Because there was also such a thing as a natural disaster.

She put her hands on broad shoulders and leveraged herself three inches away from temptation. Because Grady Roberts had all the makings of a disaster for her, natural or otherwise.

She'd heard the stories: Grady Roberts, the great ladies' man; Grady Roberts, the smooth operator.

Partially straightening her arms gained her a modicum of space, but still within the circle of his arms.

*Say something, Leslie. Say something.*

"A student with your aptitude should be able to skip several levels and graduate before you know it."

His gaze still rested on her mouth, and she felt the impact of that look like a shiver under her skin. Then he raised his blue, blue eyes to hers and she had to fight to keep from shivering in earnest.

"I, uh, mean, uh, gift giving. In the Leslie Craig School of Gift Giving."

She laughed a little. It didn't sound quite right, but the fact that she'd produced the sound at all steadied her enough to add, "If you get this enthusiastic about gift giving, you'll be a real menace come Christmas, Grady."

Another laugh, still a little forced, but a laugh nonetheless.

Grady's eyes were less readable now, more like his usual expression.

And while she was absorbing the realization of how little his usual expression *did* show of what was going on inside him, Grady released her. He made almost a caress of it, sliding his hands lightly along her back and arms, until she took a step back.

He still said nothing.

Lord, she'd like to bolt. Make up some flimsy excuse and get out of here, away from him, away from all that . . . that *nature*.

But already she could feel her equilibrium returning. He'd taken her by surprise. That was all.

And cutting the evening short would give the kiss more significance than it truly deserved. Why get so worked up, anyway? It was a kiss, just a kiss. Making a big deal of it could create awkwardness, since they would surely run into each other through their mutual friends. She didn't want that.

"So you ready for that dinner now? I know I am. Can't have us starving right here in front of the Smithsonian and in full view of our national monuments. It wouldn't seem right, now, would it?"

"No, it wouldn't. Dinner is definitely in order," he said slowly, and relief that he'd followed her light lead shot through her. Or something shot through her.

"Well, c'mon, then."

As they continued on toward his car and then back through the city to a tiny Italian restaurant up Connecticut Avenue, her spiel would have done a tour guide proud. She couldn't remember a word of it later.

She was no fool. She knew the men who found her attractive were the ones who liked a sense of humor, a sharp wit, a good listener, an undemanding presence in their social lives. And there wasn't one she didn't remain on friendly terms with after she let them know that was all it ever would be.

Grady Roberts didn't fit that mold. She knew from Tris and the others the kind of women he favored. She'd seen it herself with that redhead at Tris and Michael's wedding. Her mirror told her she was attractive enough: decent figure, clear skin, regular features, shiny hair. Her face wouldn't send small children crying for their mothers, but neither would it have strong men—especially outright handsome strong men like Grady Roberts—quaking in their boots.

Besides, Grady related to women like a shooting star—brief, intense and no residuals once it had burned itself out. No thank you.

So she ate with him and she talked with him and she laughed with him. But she insisted on paying for her dinner, so there'd be no mistaking this for anything resembling a date.

And when he pulled up in front of her building, she gave his shoulder a quick pat and threw a wave over her shoulder as she went inside, so there'd be no mistaking them for anything other than friends.

And he let her.

Twenty hours later he stared out his hotel room window at the embassy across the street flying some blue-and-white flag he didn't recognize, and he shook his head. What had gotten into him?

First, he rushed the first kiss. Then he'd stumbled through the evening like a sleepwalker, letting her rule the conversation with amusing anecdotes of her family's history without once approaching anything close to personal. All right, he hadn't expected a kiss quite that . . . quite that much of a *kiss*.

But today, while sailing the Chesapeake with a business prospect, he'd gotten a better perspective.

He could—he would—get things back on track. Because he did want to get to know her better.

He dialed her home number.

A machine with Leslie's voice, the bit of drawl warming up the succinct message about the number he'd reached and the way to leave a message, answered.

"Leslie, it's Grady. I'd like to take you out for dinner tonight, but since you're not there I'll give you a call later, or you can give me a call at my hotel." He left the number and time, then hung up with a strange reluctance.

Restless, he walked toward Dupont Circle. The soft spring evening had brought people out, couples slipping past him two by two. In every conceivable combination of humanity they sat on front steps, lolled on park benches, perched on the sides of cars, laughed in front of ice-cream shops, shared a bicycle.

Room service and a channel-hopping binge that finally located Katharine Hepburn and Cary Grant whiled away the night. Twice more he reached Leslie's machine.

She wasn't available at her office when he called late the next morning during a break from his appointments.

With fifteen minutes until his five-thirty flight, he tried one last time from the airport. She was in a meeting, did he want to leave a message? No, no message.

"And if we can get the coverage I'm hoping for in *The Post*—"

Interrupted by her own office telephone, Leslie made an apologetic face at her two visitors and answered.

"Public Relations, Leslie Craig."

"Hi, Leslie, it's Grady."

He'd caught her by surprise. The message on her machine that Sunday night she'd understood. He'd been in town, didn't know many people, probably wasn't accustomed to an evening without a date to fill it. And the message at work the next day had been polite follow-up. But that had been a week ago, and she certainly hadn't expected to hear from him now.

She'd let the silence drag on too long.

"Grady Roberts," he prompted, without sounding the least put out.

She smiled. "I know. How are you?"

"I'm fine. And I'm coming right along with that project we talked about."

"Project? Oh, the present?"

"Yeah. I contacted that landscaper I mentioned and he went by the place yesterday, right after they closed on the house. He said it's got a lot of potential. Now he's drawing up a few general ideas for them, rough sketches, so I'll have something to put a ribbon on when they have their moving-in party in a couple weeks. Then he'll work with Paul and Bette so it's just what they want."

"That sounds terrific. I don't think you could have come up with a better present."

"Thanks to you."

"It was your idea, Grady."

Tris Donlin Dickinson's head came up from where she was reading the news release Leslie had been going over with her and an architectural consultant to the historic preservation foundation they both worked for. Leslie met her questioning look with a faint shrug.

"My idea that I wouldn't have had if you hadn't insisted I actually give it some thought."

"True."

He laughed, and she smiled at the sound.

"Well, I hoped I could thank you—"

"You already did and you just have again."

"—properly. This weekend. I'm coming in to D.C. and I hope we can get together. Dinner, and I hear there's a great place to dance in Georgetown by the river, and—"

"I'm sorry, but I have a visitor coming in and I'll be tied up all weekend."

A short silence, before his cheerful response. "Ah, well. Guess I'll have to wait to make my proper thank-you, then."

"Truly, Grady, there's no need—"

"Depends on whose need you're talking about." His voice had dropped half a tone. "Talk to you later."

"I don't—"

"Bye."

She held the phone through the click and the dial tone. She considered faking a more normal conclusion to the conversation, then decided against it.

Hanging up, she turned to Tris and Dick Welsh. "Now as I was saying, the coverage I'm hoping for . . ."

Tris's eyebrows had nearly disappeared under the blond hair across her forehead, but she cooperated in the return to business. Temporarily.

Twenty minutes later, the conference had ended with a few revisions to the release and contingencies for the campaign they hoped would draw attention to a developer's plan to claw a section out of a Civil War battlefield.

Dick Welsh left. Tris rose, but only to close the door before resuming her seat with an air of settling in.

"So," she started, "that was Grady on the phone, huh?"

"Um-hmm."

"Didn't know you two were exchanging phone calls on a regular basis."

"We aren't."

"You didn't tell him who your weekend visitor is."

"Didn't I?"

"You know you didn't. Trying to make him jealous?"

"Good Lord, no!"

The vehemence slipped out and Leslie would have tempered it if she'd had the words to speak again, but Tris relaxed.

"It's not that I don't love Grady," Tris said. "I mean, really love him, as a friend. For the person he is, not for the god I'd imagined him to be as a kid."

Leslie couldn't help but smile. She'd been around to listen nearly a year ago when Tris had prepared to finally test the college crush she'd harbored for Grady for a dozen years, and she'd been there this fall after Tris realized her feelings for Grady had become friendship, while her feelings for her longtime "buddy" Michael Dickinson had deepened to love. There'd been some rough spots for Tris and Michael in adjusting to their new relationship, but that was past—as Tris's face clearly showed at the moment.

"I know, Tris. I know exactly what you mean."

"And I really just started to appreciate what a great guy Grady is in the past few months. Maybe I'm seeing him better now or maybe he's more relaxed with me because I'm not starry-eyed around him. Whatever it is, I see the good things in him, the *real* good things in him, not just his looks and his charm, but his loyalty and his kind heart and his caring for—"

"You sound like the man's press agent," Leslie murmured.

Tris frowned without pausing. "—his friends. With his *friends* he's terrific. But when it comes to the women he dates ... I've seen him, Leslie, time and time again. I know he doesn't mean to hurt anyone, and most times he doesn't because he picks women who won't be hurt because they want the same thing, but sometimes he doesn't realize, and he's so charming.... It's like he just can't help himself and—"

"Tris, let me set your mind at ease."

Leslie stopped the spate of words partly out of self-preservation; her head was spinning. Now she leaned forward and put a hand on her friend's arm, speaking with the assurance of a thirty-seven-year-old who knew she was well past foibles of the heart.

"I would not succumb to Grady Roberts's famed charms, even if he *were* intent on trying them on me, which he most certainly is not. *Is not,* you hear? It's very simple. Business kept Grady in town the weekend before you and Michael came back. He wanted to get a present for Paul and Bette's housewarming. He asked me to help. I did. He called to thank me." She straightened and smiled. "As simple as that."

Tris still wore a faint frown.

"Grady called just now to simply say thank-you?" She sounded skeptical.

"Yes."

"Are you sure—"

"I'm sure."

Perhaps she spoke a little sharply because Tris cut a look at her that reminded Leslie that Tris, while younger and perhaps a bit less battered by life's disappointments, was not stupid.

"I'm just concerned about you, Leslie."

"Bless your heart." She meant it—she valued Tris's friendship and caring, but she also used the expression that Tris got such a kick out of on purpose to lighten the mood.

Tris's frown lifted, and Leslie adroitly shifted the conversation as she continued dryly, "But if you were truly concerned about me, you would volunteer to help entertain my little cousin April this weekend."

Tris snorted. "Concerned, I said. Not stupid. I still remember that trip to the zoo two years ago."

They exchanged a look of survivors remembering a shared horror. But Leslie felt obliged to defend her relative.

"She's two years older now. Surely she's grown out of the stage of trying to infuriate the gorillas by pelting them with peanuts."

"She's probably just two years stronger," was Tris's uncomforting prediction. "Now she'd probably make them so mad they really would shake the bars loose."

By late Saturday afternoon, Leslie wasn't sure if April Gareaux was stronger, but the thirteen-year-old certainly was more sullen.

Friday evening she'd taken the girl for dinner on a boat that cruised the Potomac. Admittedly, Leslie had been a bit distracted by the earlier delivery of a half-dozen red roses with a card simply signed "Grady." Thank heavens Tris had been out of the office.

Saturday morning, Leslie took April to the Smithsonian's Air and Space Museum; the you-are-in-the-cockpit

movie left most of the audience gasping and April yawn-
ing. They ducked into the National Archives building for a
peak at the original Constitution and the genuine John
Hancock signature on the Declaration of Independence. For
lunch, Leslie took her to the food court in the Old Post Office Pavilion so there would be enough choices for a thirteen-year-old palate.

April moved like an automaton at half power.

Riding the subway north, with the afternoon stretching
before them, Leslie decided to play what she considered her
ace in the hole—a trip to an upscale mall where the District
of Columbia met Maryland.

"Okay," was all April said to the suggestion.

Leslie figured it was a pose. From what she heard from
parents and advertisers, every girl that age lived for mall
delights.

Not April Gareaux.

By the time they returned to her apartment, twenty-four
hours of single-word answers, uninterested looks and dis-
dainful shrugs had Leslie so worn out she didn't even have
the energy to suggest they go out for dinner.

"How about if I order in pizza and we see what the TV
has to offer?"

"Okay."

That was one of the two answers she'd gotten all day, the
other being "yech." At least her dinner plans elicited the
more positive choice, even if it followed a martyred sigh.
She chewed on a piece of chocolate licorice as she dialed the
pizza number and watched April flop on the sofa with re-
mote control in one hand and the TV listings in the other,
showing probably more enthusiasm than for any other activity.

The chocolate licorice provided a surefire barometer to
Leslie's low spirits. Her father had introduced her to the
treat when she was nine. Chocolate licorice had been her

father's cure for the tragedy of a broken arm that had restricted her the last two precious weeks of that summer, and she still followed it.

She straightened her shoulders and finished off a second stick of licorice.

Maybe April Gareaux thought she'd worn down her older relative, scored some sort of victory. Leslie was made of sterner stuff.

She poured them each a soft drink, slipped off her shoes and sat next to April.

"Yes, it'll be good to take it easy tonight, because tomorrow we're getting up bright and early for church, then we'll change and take the train up to Baltimore for a baseball game. I have tickets and—"

April groaned, Leslie persevered.

"—great seats and the weather's supposed to be perfect. We can cheer and yell and stuff ourselves on hot dogs. You'll love it."

"I'll hate it. I don't know why I had to come here again, anyhow," April grumbled. The most words she'd said at one time since her arrival.

Leslie had always loved kids. Whenever the numerous Craig relatives and connections had gathered—as they often did at Grandma Beatrice's sprawling estate outside Charlottesville, Virginia—she'd entertained and cared for those younger than herself.

Since leaving Charlottesville for Washington ten years ago, she'd bypassed most family gatherings. But that didn't stop Grandma Beatrice from involving her in family business. Including what she saw as the sad state of her great-granddaughter April's upbringing.

"Your Cousin Melly is making a botch of raising that girl, Leslie," Grandma Beatrice had said.

"I'm sure it's not easy for Melly, with Jeff dying like that—"

Grandma Beatrice's disapproving sound—much too genteel to be called a snort—had stopped Leslie's excuses cold.

"He wouldn't have died like that if the two of them hadn't been trying to climb some fool cliff," her grandmother retorted. "If you're a reasonable human being and you want to go somewhere, you take a road, and if there's no road there's a darn good reason. Bunch of nonsense. And Melly's gotten worse, not better. Only thinks of herself and her latest adventure, never the child, and now the child's growing up a brat."

Beatrice Waverly Craig would have torn her own tongue out by its Southern roots before saying such a thing to anyone outside the family, but with Leslie she had always been bluntly honest. Sometimes painfully so.

"You've always loved children, Leslie, and you have nowhere to direct that love. Well, this is a child who takes some effort to love. See what you can do."

"But in a weekend how can I—"

"A weekend might be the most that should be asked of anyone, Leslie."

Now, looking at April's drooping mouth and pugnacious chin, Leslie thought a weekend might be *more* than should be asked. She also thought April deserved an answer.

"You're visiting me again because I've always enjoyed kids, and our family thought we'd have a good time together."

"Well, I'm not." Leslie took that to mean April wasn't having a good time, though April might have been declaring she wasn't a kid, or perhaps that she wasn't a member of the family. "And if you enjoy kids so much why don't you have some of your own to drag around to all these stupid places instead of picking on me?"

From long practice, Leslie stifled a wince, grateful when the downstairs buzzer gave her time to regain her equilibrium. After buzzing in the pizza delivery man, she opened her eyes wide at her cousin's daughter and said, with her most exaggerated drawl, "Why, darling, April, it's exactly because I don't have any of my own that I turn to you. Because I do so looooove torturing young girls."

April's mouth twitched, and Leslie hoped a smile might follow. But April, after all, was a Craig.

"Very funny." She snarled, and her face slipped into accustomed unhappy lines as she again faced the TV.

The doorbell cut short Leslie's mental debate whether to push April toward a real conversation. She dipped into her purse for her wallet to pay for the pizza and opened the door.

It should be arriving just about now.

Grady grinned to himself.

The roses had been standard, as classic as a Tracy–Hepburn movie. And he'd send more later next week—he wondered if he could have garden roses delivered like the ones they'd seen at the Smithsonian. But some situations, some women, called for something different, and this had never failed.

The only question had been timing. He didn't want to be too obvious, but he also wanted Leslie to feel his presence this weekend. Friday would have been overanxious; Sunday might have been too late. Yeah, this would work.

He might need lessons in housewarming gifts, but nobody could question Grady Roberts's success in wooing women.

Leslie stared at the man outside her apartment door.

Instead of the familiar red, white and blue shirt of the pizza delivery, there stood a man in a neat tan uniform, man who looked closer to retirement than puberty. Instead of a flat box showing grease spots and oozing tempting smells, he held a large wicker basket with its contents hidden by tinted cellophane and its handle decorated with a silken yellow bow.

"Leslie Craig?"

"Yes."

"Delivery from Not Just Another Gourmet."

She gawked at him. She'd shopped there, but the prices were so high she saved it for special occasions. And delivery? With what they charged? Never. "For me?"

"Yes, ma'am. If you'll sign here."

Dully, she followed his order, fished out a tip and took the basket.

"That's not pizza," April accused when Leslie sat beside her with the basket on her lap.

"No."

"Well, what is it?"

"I'm not sure."

April shot her a disgusted look and started peeling back the cellophane. "Well, look."

The retreating cellophane first revealed the long thin neck of a bottle of wine—a very good bottle of wine. Then an assortment of foreign cheeses, two tins of paté, four kinds of crackers, a minibowl of strawberries and another of raspberries.

April had the flap of a small envelope opened before Leslie took it away.

"Yech." April vibrated disapproval as she rooted through the basket's contents. Leslie wished she could have appreciated that April was more interested than she'd been all of her visit. "Who'd send junk like this? What's the card say?"

Leslie had a suspicion, a fear, really. She drew the card from the envelope and read: *You wouldn't come to dinner with me, so I've sent an appetizer to you. Enjoy. Grady.*

"Well?" April demanded.

"It's from a friend."

"I know, a man," April said wisely. "Mom gets stuff like this from men, too. But only when they really want to get in her pants."

"April!"

"Well, it's true. That's when men send the yuckiest things. I like it better when they send candy. But the ones who send this sort of junk are usually the ones she gets all wound up about and goes off with. For a while." She pulled out a white bakery box and sniffed diligently. "Well, at least he sent dessert. Chocolate. So who's this guy who wants to get in your pants?"

"He does not want—" She stopped. She would not debate this with a child. It was ludicrous. She wrapped herself in Grandma Beatrice's dignity and looked down her nose. "That is an extremely unseemly topic of conversation for a young lady. Especially for a Craig, who should—"

The doorbell rang again. With the basket and its contents spread out on her lap, Leslie looked at April. "That must be the pizza. Could you...?"

April gave a martyred sigh, but took Leslie's wallet and conducted the swap of money for pizza. Leslie repacked the basket so she could get plates and napkins.

April ignored the plate and silently plowed through the pizza without removing her eyes from the TV screen.

Leslie ate more slowly, but just as silently, pushing aside thoughts of Grady Roberts by mulling over what April had revealed.

Melly had always craved excitement and variety, never settling to anything or—to be honest—anyone. Even Jeff. For better or worse, that marriage probably had lasted because he shared her love of adventure and her very fluid definition of fidelity. Neither Melly nor Jeff had been sub-

le about such things. Leslie wondered how much April had
icked up in her first six years of life, and since her father's
eath seven years ago.

With Jeff gone, Melly rushed from adventure to adven-
ure, from man to man. At first she'd taken her daughter
vith her, but more and more in recent years Melly had left
April with varied relatives.

Leslie leaned back in the corner of the couch, looking at
he girl's profile. She had the long Craig nose. Grandma
Beatrice called it aristocratic. Leslie remembered at April's
ge lamenting her own Craig nose as plain *big*. Eventually,
s her grandmother had promised, she grew into her face;
er other features strengthened, balancing the Craig nose
nd creating an attractive whole. But she could remember
he agony of waiting.

"I guess this means the ball game's off tomorrow." Be-
eath April's insultingly hopeful tone, Leslie caught dis-
omfort, and knew April had been aware of her scrutiny.

"No. Why on earth would it?"

"Because you'll be doing something with this guy." Her
one said she was addressing someone who'd flunked re-
edial logic.

"No, I most definitely will not. I am taking you to a
aseball game, that's what I am doing tomorrow. You're my
uest, and you're the one I'm spending time with."

April flopped back; just looking at her slouch made Les-
e's back ache. Had Leslie detected a flash of surprise be-
ore the sullenness slipped into place? "Well, you can force
e to go to this stupid baseball game tomorrow because I'm
ill a kid. But how about this guy, huh? He's not some poor
d you can boss around. What're you going to do about
m? Huh?"

Good question.

And one she sidestepped. Sunday she'd been too tired

from the weekend with April. Monday she'd convinced herself the flowers and gourmet basket were gestures, no more.

But today, when she got home from work, she discovered a package outside her apartment door with the logo of a local department store. She tucked her attaché more firmly under her left elbow, shifted the mail she'd just collected into the same hand and warily picked up the package the size of a truncated shoe box.

Nothing on the label except her name and address, and the store's return address. She'd have to open the thing to solve the mystery of its origin.

Juggling her burdens, she fished out her keys and let herself in, tumbling her attaché, purse and mail on top of the wide bookcase near the hallway to her bedroom. The package she handled more gingerly.

She looked at it a full minute, then tore off the wrappings. Plunging through padding, she fished out a container of her favorite scent. Not cologne or the thumbnail size bottle of perfume she indulged in only when she felt particularly rich or so blue even chocolate licorice couldn't perform a cure. What she held now was a bottle big enough for a case of the blues to drown in.

The phone rang once but she ignored it, placing the bottle carefully on the bookcase and staring at it until the phone rang again. She snagged the plain envelope that had nestled amid the padding, had the envelope open and was reading the single word on it when she snatched the receiver up as the third ring faded away.

"Hello."

*Grady,* she read.

"Hi, Leslie. It's Grady," she heard.

*Damn.* Her heart sank. She could have used another moment to consider this. Which might explain why her heart picked up speed at the same time it sank.

But Craigs didn't waffle when it came time to charge ahead.

## Chapter Three

"Hello, Grady. I've just opened the most extraordinary package from you."

"Extraordinary?"

"Yes. I didn't know perfume could be purchased by the half gallon."

He chuckled, a very masculine, very satisfied sound.

"Really, Grady," she went on in a tone she kept light and friendly, "it's most generous of you to keep thanking me for helping you decide on the gift for Paul and Bette, but totally unnecessary. I enjoyed it. So, please, no more."

In his momentary silence she read indecision over whether to deny the flowers, food and perfume had been expressions of thanks, and perhaps a bit of confusion.

"All right," he said slowly. "But then let me take you to dinner tonight."

Her eyebrows rose. What *was* the man up to? She'd told Tris he wasn't trying to charm her, but she was beginning to wonder. "You're in Washington again?"

"Yes, the client I told you about wanted to introduce me to some of his connections. There's really a need for my sort of business here in Washington. I'll have to learn more about the links between the private sector and government around here, but other than that, I think a branch could practically open itself...."

She listened to his discussion of the prospects of a branch of his business brokerage in the Washington area, enjoying his enthusiasm, while another level of her mind focused on a more personal issue.

If he was trying to charm her, why?

Surely he must see she wasn't a candidate for his usual romantic interlude. At the very least he'd recognize that the web of their mutual friendships would make the postinterlude period awkward for all concerned. And with Grady, postinterlude followed interlude as surely as day followed night—and nearly as quickly.

So, since he couldn't be after a fling, what was he after?

That's when it hit her.

He was after friendship. He just didn't know how to go about it.

Sure, he was friends with Tris and Bette, but he'd known Tris more than a dozen years and viewed her as a sort of kid sister, and Bette he'd known always as the woman who made Paul Monroe's eyes glow.

But other than those two, she would wager the family heirlooms that the only way Grady Roberts knew to interact with unattached females was romantically.

In its own way, Grady's situation was truly sad. What he needed was someone to teach him how to be friends with a woman. Someone who wouldn't be taken in by his romantic ploys. Someone who wouldn't fall for the glint in his blue, blue eyes.

Someone who over the past ten years had succeeded in helping several men see how they could make their lives happier, without making the mistake of getting dangerously involved herself.

"So what about dinner tonight?"

"Dinner? Okay—"

"Great. I know a wonderful French place—"

French? Probably tiny tables, candlelight and wine? Naturally he'd think of that first. But she'd show him another way.

"I'm in the mood for a burger. Give me twenty minutes to change into jeans and I'll meet you at this place I know on Connecticut Avenue."

"Oh." She could practically hear his plans shatter, and she grinned. But he rallied quickly. "Okay."

Two minutes later she hung up with a sense of accomplishment and great optimism that handling Grady Roberts wouldn't be so tough, after all.


"You look a little tired, Leslie. Are you okay?"

Tris Dickinson studied her with narrowed eyes; Leslie wished the blinds let less revealing sunlight in her office.

Tired? Try exhausted. But Tris was the last person she'd admit it to.

On rare occasions when her subtlety slipped she had been accused of interfering in friends' lives, though she preferred to think of it as redirecting their thoughts. For their own good, of course. Tris—darn her perception—was the most frequent accuser. Leslie counted herself fortunate Tris had been too preoccupied with the joys of newly married life these past few weeks to be her usual observant self.

Leslie had said no to nearly half of Grady's invitations but since he wanted to get together every day, she wondered if cutting their outings in half was enough to let a friendship grow slowly, naturally. Though she persisted in making their encounters unrelentingly casual, paying her own way as often as she could beat him to it, talking about strictly impersonal matters and avoiding situations he could turn toward a more romantic bent.

That took a lot of energy. Grady did not give up, and he was adept at turning a look into a potential bone-melter, a touch into a possible skin-burner. He'd had a lot of practice at this romance stuff.

Remembering that kept her knees locked the couple times she'd been on the verge of slipping under his spell.

Some people cracked their knuckles or twirled their hair; Grady flirted. Things like that made no difference in your feeling about the person, if you liked them.

Ah, that was the question. Did she like Grady?

If Grady Roberts were merely handsome—could anybody that good-looking be considered "merely" anything? she wondered with a wry face—he'd be easy to dismiss. If he were merely successful he'd be easy to forget. If he were merely charming he'd be easy to write off. But there was the evidence of his friendship with Tris and the others, and Leslie's own observations of him....

"Are you all right, Leslie?"

Tris's question jerked her back to the present.

"Of course. Why ever wouldn't I be all right?" She smiled brightly.

"Well, I don't know why, but you just made this strange face, and I've had the feeling you aren't really listening to me. Is something wrong?"

"Noth—"

"Are you still worrying about April?"

"April? Yes, I suppose I am." It wasn't a lie. Since her young relative's visit nearly two weeks ago, her concerns had remained, just below the surface of her mind.

Tris frowned. "Leslie, you can't solve everybody's problems. As much as you'd like to mother two-thirds of the world—"

"I wouldn't have enough place settings for dinner," she demurred, "and Grandma Beatrice would never approve of paper plates."

The frown tightened as Tris fought a grin, and Leslie was satisfied.

"All right, I won't lecture—"

Leslie thanked her with a heartfelt, "Bless your heart," and the grin defeated the frown.

"But I'm going to agree with Michael and insist you come with us this weekend to the beach. Until last night I thought...well... But now I see how much you need the rest. And we'll make sure you don't think of anything more demanding than whether to sit in the sun or the shade."

"That sounds wonderful," she said. A lazy weekend by the ocean could cure many ills. "But I am not about to intrude on you and Michael. You'll want to be alone and—"

"You will definitely not be intruding, so it's settled—you're coming. If you can get Friday afternoon off, we'll leave around lunchtime. And see if you can get Monday off too."

Leslie decided she must be more tired than she knew, because she found herself nodding in acquiescence. The foundation director had been fretting about the vacation time she'd built up, though out of concern for her well-being or his record keeping she didn't know. Either way, she wouldn't have trouble getting the time off.

"Besides," Tris went on, "it would be impossible to be alone, since Paul rented the beach house. He's not allergic to making plans the way he was before Bette, but he still has his impulsive moments. He decided a weekend at the beach was a perfect way to celebrate wrapping up the installation of the exhibit—you are coming to the opening, aren't you?

"Uh, yes."

She'd returned her RSVP for the Thursday evening reception, and she'd turned down Grady's suggestion they go together. She didn't want him or anyone else to see them as a couple; that would defeat her whole purpose. But what about at the beach? Where Paul, Bette, Tris and Michael went, would Grady be far behind? But could she back out now without being terribly obvious?

"Good. And don't worry about a thing this weekend. I know you're not the type to get all bent out of shape about being a single woman along with just two married couples for company." Tris looked at her intently, and Leslie thought she understood; Grady wouldn't be there. That's what Tris had found out last night. "But just so there's no mistake, we really want to have you along."

Tris stood and gathered the coffee mug she'd brought with her. "So that's settled. You'll drive out with Michael and me on Friday. But first we'll all be together Thursday night at Paul's reception."

Grady listened to the man next to him, but his eyes followed Leslie as she accepted a glass of wine from a thin man with even thinner sandy hair. The exhibit light, meant to bathe details of handcarved toys and the patina of two-hundred-year-old wooden games, also caught Leslie's high, wide cheekbones, leaving shadowed hollows before picking out the sharply etched line of her jaw.

A movement subtly shifted the sheen of her royal-blue silk dress, and halfway across the exhibit area Grady swallowed at the intimation of the curves below.

She moved closer to the sandy-haired man and Grady's muscles tightened fractionally; it wouldn't take but a minute for him to reach them, less than that to send this guy on his way. Then a turn of Leslie's head showed him her smile. He thought he read tolerance in it and relaxed.

Even though he kept his conversation with the brother of a Chicago client short, he'd lost sight of Leslie by the time he shook hands and started off.

Paul was by the exhibit entrance, surrounded by officials, complimenters and questioners. He handled them with almost careless ease. Grady had caught Paul's interview on local TV as he'd changed for this reception, and marveled at his friend's naturalness.

Opposite Grady, Michael stood back from the crowd, watching the comings and goings with his usual quiet intensity. But Grady noticed Michael seldom stood in his out-of-the-way spot alone. Sometimes in pairs, often singly, others made their way to Michael, and when he spoke they listened.

A shift in the crowd opened a new line of sight and he saw Leslie, alone for a moment, like him. Without moving her head, her gaze came around to meet his. He lifted his glass, and her eyebrows rose as a smile pulled at her lips.

He took a step toward her, then stopped as she turned away, and he saw Tris had placed a hand on her arm.

Meeting Bette Wharton Monroe's eyes then, Grady altered his course to where she stood, cornered against a display case by a bushy-haired man, short and rotund in a tweed jacket whose weave had caught crumbs from his repast. Grady traced crackers, cheddar cheese, flaky pastry, a dollop of creamy dip and smear of strawberry juice.

Bette had to interrupt to introduce the man as Professor Whicken. Assessing Bette's pale face and the professor's renewed conversational flood, Grady took action.

"I think it's time for all pregnant ladies to be sitting down," he announced, grasping Bette's elbow and drawing her away.

"I'm just telling Mrs. Monroe—" The professor, who showed an inclination to follow, halted when a hand met his chest.

"We appreciate your concern, Professor," said Grady to the man who'd expressed no concern. "But I'll be happy to take care of Mrs. Monroe from here. Thank you."

Out of earshot, Bette added, "Thank *you*. That deserves at least a knighthood."

Halfway to the chair Grady had spotted, Michael joined them. "You beat me to it, Grady. How're you doing, Bette?"

"I'm fine. And I don't need to sit down." She hung back a little. "Really."

"Sure you do," Grady disagreed amiably, still homing in on the chair. It happened to be occupied by a white-haired lady, but that didn't matter.

"What's wrong?" Paul arrived a little out of breath, a wake of surprised looks behind him.

"*Nothing* is wrong. Go back to your conversation, Paul," Bette ordered as Grady ceded his hold on her arm to her husband.

Paul ignored her. "Michael? What's up?"

Not even particularly surprised it was Michael that Paul presumed would know, Grady simply continued to the chair, stopping in front of the white-haired lady.

"Excuse me, could we possibly have the use of that chair? As you can see, our friend is pregnant, and with all the excitement and everything..." He let it trail off and smiled, a man smiling at a woman, sharing an understanding of the world and humanity.

"Of course, of course." The white-haired lady fluttered up, joining her insistence to the three men's until Bette sat.

"Thank you," Grady told the woman, and smiled again.

She smiled back, then headed off, but not before she tossed a distinctly saucy look back over her shoulder.

Bette covered her mouth with her hand, but the amusement colored her voice. "Grady, you are incorrigible."

"What?" he asked innocently. "I just asked if we could have the chair."

"Hey, I don't care if he tangoed with Grandma Moses in front of the Supreme Court," said Paul. "He got you a chair."

"Yes, he did," she agreed. "Thank you, Grady. It was very nice of you."

"You're welcome."

"I think we should leave," Paul said abruptly.

"Leave? But the reception's only half-over. We can't leave," Bette objected.

"Sure we can."

"Well, I don't want to. I came here to bask in the glory of your accomplishment, and I'm not done basking." Husband and wife exchanged a look. "I'm all right, Paul. Honestly."

Paul seemed to relax, moving his hand from Bette's shoulder to stroke her cheek.

"Is something wrong?"

"Are you okay, Bette?"

The questions from Tris and Leslie tripped over each other as they joined the group.

"I'm fine. Just a little tired. Grady rescued me."

Grady felt the look Leslie flicked at him, but was too late to meet it. By the time he turned to her she was assessing the situation. She looked at Bette closely, then to Paul's still-stubborn expression, then over her shoulder at the important people Paul had deserted.

"Well, she looks fine to me," Leslie declared, then dipped deeper into her drawl. "And if there's one thing a Southern woman knows, it's the vapors."

Bette gave her a grateful look, turning to her husband she said, "See? The words of an expert. Now will you please go back to the others?"

"I don't think—"

"Bless her heart," Leslie interrupted blithely, "Bette simply had the common reaction to being near talked to death by Will-He-Ever-Be-Quiet Whicken."

Everyone chuckled except Paul, but even his face eased.

"Whicken is a notorious windbag," added Tris. "Everybody who knows him stays away, so he picks on newcomers like Bette."

"Especially slow-moving ones like me," she said with a rueful look at her girth.

This time even Paul chuckled. In three minutes he'd been persuaded to return to his conversation, though it took both a promise that someone would stay with Bette, and Michael's taking him by the arm and leading him away.

"Professor Whicken is the source of a good deal of conjecture in some circles in Washington," Leslie informed the group that remained around Bette's chair.

"What sort of conjecture?" Bette prompted.

"Well, nobody's ever actually seen him stop talking long enough to breathe, so we wonder if he ever does."

"He must." Grady waited until all three pair of eyes were on him, especially the hazel pair. "He's got to stop talking in order to eat, and we know he eats from the evidence on his jacket. In fact, the evidence showed he'd stopped talking long enough while he's been here to eat."

"Couldn't be," objected Tris. "Must be old stains."

Grady shook his head. "Crackers, cheese, dip, pastry and strawberry from those little tarts—in other words, a good portion of the menu here."

"I think Sherlock Roberts has you, Tris." Leslie turned to Bette. "What do you think? You spent the most time with him."

Bette looked from one face to the other. "I think it does not behoove someone who's seven months pregnant to comment about someone spilling food down their front."

As the laughter died down, Bette said, "Someone's trying to get your attention, Tris. Or maybe Leslie's?"

The sandy-haired man Grady had seen earlier with Leslie looked over at their group.

Tris smiled at him as she said to Leslie in a low tone, "Did you—?"

"Yes, indeed. Consider the way paved. Now go to it, kid."

Tris hesitated. "Will you be okay, Bette?"

"Of course, as long as Leslie sticks around to tell me what this is all about."

"It's about being a foundation with not very much money trying to do work that costs a lot of money." Tris sighed, but her smile didn't falter as she headed off.

Grady gave in to the urge to grin as Leslie explained that the sandy-haired man had a bank account as fat as he was thin, and the historic preservation foundation she and Tris worked for was courting a large donation. Leslie had softened him up, now Tris would hit him with the facts and figures of how much they could accomplish with his check.

Business, that's why Leslie had been so attentive to the man. He could understand that.

"A nonprofit foundation's work is never done," Leslie said, "especially when it comes to getting donations. But in this case, he's really a very nice man."

Grady turned away from where Tris and the man were in earnest conversation and looked at Leslie.

"Have you seen all of the exhibit?"

His abrupt question didn't faze her. "Yes, I have."

"Good, then you can show me. I haven't had time to get all the way around."

"Don't forget to show him the section with those handmade chessboards from the backwoods," instructed Bette. "Some of them are amazing."

Leslie flashed her a look Grady couldn't see. Bette smiled blandly.

"You should probably go take a look around now, before it's too late, Grady. But I'll stay here. We promised Paul someone would stay with Bette."

"There is no need for anyone to stay with me. I'm—"

"I'll be happy to," said Michael, rejoining them after depositing Paul amid a crowd of well-wishers. "We've hardly talked because of the opening. This is our chance."

Leslie had been taught well. She gave in so graciously, Grady could almost pretend she had really wanted to go with him. That ingrained graciousness was one of the things he liked about her. As they studied the displays that drew the viewer along with an appreciation of humanity's deep-seated desire for diversion and its ingenuity in meeting the desire, Grady detoured from the thought that there were a lot of things he liked about her.

*Almost pretend she had really wanted to go with him.* Almost, but not quite, because clearly she'd been reluctant.

Maybe pure stubbornness prompted him then to lead her away from the activity around Paul's exhibit. A couple twists and turns later and they were in quiet, shadowy isolation with only unlit display cases for company.

"We must have taken a wrong turn somewhere," Leslie said. "Maybe we can follow the bread crumbs back."

"Wait a minute. I want to talk to you."

Caution replaced cheerfulness. "Oh? About what?"

"About this weekend . . ." She looked away, but not before he'd caught a shadow of expression, almost hunted, on her face. He went on slowly, turning that over in his mind. "I'm planning to head to Denver to check something for a client. Then I've got things in Chicago that need attending, so I probably won't be back until the end of next week."

"Oh. Well, have a good time. Hope all your business goes well."

The relief in her voice hit him low and hard. He'd considered accepting Paul's invitation to the beach this weekend, then trying to wrangle it so Leslie came, too. But he'd decided a week apart might make her appreciate him more. And might give him a chance to figure out what she was playing at. He'd heard about hard to get, but he hadn't seen it often, and it didn't seem Leslie Craig's style.

Now he had another answer—she didn't want to be around him.

"Thanks." He didn't examine his curt tone or the raw sensation low in his stomach. "Guess we should get back."

He took her arm, maybe with a little more force than necessary, and she pulled back automatically. But he already had his hold, so the momentum of her countermove simply pivoted her until she came up against him, one open hand on his chest.

She was in his arms, the way she had been in the rose garden not so long ago. She smelled as sweet. She felt as good. And her mouth . . . her mouth was right there . . .

It took no thought, just the following of a need. He bent his knees and ducked his head; he had to because she hadn't looked up at him, but he caught her mouth.

He dropped his hand from her arm, holding her only with the kiss. She tasted of warmth. Sweet, sweet warmth that seeped into him and fired his blood. And she tasted of hesitation. But she didn't pull away.

Wanting to crush her to him, he instead touched his fingertips lightly to her jaw. She raised her chin, and he deepened the kiss, sliding his tongue through her slightly parted lips as his hands tunneled into her hair to cup the delicate curve of her skull.

It took only the slightest pressure to urge her tighter against him. Her hands slid up to his shoulders. Better, but not enough. He didn't want those elegantly capable hands on his damn suit coat, he wanted them on *him*. Then, as if in answer to his desire, she moved one hand to his neck, the tips of her fingers stroking the skin.

He swirled his tongue deeper into her mouth, exploring the warmth, barely holding back the fire.

Her tongue touched his—almost, it seemed, by accident—and started to retreat. But he caught it, drawing it into his mouth with an insistent need he was too absorbed in meeting to analyze. He felt more than heard the soft sound deep in her throat, the same way he experienced his own groan at her delicate touches. He wanted more... more... And he wanted so strongly he started to feel light-headed with it.

He raised his head to gasp in the oxygen his lungs demanded, but he kept his gaze on her lips as if a look could sustain the physical link.

"Grady."

Uncertainty clung to the word. It certainly wasn't an invitation, so when he took possession of her mouth once more, it was all his own doing. For an instant she met him, a glimpse of what she held back from him, enough to make him know he wanted it all. Desperately.

And then she withdrew. Even before their lips parted.

"Grady, no."

He felt the breath of her words on his lips, absorbed the impact of them in his tight muscles.

He raised his head, so the differences in their heights put distance between her lips and his. He watched the slumberous desire in her eyes give way to a haze he didn't understand.

"Why?"

"Because I want us to be friends."

"Friends?" The word didn't register immediately, but when it did, he grinned a little at her, the blood still humming through him in a most *un*friendly way. "It would be a hell of a waste of chemistry for us to be friends."

Where had she gotten the notion they should be friends? A kaleidoscope of the past few weeks flickered through his mind. Wherever she'd gotten it, it certainly explained a number of things, and he sure preferred that explanation to the idea that she just didn't want to be around him. Besides, now that he knew, he was certain it wouldn't take him long to change her mind.

Not with this encounter as proof of the charge between them.

"That's just . . . just hormones." She waved away a millenium worth of powerful instinct with one hand. "It's much more important that we be friends. I think we've made a good start toward that these past few weeks. I'd hate to see it ruined by something so ill-advised."

Ill-advised? No woman had ever called kissing him "ill-advised." He frowned. "You're serious about this."

"Yes. Yes, I am. I most certainly am. I know you're not accustomed to friendship with many women, but think of me like Bette and Tris."

He stared at her. If he'd ever had a quarter—an eighth—of this reaction to Tris or Bette, Michael or Paul would have shot him.

What he felt for her had nothing to do with the easy, accepting warmth of his deep affection for Tris and Bette. How could it? He shifted his weight to one foot, brushing his right hip against Leslie.

There was no denying the desire he felt for Leslie Craig, so she must fall into that other, much more populated category of women in his life. He couldn't get confused by the warmth he also felt. He'd spent more than half his life exploring the attraction between men and women, and he couldn't mistake it. Relieved to have that settled, he leaned forward to demonstrate the matter to her. But before his lips did more than brush hers, she backed up, out of reach.

"You're sort of stuck, aren't you, Leslie?"

"What do you mean?"

"You can't convince me we're just friends if you're afraid to kiss me. And you can't kiss me because it proves there's more between us than friendship."

A stubborn expression settled over her features and he remembered her account of her couple-of-times-great-grandmother who had single-handedly held off first a Yankee patrol and then a band of renegade Rebels. He didn't doubt it for an instant.

"Friends, Grady. That's all we are. That's all we ever should be. That's all we ever will be."

With the sensations still alive, he stared at her. "We'll see."


Any given warm-weather weekend, beach-bound traffic stretched from Washington, D.C., to the Atlantic shores of Maryland and Delaware like an army of ants on the march. At least being toward the head of the column spared Leslie, Michael and Tris the sort of backup at the Chesapeake Bay bridge that overheated engines and tempers.

They reached, in decent time and good spirits, the house Paul had rented just over the Delaware border. The house, weathered but solid looking, had its back to the street so it could turn its face to the ocean. A porch edged with a railing wide enough to sit on encompassed the entire building. Unloading their bags, they followed the path around to the oceanside.

Turning the corner to the front, Leslie caught a glow of gold amid the shade of the porch's overhang, on the far side of where the path met wide stairs leading up to the porch.

Grady. Her steps faltered at the sight of him sitting on the railing. He'd looked too good for comfort in his perfectly tailored suit, immaculate white shirt and discreetly expensive tie at the reception last night. So good she'd given in to the urge to kiss him back for those few, unthinking moments in the shadows.

He looked even better with his hair ruffled, his shirt faded from the open collar to the loose tails and his shorts frayed at the hem.

He smiled at her, and her heart sped up.

Well, of course it did. He was a very good-looking man, and she hadn't lost the instinct that made her as aware of that as the next woman. Which also explained giving in to the urge to kiss him last night. It didn't mean any more than that, though.

"Oh." Tris, walking next to her, flashed her a look, then frowned at her husband and said almost under her breath, "I thought Grady wasn't going to be here."

Michael gave a slight shrug. "Last I heard he wasn't coming. Guess he changed his mind."

"Hey, you guys! Glad to see you could finally tear yourselves away from all that Washington power and glory." Paul's shout ended any further discussion.

He and Bette stood at the top of the wide stairs, grinning and exchanging greetings and hugs as the three newcomers joined them on the porch. Grady took his eyes off Leslie only long enough to clap Michael on the back and give Tris a quick hug before he resumed his perch on the wide porch railing, elbow hooked around one upraised knee.

She turned to him then, steadily meeting his bland gaze.

"I thought you had business in Denver."

"Changed my plans. Something more important came up."

"I see."

"Leslie, c'mon in here and let me show you where to stow your bag before we all collapse in decadent abandon on the beach chairs."

She started after Paul, but still heard Grady's murmured response: "No, you don't see yet. But you will. We both will."

## Chapter Four

They delayed Paul's promised decadent abandon on the beach chairs to take a long, slow walk along the waterline. Clouds piling up on the horizon and blocking out the warmth of the sun discouraged any thoughts of swimming. But they splashed along the edge, occasionally wading deeper to gauge how much spring had warmed the water.

Leslie would have preferred not to have stated her plan to keep their relationship at the friendship level; the last thing she wanted was to set herself up as a challenge for Grady Roberts. But subtlety couldn't stand up to that kiss at the reception. She'd thrown down the word "friends" to make Grady take a step back, and give her room to breathe.

It worked. For the moment.

She'd figured he'd be half a continent away in Denver and would find other targets for his attention.

But he wasn't half a continent away. He was right here. And come tonight, he'd be right down the hall, sleeping on a couch in the living room.

Paul had cheerfully announced that arrangement when he'd shown her to her room. Not by a flicker did he indicate she might appreciate reassurance on that point. "With three bedrooms, we figured the latecomer should be the one to camp out on the couch."

She would have preferred half a continent between them instead of a hallway. It struck her as ominous that Grady's final words had gone from yesterday's, "We'll see," which she'd optimistically interpreted as meaning he'd consider being her friend, to essentially saying today, "You'll see," which no amount of optimism could twist to mean that.

So Leslie braced.

And Grady did nothing.

At least, nothing objectionable. During the walk, he didn't once try to touch her. He didn't single her out to walk next to. He didn't even make eye contact.

It was darn annoying.

She lugged out the emotional sandbags in preparation for a hurricane, then ended up with a drizzle.

Actually, they all ended up with a drizzle. The clouds completed their takeover of the sky as the six of them neared the house.

From the porch, they watched the drizzle turn to steady rain, and enjoyed the coziness of their shelter. Bette sat in the circle of Paul's arm on the swing they shared. In a nearby chaise longue, Michael's light hold drew Tris's back against his chest.

Fighting a twinge of isolation, Leslie sank into a canvas deck chair. Rather to her relief, Grady didn't take its twin, but returned to his spot on the railing.

"So, Tris, how did your talk with the potential donor go last night?" he asked as he settled comfortably with his back against the roof support.

"It went fine, but it didn't go far enough."

"What does that mean?"

From long experience, Leslie knew what it meant. The prospect was still a prospect, which was better than no prospect but not as good as a check. She'd already heard these details, so she let her mind and her eyes stray.

From a contemplation of the mesmerizing rain, her focus turned to the foreground—the man perched on the railing. The position emphasized the strong lines of his neck. The open collar of his shirt revealed a dusting of hair that showed golden even in the dim light.

Grandma Beatrice had long blamed curiosity for leading Leslie into numerous scrapes. Now that regrettable curiosity prompted her gaze to follow the line of his broad shoulders down a rolled-up cotton sleeve to his forearm. With his right foot on the railing, his bent knee propped up his left forearm. She had a clear view of a thicker covering of hair there, but of the same golden color, almost a delicate tint. His forearm was well muscled and his wrist thick with tough bone—nothing delicate there.

Below the ragged line of his shorts, the same golden glint was visible, but the long, defined muscles were just as tough as his arms and wrists. Maybe more so, she thought as she noticed a number of lighter-skinned scars.

His golden perfection being marred by something as mundane as scars seemed incongruous.

"Wondering where I got them?"

She looked up sharply and met his gaze. How long had he followed her survey? Her neck heated with rising color. She countered the embarrassment with wry humor.

"That's all right. This way I can let my imagination run wild."

His face seemed to tighten. "Don't let it run too wild. They're very prosaic scars."

She opened her mouth to repeat that she didn't need to know, didn't want to know how he got them. But he seemed to feel a need to explain them to her.

"I got them playing tag football."

"Oh, with your family?" That surprised her, and she had no idea why.

"No." He clipped the word uncharacteristically. "Tag football's not their style at all."

"No," said Paul. "Mayhem on the lawn is more my family's style." Despite his humorous tone, Leslie thought she detected a bit of protectiveness in his interruption.

Grady said nothing. Without changing his relaxed position, he seemed to tighten. She wasn't surprised Paul took over the conversation; it was clear the tense figure on the railing wasn't going to continue.

"We used to have marathon games in our backyard. Dad swears he never could keep grass until I left for college."

"Even after that," said Michael. "I've played in some Thanksgiving Day games that came long after high school."

"And not just football," Tris added. "Volleyball and badminton."

"Badminton! My sister's a badminton fiend," Paul said. "You met my kid sister at Tris and Michael's wedding, didn't you, Leslie?" She nodded. "Well, Judi may look like your everyday college student, but don't ever get around her when she's got a badminton racquet in her hand. She plays to the death."

"Look who's talking," Bette interjected, then turned to Leslie. "I never knew sailing could be a contact sport until I went out with Paul last spring. He told me we were going sailing with Grady, but what he really meant was we were in one boat and Grady was in another and then each tried his damnedest to sink the other. I was expecting skull and crossbone flags to be unfurled any moment.''

"Just a little friendly competition," said Paul, but with a grin lurking. "Right, Roberts?"

The odd tension had left Grady. Even before he chuckled and started an anecdote of the boyhood competition he and Paul had indulged in, Leslie knew the conversational diversion his friends had constructed had served its purpose; he was back to being himself.

She didn't doubt that Grady had been disturbed. She didn't doubt his friends had stepped in to both give him time to recover his equanimity and to direct the conversation away from whatever had triggered his reaction.

She was surprised by his reaction. And she didn't have a clue what had triggered it.

She'd outsmarted herself, and Grady took full advantage of it.

After a dinner that turned out surprisingly well despite the chaos of six chefs bumping into one another in a one-person kitchen, the rain-cooled air prompted them to settle in the living room.

He deliberately chose a corner of the love seat, then watched Leslie pick a chair at the opposite end of the conversation area—not far in the compact arrangement.

He recognized the exact moment she realized that sitting opposite him meant she looked right at him, and he looked right at her.

But he refrained from making obvious eye contact as the talk flowed. From plans for the next day—all agreed to let the day develop as it would; "Paul's favorite kind of plans," teased Bette, "no plans.''—to the success of Paul's exhibit to Michael's work as an aide to a senator from Illinois to Bette's arrangement to make her longtime assistant a full partner in Top-Line Temporaries.

"It's ideal. Darla says that with her youngest child going off to college this fall, she wants to go full steam ahead with her career so—"

"But she's too smart to work the kind of hours you were working," interjected Paul.

"Are you saying I wasn't smart?"

"I couldn't ever say that, since you picked me. Let's just say you were in need of some diversion."

"And you are very diverting, Cousin Paul," contributed Tris, catching the peanut he tossed and popping it in her mouth.

"To get back to what I was saying," Bette resumed sternly, but with a smile, "Darla's going to run Top-Line full-time the first few months while I stay home with the baby. After the first of the year, I'll go in a couple days a week, and work from home through the computer linkup Grady's setting up for us." Grady was aware of Leslie glancing at him, but when he looked at her, she'd already turned back to Bette. "That way I can spend more time with the baby."

"Have you decided on names?" asked Michael.

Grady slipped away from the current of the conversation. Was Leslie surprised he knew enough about computers to help Bette set up? Not very flattering. Even less flattering, was she surprised he would help?

He stared at her, and gradually awareness of her discomfort surfaced. Too bad, he thought, tuning in enough to know the talk still centered on the baby. On the creation of a family that Paul and Bette were embarking on.

A family. Paul and Bette having their own family.

A sourness trickled through him. He'd never felt this before. He wondered, dispassionately, if this was what envy felt like. If so, he understood a lot better the bitter expressions of some who'd looked at his money, his looks, his lifestyle. Not a pleasant sensation at all.

Not that he wanted to get married. He wasn't ready. Far from it. Still, to have a family...

He jerked his mind away from the thought. He waited until Leslie looked at him, a faint belligerence in her expression, then he let his eyes trail down her. Throat, curve of her breasts under the cotton shirt, slanted torso as she sat on one hip in order to tuck those long, slender legs to one side. From her bare feet, he started the return journey, noting this time that her right hand clenched the arm of the chair.

When he reached her face again, he saw the expressive brows raised at him, the glint of anger in her eyes, and fought an urge to apologize.

Too bad. He didn't care. Better to focus on sexual flirting—something he knew a damn lot about—than think about other things.

After a swim the next morning, Bette retired to the shade of the porch, proclaiming an itchy sunburn was the last thing she needed. Grady started a ball going among the rest of them. When Paul added a Frisbee, their five-pointed catch became a real challenge, especially when the ball, the Frisbee and a wave converged on one person.

Leslie felt something akin to relief that Grady seemed lighthearted, untroubled by whatever had caused, first, that odd moment on the porch and, later, that provocative survey of her. She'd been lost in her own thoughts—not of the cheeriest variety, either—when she'd caught his look.

It had surprised her. First, because he looked at her the way she would expect a man with his lady-killer reputation to look at a woman. Then a second jolt *because* she was surprised—because it wasn't something she would have expected from *Grady,* no matter what his reputation.

Grady emerged, spluttering and streaming water from his body but triumphantly holding aloft the ball in one hand and Frisbee in the other.

When she stopped laughing, Leslie announced she was going to sit out for a while. "I didn't come to the ocean to spend all my time in the water."

"I'll come with you," Grady declared. "I didn't come here to spend all my time drinking the water."

They slowly made their way to the shallows, pausing to brace for enthusiastic waves that broke around them.

"Here comes one."

Just as Grady spoke his warning, Leslie caught sight of a small boy a few feet in front of them. He didn't look more than five; he seemed to be alone, and he was facing the oncoming waves with eyes wide and mouth open.

"Look out!" she shouted as the wave hit her and rushed on toward the boy.

The boy didn't move, but the man next to her did. Halfway to the boy before the words were out of her mouth, he still couldn't beat the wave.

The force of the water caught the child, pulling him under and dragging him along in its race toward the shore. Leslie pushed her hair out of her face in time to see Grady scoop up the boy before he could be caught in the wave's return trip.

The child came up coughing the water he'd taken in. But in the seconds it took her to reach them, he'd cleared his lungs sufficiently to get down to the serious business of crying.

Grady stood in water now placidly lapping his calves, holding the small body almost gingerly. The boy wasn't as wary. He had his arms wrapped around Grady's neck and held on with all his might.

"Is he all right?"

"I think so. I think he mostly got scrapes from being pulled along the bottom."

Leslie saw angry red marks on the tender skin and several scratches. "That and a huge scare."

"Brian! Oh my God, Brian!"

They looked up to see a man and woman followed by an older boy racing toward them.

"He's all right," Grady said, almost shouting to cover the distance and the panic. "He's all right."

The man reached them first, splashing into the water and skidding to a halt.

"Brian?" The boy lifted his head from where he'd buried it against Grady's shoulder and stretched out his hands to his father without abating his crying.

The woman arrived as they all reached the water's edge. She ran shaking hands over the boy's small body, reassured through touch that he was all right.

The older boy came up, pale faced and anxious. "Is he okay?"

"Yes, he's okay," his mother said firmly.

"We don't know how to thank you—"

The man's words ended in a deep gulp as his wife's eyes filled and spilled over. Grady waved away the need for any words. The man shifted his son's weight to one arm and reached out the other to shake Grady's hand.

"Thank you. You'll never know— Thank you." He swallowed. "C'mon, Brian, let's get you dried out, okay?"

As the family group started off, they heard the older boy say, "He was right there. I only looked away for a minute, Mom, honest!"

The mother hesitated before she said very quietly, "We'll talk about that later, Kevin." But she put an arm around the slumped shoulders of her older son.

Grady stared after them, his face unreadable.

"Grady?"

He didn't blink, he didn't respond, he just watched the family's progress across the wide expanse of sand.

Feeling as if she were prying, Leslie slipped away to where they'd left their towels and sunscreen lotions.

She dried herself, then spread the towel and sat down. A glance told her Grady was no longer where she'd left him. She scanned the beach in the direction the family had gone without any sight of him. In the water, she spotted Tris, Michael and Paul grouped together, but no sign of Grady's golden head. She turned and saw him. Jogging steadily, head bent as if in contemplation of his next footfall, in the opposite direction.

She laid back and wondered what had been going on in Grady Roberts's head when he'd stared after that family.

She wasn't sure how long she'd been lying there, but she was aware of the increasing warmth of her skin. As she turned over, she caught sight of Grady walking back along the water's edge. Beside him was a young woman whose fall of shining brown hair hid more of her model-thin body than her bathing suit did. The young woman had her hand on Grady's arm, and he was looking down at her.

Tucking her own salt-stiffened hair behind her ear, Leslie turned away and rested her cheek on her arm.

"Hey, Leslie, you're starting to get pink."

She opened her eyes to see Tris toweling off and looking over her shoulder toward Grady and his companion.

"Are Paul and Michael still in the water?"

"Yeah, they're swimming laps—as much as you can with the waves coming in. But I've about had it for this afternoon. I want to shower, wash my hair, then sip a tall drink on the porch. How about you?"

"I've about had it, too. Your itinerary sounds great. Let's go."

* * *

"Sometimes I could shoot Grady." Leslie heard Tris's voice, and hesitated before turning the corner that would take her into the kitchen. "He's never going to change."

"Oh, I wouldn't say that."

"You didn't see him, Bette."

"Actually, I did. I saw the whole thing from the porch, and it was the girl who approached him. And it didn't take him long to head back to the rest of you. But by that time you and Leslie were nearly to the house."

Leslie backed up a couple steps, then scuffed loudly along the hall, emerging into the kitchen with a bright, "Hi. What's everyone up to?"

Tris gave her a wide smile. "Getting that drink we talked about and starting to talk about dinner. What do you think of shish kebab?"

"We were talking about Grady," Bette contradicted. "Of course there's one thing you've got to understand about Grady."

Leslie could see Tris consider trying to override Bette, then decide to go full speed ahead. "Yeah," Tris said dryly, "his emotional life's like a firecracker. His relationships start off as if they've been shot out of a cannon, burst into their brief, shining moment, then fade out of sight, leaving only ashes."

"Very nice image, Tris." Leslie knew her light tone was perfect, though it cost her some. "If you're that good I'm going to start having you write your own news releases."

"Oh, no—"

Bette ignored the byplay and said, "I'm not talking about how he's dated in the past. I'm talking about something more basic. Grady has had the disadvantage of being handsome, wealthy, smart and successful."

Leslie fought the truth of that with dry humor. "We should all be so disadvantaged."

But Bette wasn't sidetracked. "What do you think happens when someone like Grady meets people?"

"They look at the package and not the person."

Both Bette and Tris stared, and Leslie deeply regretted the impulsive words. She didn't want them thinking...well, what they both looked as if they were thinking.

Bette recovered first. "Yes. That's exactly what happens. People are so impressed with the outside, they don't bother looking to the inside. I guess for some people that's a blessing. But what happens when a person with a great outside also has an impressive inside? And day after day, year after year, nobody bothers to look for it."

Tris's eyes lost their focus. "That's exactly what it was like in school. All the girls who were crazy about Grady, none of them talked about what a great guy he was, how funny he could be, how nice. They only saw the looks and the charm. God, even me."

She blinked, and looked from Bette to Leslie. "Those years I had the crush on him, I wasn't really looking at Grady. It wasn't until the week we were all together before your wedding, Bette, that I saw him as a person, a friend. No wonder that's when he started keeping in touch."

"That's right. So is it any wonder that he's conducted his relationships the way he has?"

"Oh, now wait a minute, Bette. I think that's going too far. Grady has a short attention span with women. He always has. I don't mean the other might not contribute in a way, but I think it's more an ego thing. That and the old male standby of fear of commitment."

"I've been right before, haven't I, Tris?"

Leslie knew a challenge when she heard it, though she didn't understand this one.

"Yes, but that was different. That was—"

"That was Michael, whom you'd viewed in certain ways for too long to see clearly," Bette interrupted firmly.

"What are you two talking about?" At first she'd been glad to drop out of the conversation, but curiosity could itch like crazy.

"Tell her, Tris."

"Tell me what?"

"It's not anything awful, Leslie. It's just something never told you about that week before Paul and Bette's wedding, the week I realized how I feel about Michael."

"There's a *lot* you never told me about that week, Tris. When you came back you weren't talking at all."

Tris waved off that period of misery. Michael's love had washed it away.

"Bette was the first one who opened my eyes about Michael, to see him the way he is instead of the way I'd gotten in the habit of thinking he was. But—" She spun around to face Bette. "That was Michael. And this is Grady."

"Yes," Bette agreed placidly. "But the question is, who is Grady?"

They hadn't come up with an answer to that one.

They hadn't even had time to try before Grady, Michael and Paul returned, ready for their turns at the showers. Before long all six of them sat on the porch sipping wine coolers Michael had concocted, building up the energy to fix dinner.

"We could go out to eat, you know," said Grady.

"Too crowded," objected Michael. "Saturday night everywhere's packed."

"How about if we just eat cheese and crackers," suggested Tris. "Then all we need is one volunteer to walk all the way back to the kitchen."

In unison the three men moaned as if in the later stages of starvation.

"Okay, let's divide and conquer this project. We need fire in the grill so we can cook, we need the skewers threaded with all those goodies we've got in the fridge and we need a salad and rice. Then we need the table set and the wine poured. Sound about right?''

Everybody murmured agreement with Bette's assessment, happy to let her organize.

"Okay, how about if we divide up into teams. One team gets the fire going, then sets the table and pours the wine. Another team threads the kebabs and cooks them. And the third team makes the salad and cooks the rice.''

"Sounds good," said Grady over the general assent. "Leslie and I will be team one, with the fire and stuff.''

Even if Leslie wanted to object, which would have been making a big deal out of nothing, she didn't have a chance.

"Okay," said Michael. "Tris and I'll do the kebabs.''

"Rice and salad, it is," agreed Paul. "C'mon, Bette, let's get to it.''

A few minutes later, Leslie watched Grady place charcoal briquettes in the bottom of a grill by the back door.

"Here are the matches.''

"Good." He splashed on lighter fluid and lit a match. He didn't pull his hand back from over the grill until long after she would have.

"Hey, be careful!''

"It's all right. You have to start the fire at the bottom or it takes forever to get going.''

"I'm a firm believer in light the match and toss," said Leslie, the vision of those flames so close to his arm uncomfortably vivid. "If the choice is burning your arm like a marshmallow, I'll settle for a slower starting fire.''

He grinned at her. "Nice to know you care.''

"I just don't want to delay dinner by having to take you to the emergency room," she said tartly. "I'm hungry.''

"That's why I went with the quick-starting method.''

She gave him a disapproving look before going to the wooden kitchen steps to sit down. As she sat, she slid her hands under her shorts to smooth them.

"Ow!" She instinctively put the side of her finger to her lips.

"You okay?" He sat next to her and drew her hand down from her mouth, turning it palm up and bringing the side of her index finger close to his face so he could inspect the damage. Stretching her skin between his thumbs he examined it. "You've got a splinter. It's not deep. If I had fingernails, I could pull it out."

"Oh. I better go in and get tweezers— What are you doing?" He'd bent his head over the finger he still held fast. His breath across her palm sent shivers up her arm. "What are you— Oh!"

He released one of his hands from hers, took something from between his teeth and threw it away, then smiled.

"You didn't—?"

"Sure I did. No fingernails, but I do have teeth."

She shook her head, unwilling to acknowledge that her reaction was anything other than amused disbelief.

"Better?"

"Yes, thank you," she said solemnly. She tried to ease out of his light grip, but he didn't release her hand.

"Good. You should be more careful with your hands." Her eyebrows rose at his admonition. Was he kidding?

"You have beautiful hands." He took a hand in each of his and spread them over the warm, soft denim just above his knees. He wasn't kidding. "I remember thinking that the day we went shopping for a housewarming gift for Paul and Bette—that your hands are remarkable. Delicate and capable."

She wished he was kidding.

He rested his hands on hers, his palms warm against the backs of her hands. Then he lightly drew his fingertips from her wrists to her spread fingers, interweaving with them while his thumbs stroked the tender arch between her index finger and thumb.

Sensation centered in her hands, in the few inches from wrist to fingertip that Grady's touches cherished. Every other part of her was left with only the memory—no, the imagination—of sensation. But imagination was plenty.

Unwelcomed and unstoppable came the question of what it would be like to be Grady Roberts's lover, to have all this sensual concentration on areas beyond her hands. Equally unwelcomed and unstoppable came the flashes of images that answered the question.

He released her fingers to stroke the edges of her palms, rhythmically, slowly.

All those women who had enjoyed the full powers of Grady Roberts... for an instant she envied them.

But his stroking touched the sore spot on her finger, and pain brought a return of sanity.

She pulled her hand away.

"Now, Grady," she started in a tone she wouldn't have used to April because the thirteen-year-old would have been insulted to be addressed like a child. She didn't bother to untangle whether it was him or her own feelings she wanted to put firmly in their place. "I know old habits die hard, but that's not the way to treat a friend."

Deep in his blue eyes she thought she read hurt and disappointment—in her. As if he felt she'd misjudged him and he'd been hoping—counting on?—a fairer hearing from her. Could she be that wrong about him, that wrong about his intentions? But if she was...

"I never said anything about friends," he said flatly.

Then he blinked, and what she was coming to think of as the curtain of his charm slid back into place, and her doubts slid away.

He was a man used to getting what he wanted, but not accustomed to wanting anything for long. She would simply point out—in the most reasonable way—the impossibility of their being any more than friends, and eventually—soon—his interest would go on to the next woman.

"It's really the only practical possibility."

"Practical?" His tawny brows quirked.

"Practical." She staunchly stood by the choice with firm repetition. "After all, you live in Chicago and I live in Washington—a thousand miles apart—and that doesn't—"

"Two hours on an airplane. Less. Barely time to read a couple reports and make notes. I know."

She had to take another breath, but she continued with the thought she'd started. "And that doesn't seem likely to change. I certainly intend to keep working for the foundation, and that means living in Washington, so—"

"But I might not continue living in Chicago."

"What?"

The syllable rose too close to a squeak for her dignity's comfort. Grady looked mighty pleased. She brought her voice down to mild interest. "What do you mean?"

"I mean that I have definitely decided to open a branch of my business brokerage in Washington. And I'm going to do it as soon as possible, because the past few weeks have shown me there's even more potential here than I'd thought when I started exploring the idea.

"And with a branch here, I'm going to buy a place because I've spent enough time in hotels to last my lifetime." She heard an underlying bitterness in the last phrase stronger than she would have expected. "I want a home. And if I find the right one, and if the business goes the way I think it will, who knows, I might move my base of operations here. My assistant could keep the Chicago office running fine, because our reputation's already built there. But here where we'd be new..."

He'd spoken almost to himself at the end, gazing off to some future she didn't see. Then his look sharpened as he faced her, and his words turned deliberate. "Yes, I would seriously consider moving to Washington permanently."

"Grady! Leslie!" Tris called from the kitchen. "How's the fire? Ready for cooking?"

"Ready," Grady called back.

Leslie stood and started up the steps. "Table setting time."

But Grady stopped her with a hand on her forearm.

"I am seriously considering a move," he repeated. "So that shoots down your excuse."

"It's not an excuse—"

But her retort lost its impact since he'd already moved ahead of her and was taking the stairs two at a time.

## Chapter Five

Having learned her lesson the night before, when they re
turned to the porch after dinner, Leslie chose a spot at righ
angles to Grady, so there wouldn't be any "accidental"
meeting of eyes.

Stupid, stupid, stupid.

All that did was give him free rein to contemplate he
profile. She could feel his look, feel it as clearly as she had
felt the brush of his arm, the nudge of his knee, the warmtl
of his breath as they had set the table. Set the table and un
settled her, that's what they'd done, as he had brushed and
nudged and warmed.

Well, she vowed inwardly as she outwardly joined in th
talking and joking, tomorrow she would avoid this sort o
scrutiny if she had to sit in the damn attic by herself.

Then the following morning they'd all go home, and tha
would be the end of it. And she would not, absolutely not
entertain any shreds of regret.

\* \* \*

Sunday, Leslie clung to the group like a limpet.

A couple times he tried to maneuver her off by herself, but she foiled the efforts, so he accepted that the day would be spent en masse. From the lazy perusal of the Sunday paper, with much passing back and forth of sections and a joint effort at the crossword puzzle that left in doubt whether six heads were better than one, but definitely proved they produced more erasures. To the afternoon spent enjoying waves and sand that rapidly emptied of crowds trying to beat the traffic back to the city.

For dinner, they decided to drive up the coast to the next town, which boasted several choice restaurants and a compact boardwalk. The night before, both restaurants and boardwalk would have been packed. But Sunday night had a distinctly laid-back air they all enjoyed.

After a leisurely meal, they strolled the boardwalk often lashed by storms but still surviving. They discussed the merits and difficulties of various games of chance and skill in great detail.

When Leslie showed ability at the "shooting gallery"—at least in comparison to the rest of them—Paul had an explanation. "It's because she's from the landed Virginia gentry. Fox hunting, you know. Probably been doing it since she was just out of diapers."

"Fox hunting is done with a horse, not a gun," pointed out Michael while the rest of them laughed.

"Same difference." Paul dismissed it with a wave.

Michael's picks proved particularly unlucky when they all bet on tiny mechanical horses racing under tiny mechanical jockeys around a slotted metal course. Michael's choice invariably came in last.

"Dickinson, this finally explains something to me," Grady said. "I've always wondered why they said a horse was dead last—it's because they look like they're dead."

When Michael withdrew from the ranks of the bettors because he was out of change, Paul chortled, "Wouldn't the tabloids love that—'Senate aide leaves racetrack without a quarter to his name.'"

"Now there's a game I want to try." Tris pointed to a sign advertising Whack-a-Mole.

"How does it work?"

Michael answered Bette while Tris handed over her money. "For a token fee, the player gets a rubber mallet. When the game starts, plastic moles pop up from those holes at random and the player tries to whack them before they disappear again. For each mole whacked you get a point."

"I'm going to mash 'em all," Tris declared.

"Your wife sounds damn bloodthirsty, Dickinson. I'd be careful not to leave any rubber mallets around the house if I were you," advised Grady.

Michael shrugged. "As long as she sticks to moles."

"But, Tris, you're a softy, why do you hate moles?"

"Because they dig up my lawn, and my garden. And they won't go away."

"It's a long-standing feud," Leslie explained to Paul, Bette and Grady. "From the time she bought her row house and started trying to tame that jungle of a yard—"

"A postage stamp," murmured Michael.

"Maybe a postage stamp, but when I started on it, two-thirds of the mole population of the Metropolitan Washington area was concentrated on that postage stamp!"

"Anyhow," resumed Leslie, "every Monday at work we'd hear about her travails with the moles. The square footage they'd dug up, how much work they'd undone, the number of bulbs they'd devoured. So one guy went to the hardware store, got a trap and wrapped it as a present for her."

"Dead moles in traps." Tris shivered and got a sympathetic look from Bette and grins from Paul and Grady.

"And another guy brought in this article about how you could put fresh chewing gum down their holes and the moles would eat it and then they'd die."

"They'd *starve* to death," Tris elaborated. "I didn't want to kill them, I just wanted them to go away. So then Leslie called an agriculture expert and found out that if you got rid of the grubs they eat, they'll go away. So that's what I've been doing. But it takes so darn long, and they tunneled through another corner of the garden this spring and it's so annoying—"

"You're up, lady," called the game attendant.

Tris gave it her all, but she had more enthusiasm than technique and when the game ended the population of plastic moles was none the worse for wear.

"They're crafty critters, aren't they," said Paul, pretending to console his cousin with a shake of his head. "Boy, I'm glad we don't have moles in Illinois." He stopped abruptly. "Do we? I better check with Charlie."

"Oh, no." Bette gave a mock groan. "Grady, do you know what a monster you've created with that gift of landscaping for the house? Any second now I expect Paul to turn into Mr. Greenjeans. He and Charlie get together and they start talking this lingo about friability and sun hours and pH levels and root systems."

"You'll love it when we're done, Bette."

"Yes, dear."

Paul's fake swipe at his wife's bottom turned into a hug.

But Tris's attention hadn't strayed from the game. "Darn! I wanted to get more of those little devils."

"How about you, Michael?" Leslie asked. "That's your yard they're digging up, too. You want to take a whack?"

"Not me. I'm the easygoing type." Tris slanted him a look, and he grinned a little lopsidedly. "Besides, they've been there a long time. I like continuity. My wife says I'm not fond of change. Maybe she's right."

A look passed between Michael and Tris, and Leslie could almost imagine she saw the electrical charge that bridged the four feet between them. She swallowed, not sure if her throat had tightened at the power of their love or at the remainder of a chasm in her life.

Grady stepped forward and swept Tris a deep bow. "I would be honored, milady, if you would allow me to enter the fray and whack in your stead."

Tris assumed a serious expression as she gripped the cuffs of her shorts for an answering curtsy. "I accept your brave offer, Knight Whacker."

Under cover of more flourishes and encouragement from the rest, Grady leaned close to Leslie. "Thursday, Bette said I deserved a knighthood for rescuing her from Whicken. Now Tris. I seem to be everyone's knight in shining armor except yours, Leslie."

She didn't have to answer because just then he was handed a mallet and swept up to the game.

From one side, she watched Tris, Michael, Paul and Bette crowd around Grady, the kidding fast, affectionate and good-humored. They truly were good friends. This was why she enjoyed their company so much. This was what she stood to lose if she were ever foolish enough to let errant thoughts about Grady Roberts lead to foolish actions.

The whoops and hollers of encouragement soon drew a crowd around them as he played a second game, then a third.

From her position, Leslie could see Grady, intent, yet grinning, as well as faces in the half circle behind him. She noticed many of the males first looked faintly contemptuous of Grady's good looks, then gradually impressed by his performance, even jousting a mole with a rubber mallet displayed his strength and agility.

And she noticed the admiration of the females. It was there from the first moment they looked at Grady, and it only deepened. It should have been comforting to have her earlier thought confirmed that she'd reacted to him the way any woman would. It wasn't.

She sighed when a college-age girl wormed her way into the front row by the simple method of pushing Leslie back. The attendant gave her a wary look at the intrusion of his territory, but with space at a premium—and crowds good for business—he didn't object.

From this new vantage point, Leslie looked over the gathering, and something new struck her. Grady was the center of the group, but not really part of it.

He didn't share jokes with the newcomers the way Paul did. He didn't share assessments of his progress toward the grand prize the way Michael did. He seemed to detach himself from the people all around him, focusing solely on his objective. A performer vying for the applause of his audience, yet separate from them.

She thought of her observations of how people reacted to him, and Bette's question of how having people judge only on the outside would eventually affect someone inside.

Another impression struck her with enough force to tighten her throat and sting her eyes. Loneliness. Deep, soul-parching loneliness. A loneliness he hid from himself, as well as others.

The crowd erupted into a roar.

Leslie blinked, adjusting to Grady as he was now. His arms lifted in triumph, a slight sheen of concentration making his face even more appealing, and his eyes zeroed in on her. She shivered with the impact of that look.

"Grand prize," acknowledged the attendant. "You can have the big 'un." He jerked a thumb to a man-size rendering of a mole in shaggy brown plush that suggested the creature was molting. "Or five of your choice."

Calls from the crowd divided equally between the options.

He looked the huge mole up and down, then solemnly told the attendant, "I cannot justify depriving you of such a useful marketing tool. I'll take the five."

He made the choices quickly, and just as quickly distributed each. Something that was either a plush football or a toy mole to Tris. A yellow stuffed rabbit with floppy ears to Bette. A smaller version of the same in green to a lady in the crowd in an even more advanced stage of pregnancy. A lumpy hand puppet of a bucktoothed beaver for a little girl in a stroller.

And finally, a teddy bear no bigger than the palm of his hand. This he slipped into the pocket of his shorts as he stepped back from the game, allowing a tide of others in to try their skill. Separated by the flow of the crowd, Grady looked over the tops of heads to her.

"Can you fight your way out?"

"Sure. I'll meet you over there on the boardwalk."

In two minutes and fifty "excuse me's" she caught up with the rest of the group in animated discussion.

"We're having celebration ice-cream cones, Leslie," Michael said. "Tris and I are going to go get them, so tell us what flavor you want."

"Anything with chocolate and nuts."

"Mmm, sounds wonderful," said Bette. "A great finish to those crab cakes Leslie and Tris convinced me to try."

"So far you've said everything sounds wonderful. You've got to make a choice," said Paul.

"How can I decide without knowing the options? I'm coming with you guys."

"Then I am going, too. Or you'll order something outrageous and keep the baby and me up all night."

Bette turned to Leslie. "You know, I only ate vanilla until I met Paul Monroe, and now all he does is complain about my exotic tastes."

But the look she gave her husband as they started off with Tris and Michael for the ice-cream shop was so full of love that Leslie smiled, despite another clutch of pain deep, deep inside her.

"Here."

She turned back from her own thoughts to find Grady holding out his hand to her.

"I considered the puppet for you—that was one cute beaver—but it would be a shame to hide hands like yours. So I got this guy. I hope you like him."

She looked down to the teddy bear resting in his wide palm. A wise and smiling face looked back up at her.

She shouldn't take it. She'd be much better off without any whimsical teddy bears around to remind her of Grady Roberts. Definitely she shouldn't take it.

"Thank you, Grady, but—" She looked up then. Somewhere under the surface blue of his eyes she thought she saw a shadow of that vast loneliness she'd sensed earlier.

If it had been there at all, it was gone in an instant. Maybe she'd imagined the whole thing. She should still say no thank-you.

"Thank you, Grady. I love him."

Paul and Bette drove back. The rest of them decided to walk. They followed the shoreline, shoes off. Sometimes single file so each could let the waves wash over their feet before pulling back to the dark ocean to their left. Sometimes they walked four abreast as they talked easily.

Eventually Tris and Michael, holding hands, fell back, leaving Grady and Leslie to walk on as a couple.

Whether she liked it or not, he thought with satisfaction.

But he made no effort to break the silence until the lights of their destination glowed in front of them.

"Looks like Tris and Michael will be a while," he said, with a nod of his head back to where two barely visible forms sat on a dune looking out to the water.

"Mmm-hmm," she agreed. "Understandable that they'd want time alone."

An opening like that couldn't be passed up.

"Paul and Bette, too, probably."

"What?"

"They probably want time alone."

Two figures sat close together on the porch swing. No creak reached them over the sound of the waves, but from the movement, the swing was swaying gently.

"How about if we give them some time alone," he suggested, fully aware of producing time alone for another couple, as well. "We can walk to the other side of the house and sit for a while."

"Okay. For a while."

Her easy acceptance surprised him, and put him on guard. So when they found a comfortable natural hollow in the side of a hillock of sand, he was prepared for her opening comment.

"I'm glad we've settled this, so we can be comfortable being friends, Grady."

"We haven't gotten anything settled." He echoed her reasonable, even tone precisely.

She arched her brows at him. "But yesterday—"

"Yesterday you said it was impractical for us to get involved for geographic reasons, and I demolished your argument. So there's no reason—"

"There *are* reasons."

He shook his head. "Face it, Leslie, I'm going to be in Washington a lot. And I'm going to be calling you a lot. And I'm not going to be calling you 'friend.'"

"Well, even if you were going to be in Washington every minute of every day, there's nothing you can do about the fact that I'm older than you. Not even Grady Roberts can do anything about birth dates.''

Smug, that was the only word to describe her expression. She'd been waiting to deliver that line. He had all he could do not to laugh at her. But she apparently read his silence as a triumph for her logic.

''How much older than me are you?'' he finally asked.

''Let's just say I could be your older sister.''

He shook his head. ''That's no good. Lots of women could say that. Let's get down to facts and figures. I'll be thirty-four in October. How old are you?''

''That is not a question to ask a woman.''

''You're going to have a hard time convincing me you're too old for me if you won't tell me how old you are.''

He had a point, and her expression in the soft light of the moon showed that she knew it.

''Let's just say I have wrinkles.''

''Character.''

''And grey hair.''

''Where?''

Defiantly she swept back her hair over her left ear. Against the darker mass he saw strands of silver. Maybe five.

He reached up, gliding his fingertips into her hair, letting his hand graze on the top of her ear. She shivered, trying to hide it by shifting and dropping her hand. But he held her hair back and leaned forward to touch his lips to the exposed skin just behind her ear. Only a touch, but a long, slow one.

''I'll buy you some Clairol.'' His voice carried a trace of huskiness.

She glared at him.

''Are you frowning at the kiss or the comment?''

''Both. You aren't taking me seriously, Grady.''

''Sure I am.''

"We're from different generations."

"Then we've bridged the generation gap because we've spent the whole weekend doing the same things, and enjoying the same things. I haven't noticed you having to make any concessions because of your advanced age."

She studied him a long moment, then apparently reached a decision.

In the tone of one prepared to take extreme measures, she said, "I can remember when the Beatles were on the *Ed Sullivan Show*."

He laughed. He laughed until he dropped back flat on the sand.

"Grady!"

He sat up, but the chuckles still rumbled. "Sorry. Really, I'm sorry. But you made it sound so heinous."

"Well, it proves how much older I am. You probably don't even remember Paul McCartney before he went solo."

"Hardly that, Leslie. But even if I were that much younger than you it wouldn't matter."

"It does matter. It means—"

"Because I've always had a hankering for a Mrs. Robinson sort of character in my life."

"Mrs. Robinson! I said I'm old enough to be your older sister, not your mother!"

"She wasn't Dustin Hoffman's mother."

"Or your girlfriend's mother!"

She tried to look incensed, raising her eyebrows and looking down her nose at him. But she wanted so badly to grin that her mouth trembled.

And looking at her mouth made him want badly, period.

He scooped her to him with one arm before he could think or she could protest. Her lips were cooled by the night air and tasted of salt, lingering ice cream and surprise. But only for a moment. Because then the chemistry, the hormones, the sparks, the whatever she wanted to call it, fired between them, and he tasted on her lips what she must be tasting on his. Desire.

"Two, three years difference doesn't stop us from feeling like this." He'd meant to make the words a smooth persuasion, but they sounded gritty even to him.

"Almost four years, and—" She protested, though her hands rested on his shoulders without pushing him away.

"I don't give a damn, Leslie. This is what's important."

His other arm completed his circle of her as he bent to her mouth. Her lips weren't parted at first, but she didn't resist his invasion. He delved more deeply, feeling his own heart-beat's hammer skip to a harder rhythm. For an instant that was nearly longer than he could bear, she remained absolutely still. Not withdrawing, not responding.

Something much deeper than his pride ached, but he knew he would release her if she remained passive. He would let her go in a second. One more second of tasting her . . .

She made a soft sound in the back of her throat that he *felt,* not just heard. And then she was kissing him back, meeting his tongue, leaning into him, sliding her arms around his neck.

He shifted so he bracketed her between his legs, her back against one of his bent knees, her legs stretched under his other. He needed her closer. He had to have more.

He touched her, tracing the curves and hollows of her body through the soft cotton of her shirt. The straight, clean line of her collarbone, the swelling curve of her breasts. More than flesh and blood and bone, he felt as if he were touching liquid fire briefly transformed to human form. Under his breath, as his mouth followed the descent of her satin throat, he muttered a prayer that she was half as close to drowning in the sensations as he was.

How had he gotten so far so fast? And without any consciousness of the gradual escalations whose timing he prided himself on judging to perfection?

Had he simply vaulted from meeting her lips to near explosion or had the heat of the kisses, of her fingers in his hair, her palms on his cheeks, seared the intermediate steps from his memory?

It didn't matter. *This is what's important.*

Her shirt had ridden up, so they were skin to skin where his arm circled her back, where his hand caressed her midriff. His fingers grazed the silky material at the lower curve of her bra, and he craved much more. With his free hand on her legs, he pulled her tightly against him, the pressure of her hip against him a pain that made him groan with pleasure.

He stroked the long line of her thigh, dipping inside the wide cuff of her shorts. He spread his hand, marveling at the smoothness. But he wanted more. He pushed the shorts up, delving nearer the mysteries Leslie hid.

She made a sound he could almost tell himself was surrender, but an instant later she shifted in his hold, moving infinitesimally away from him.

"Grady—"

He moved with her, following her, taking her mouth, sweeping his hand lower, lower, until his fingertips encountered the silky material of her panties.

But she retreated again, and this time he did not follow. Though he didn't give up her lips until she exerted firm pressure against his shoulders.

"Grady. Stop."

"You really want me to stop, don't you."

"Yes."

He didn't understand her at all. "But you are attracted to me."

Her body had told him that, but he waited for her lips to try to lie.

"You're a very attractive man."

If she'd denied the power between them, he could have proven her wrong. But how could he argue with agreement?

"Then why?"

"Because it wouldn't be right."

"Why not?"

She shook her head a little—he guessed at his stubbornness—but she answered evenly. "Because I don't believe in short-term flings. And even if I did, with both of us being friends with all of them—" Her gesture took in the house behind them. "It could only lead to strained feelings, at best, when it ended."

"What's to say it would have to end?" he demanded boldly. His question must have surprised her less than him, because she answered calmly enough.

"Two things right off. First, we don't have anything in common. And second, your history."

Her voice held no condemnation, yet he felt like a condemned man. He couldn't even claim he was innocent.

He couldn't deny that short-term romances filled his history. When he'd been younger that had made him no different from most of his contemporaries. But now he found most men his age had something deeper with one person, while he still jumped from relationship to relationship. He'd felt vaguely uncomfortable about that for some time. Most often when his friends teased him—because he valued their opinion of him, and he discovered he wasn't particularly proud of this aspect of his life. And lately he'd found the chase so much more of a burden than a pleasure that he hadn't bothered. Though the reputation had lived on.

But never before had it made him feel so shoddy.

He didn't look at Leslie as he stood, brushed the sand from his shorts and extended his hand to her.

"Guess it's time to call it a night."

Good-nights were brief. Only minutes after Leslie and Grady reached the porch, Tris and Michael arrived. Before long, everyone was heading off for bed.

But an hour later she sat on the edge of the bed, staring at a framed print of daisies in an earthenware jar.

She decided to pack.

She'd have time in the morning, but she had time now, too, along with too many thoughts and too many nerve endings still singing a siren's song.

She'd folded everything except her robe and what she'd wear tomorrow and started sorting through her cosmetics bag when she realized she'd left her brush on the porch.

The only way to the porch was through the living room, where Grady slept on the couch.

Her heart started beating more quickly and her breathing grew shallower.

How ridiculous! Afraid to walk through a room because of a man! She resolutely pushed aside the question of whether fear was an accurate description of her reaction.

She put on her robe, allowed herself a deep, steadying breath, then eased open her door. Finding her way through the dark living room, she kept her eyes from the couch.

But opening the front door produced a squeak that jerked her head around to see if it had trumpeted as loudly to the couch's occupant as it did to her.

Moonlight picked out the white of the sheet that draped across his hips and one leg, leaving bare the other leg and his chest. From where she stood, it was entirely possible that he was naked under that sheet.

More important, she reminded herself, he wasn't moving.

She slipped outside and padded barefoot to where she'd left the brush. Back through the open door, with one hand on the knob and one on the frame, she closed it inch by unsqueaking inch. When the door was closed and locked, she released a breath, but she did that quietly, too.

Two steps away from the door she stopped.

She turned back and looked at Grady. His position hadn't changed. But something about him suggested movement. She counted to ten. Nothing. Letting out a breath, she relaxed.

Maybe too much, because that's when it struck her, with the golden body she'd seen being bronzed by the sun now shining silver in the moonlight. Lord, he was an attractive man, with a smoothly sculpted body to match his handsome face. A smile that heated cool blue eyes. A touch that knew how to please a woman. And heaven help her, she was attracted to him, though she'd fudged her answer to him.

Well, of course she was attracted to him. And of course she fudged her answer. She needed distance from him. Even at the cost of producing that bleak expression on his face when she reminded him of his pattern with women. An odd reaction, she thought again; she would have expected a veritable Don Juan to be proud of his conquests.

She shook her head. He was an expert at making himself attractive to women and he had all the raw material to work with. He also was far from stupid. He'd recognize that his reputation wouldn't appeal to her; he couldn't hide it, but he could make her wonder, so his other appeals came through. And she did, and they did. Yes, she was definitely attracted.

Physically.

Lust, that's all. Little case of lust never hurt anybody, as long as you didn't act on it.

*I seem to be everyone's knight in shining armor except yours, Leslie.*

There was his kindness to friends. His humor. His need
for remedial gift-buying lessons. His pleasure in pleasing hi
friends. And, most disconcerting of all, that aura of basic
isolation.

All right, maybe lust was complicated by less clear-cut is
sues.

That didn't change the bottom line. The reasons she'd
told him for remaining strictly friends were as strong as ever
The one she hadn't told him was even stronger.

"You better hurry back, Leslie. Back to the safety of you
room." She jumped at his voice, but he didn't move. As fa
as she could tell he hadn't even opened his eyes. But hi
whisper in the dark was very sure. "And you better do i
fast."

She hesitated, adding another ounce to his discomfort o
lying still and silent under the weight of her regard. Then she
left without a word, without a sound, except, finally, the
click of a door closing down the hallway.

"It wouldn't hurt to lock it, too, Leslie," he whispered
into the shadows that still carried her scent.

With Paul and Bette staying on at the beach a few day
before flying back to Chicago, Grady joined Leslie in Mi
chael's and Tris's car for the return to Washington.

Grady watched Leslie arrange herself in a far corner of the
back seat and turn to watch the scenery out her window
Then he stared unseeing at the view out his. Tris looked
straight ahead, answering Michael's comments with mono
syllables. As thickening traffic required more of his atten
tion, Michael stopped carrying the conversational ball, and
it dropped with a thud.

Grady preferred it that way. He'd had enough of talk i
the past twelve hours. First, that exchange with Leslie las
night. And this morning, Paul.

They'd been alone in the kitchen, drinking the strong black coffee they'd needed to revive on many a morning during college. The only hangover this time, though, was from a night of tossing and turning.

"Leslie Craig's a very nice woman," Paul had started.

"Yeah," he'd said, wondering where this was going.

"Glad you agree. You know, Grady, I've never known you to deliberately hurt anybody. Oh, sure, you've hurt people—by accident, from misreading them, from honest thoughtlessness. I guess we all do that sometimes. But never when you realized that what you were doing could hurt somebody, and especially never somebody nice."

Then the man who had been his friend since they were boys clapped him on the shoulder and walked out of the kitchen, leaving Grady feeling as if he'd been blindsided.

"Let's drop Leslie off first."

Tris's suggestion—an order really—brought Grady's attention back to the present. He didn't know the area well, but he knew that dropping off Leslie, then him before Michael and Tris returned home, would be a roundabout route.

But no one protested. Leslie wasn't transparent enough to look openly relieved when they pulled up in front of her small apartment building, but the tense line of her shoulders eased.

"Thanks for the weekend, it was wonderful." She addressed the car at large. Michael got out to retrieve her bag from the trunk, and Grady started to follow. "No, please don't get out." Their eyes met an instant. "There's no need. Goodbye, Grady, good luck with your business. Tris, I'll see you in the office tomorrow. Thanks again."

The door closed. He heard her exchange goodbyes with Michael, then she was gone.

Michael turned into the hotel's driveway. But before Grady could put his hand on the door handle or marshal words of cheerful farewell, Tris slued around to face him.

"Grady, stop trying to seduce Leslie."

Her distrust was like a slap; the unfairness only added to the sting. He could have tried to seduce Leslie—and probably succeeded—but he had released her. And later, when some sense they didn't have a number for had told him her resistance was weakening, he had warned her to run back to her room.

He said none of this. He stared at the woman who'd been his friend, who'd once idolized him, and said nothing.

"How can you do this, Grady. Another piece of the Grady Roberts legend? You don't need more notches. What are you trying to accomplish? When I introduced you two last fall, I was so happy that two people I love seemed to get along. But now... This isn't right, Grady."

"It's none of your business, Tris."

"Yes, it is my business because Leslie's my friend. And if it weren't for me, you never would have met her. You never would have made her a target for one of your all-out campaigns. The flowers and candy and wine— No, she didn't tell me. She probably thinks I don't know. But I do. And even if I didn't I saw you at the reception and this weekend. Remember, Grady, I've been around you a long time. I know the signs. And I won't stand by and watch you treat her the way you always treat the women you date."

He said nothing, afraid of what he would say if he started.

"Why can't you just leave her alone?"

He shifted but still said nothing.

"Grady, you've always been careful to try to pick women who won't be hurt when you leave, but Leslie's not like that."

"I know that."

"Then how can you do this to her? How can you go after her like any other woman?"

"It's different."

"Different? How? It looks like a standard Grady operation to me, except Leslie's holding out."

"I don't know, Tris," Michael interposed quietly. "I don't remember Grady seeing a woman for as long as he's been seeing Leslie."

As much as Tris had hurt him, Grady was nearly as disconcerted by Michael's thoughtful eyes.

"That's because he's never had a woman resist the way Leslie's resisting. He's not 'seeing' her, he's pursuing her. And only because she hasn't fallen into his lap."

"Tris—" He bit off the words, but couldn't purge the anger from his muscles as he shoved open the car door, or from his tone. "Just back off, Tris."

She leveled a stare at him. "That's exactly what I'm asking you to do. Back off."

He slammed the door behind him and waited impatiently for Michael, moving in his unhurried way, to come around to open the trunk.

When he had his bag, he issued a curt, "Thanks," and started around Michael.

"Grady—" He might have kept going, but a hand on his arm stopped him.

He glared into Michael's unperturbed eyes. "You, too, Dickinson? You want to take a shot, too?"

"Not particularly. But I do want to say something."

"Doesn't everybody?"

Michael ignored that. "We haven't been as close as you and Paul, but I've known you a long time, Grady, so in a lot of ways I think I know you very well. And there's something you said just now that I think you should think about carefully."

"Yeah, what's that?"

"You said it's different."

Grady looked at him without saying anything, not understanding immediately, then not sure he wanted to understand.

"Tris asked how you could go after Leslie like other women you've gone after, and you said, 'It's different.'"

"So?"

"So that could mean one of two things. It could mean you have different feelings about Leslie than you've had about the other women. Or it could mean Leslie's different from those other women. Or it could mean both."

Under Michael's intense look, Grady remained silent.

"I've seen a good number of the women you've dated over the years and I've gotten to know Leslie the past few months, so I can say she is definitely different from your usual choice. About your feelings, well, only you know that, if anybody does. That's what I want you to think about. That's all I had to say. See you later, Grady."

Grady was standing in the driveway when they pulled away.

## Chapter Six

Over the next hectic few days in Chicago, as Grady finalized plans so that operations would roll smoothly while he devoted himself to establishing a D.C. branch, he thought about what Michael had said. He could think about that without the lump in his gut that formed if he let memories of what Paul or Tris had said creep into his consciousness.

At least, he thought about Leslie being different from other women he'd dated. The stuff about his own feelings he decided wasn't worth thinking about. If he was acting different—and God knows Michael was the only one who thought he might be doing that; Paul, Tris and Leslie had told him often enough he was acting right in character—it was simply because Leslie was a different type of woman.

And since she was different, what he needed was a different approach.

Stripped of the standby gifts of flowers, candy, wine, perfume or jewelry, Grady felt naked. But far from defeated.

After all, Leslie might have given him the key herself. What had she told him about finding the right gift for Bette and Paul's housewarming? Think about their lives, think about their likes. Then think about what he could give them that would make them feel good.

So he thought hard about Leslie Craig's life and likes, and when memories of her laughter and her lips intruded, he resolutely pushed them back.

At 2:45 Friday afternoon it hit him. He got his personal assistant started gathering the information he'd need—by fax or express delivery or any other means before he returned to Washington on the next Thursday.

And then he dove back into the work he needed to complete before he could leave, and start a new kind of campaign. To get to know Leslie Craig. Really know her.

The toughest part was getting Leslie in his car.

He'd felt like a maniac lurking around her apartment building Saturday morning, but talking to her phone answering machine wouldn't do. This had to be done face-to-face. So he lurked. And, finally, he was rewarded.

Leslie came around the corner carrying a bag of groceries in one arm and dry cleaning in the other.

In jeans and sneakers, her hair pulling free of the clip at her nape, she looked more like a waif than anyone seeing her professional image would believe. This was the woman from the beach, the one he'd held and desired. He might have preferred a layer of her professional polish between them right now. He felt a lurch in his chest that had to be nerves.

He moved quickly to intercept her, relieving her of the groceries during her moment of frozen surprise.

"Grady. What are you doing here?"

"I'm here to make amends."

"Oh?" The syllable vibrated with wariness and curiosity.

"I told you when I first called that I wanted to get to know you. And then when you gave me the opportunity, I tried to push you into something, uh, different." This was tougher than he'd expected. "So to make amends, I figured since you don't have a car, I could take you places you wouldn't ordinarily get to visit."

"Grady, I don't—"

He pushed on before her "no" solidified. "Starting today. It's a beautiful day. I thought we'd go to Manassas Battlefield. Unless you'd rather see Mount Vernon."

"Manassas?"

"Sure, you know, site of two Civil War battles. Being a Southerner, you probably call them the Battles of Bull Run. It should be a great day to see it. There's a slide show, and park rangers give talks, then we can wander around on our own, really get a feel for the place. But, as I said, we could make it Mount Vernon. Or Gunston Hall or—"

"How do you know about Gunston Hall?"

"Gunston Hall, home of George Mason, Virginia patriot and principal architect of the Bill of Rights. Called by Thomas Jefferson the wisest of his generation. Built Gunston Hall in 1755, down the Potomac River from Mount Vernon," he recited. A grin, partly relief, escaped. "I've been doing my homework."

An answering smile started, but she clamped down on it. "It's a generous offer, Grady, but I have plans this evening, so—"

"So I'll get you back in good time. That probably would make Manassas best. It'll be closer than Gunston Hall and less crowded than Mount Vernon."

"Grady, I really think—"

"Please."

They looked at each other for what felt like three-quarters of an hour, but what he supposed couldn't have been even a minute. But it was enough time to read a flurry of emotions in her hazel eyes, then a growing determination.

He made another try, "It's my way of saying I'm sorry and—"

"That's not necessary, Grady." She reached for her groceries, but he held on.

"I want to say I'm sorry," he repeated, "and that I'd like a second chance—"

"But—"

"On your terms."

That stopped her. "My terms?"

"Yes. Friends."

"Friends?"

He nodded. "Friends. Strictly hands-off friends." He raised his free hand palm out and met her eyes directly. "I mean it, Leslie. I'll try my damnedest."

The multiple colors in her eyes shifted and started to take on a new hue. But before he could read the secrets she hid, she turned her head. His hand started reaching, prepared to cup her chin, to turn her back to him so he could see her eyes.

He let it drop to his side. Hands-off, he'd promised. Strictly hands-off. So if she wanted to contemplate the line of begonias that flanked the apartment building's door, so be it. But he hadn't promised he wouldn't talk.

"You were right that being friends is new to me. I'll need your help to pull it off. But I usually do pull off the things I put my mind to." He said it flatly; fact wasn't bragging. "Give me a chance to show you, Les."

Slowly she brought her eyes back to his face, and he didn't have a clue what would come next.

"I have to be home by four-thirty. And nobody calls me Les."

He bit back the inclination to reply that he'd be happy to all her more. It wouldn't have been an auspicious beginning to his new attitude.

He returned her to the front door of her apartment at :34, but she didn't seem to hold it against him.

By then they both sported sunburns around pale raccoon yes left by sunglasses, and weary legs from tramping over he countryside that witnessed the turning tides of a country and the ebbing lifeblood of thousands of men.

They watched a slide show and map program, then listened to the talk Grady's research had promised. He soon realized the background was for his benefit, not hers.

They took the fruit and bottled water he'd brought to a antage point and he tried to translate the images he'd just bsorbed onto the landscape spread out before him.

Leslie spoke of the first battle—the first full battle of the var—as if she'd been there. July 21, 1861—when Washingonians, led by some of the day's highest and mightiest, rove buggies out to observe a bit of history, though mostly rom five miles or so. When Union troops, panicked by Confederate shelling and rumors of atrocities, reached the nlookers in late afternoon, there was a wholesale flight ack to the capital. Some kept going, thinking the Confederates would march on the city. If Stonewall Jackson had ad his way, they might have tried. But the Confederates ere too exhausted and disorganized to pursue the fleeing Jnion soldiers, much less engage a large reserve force and ross the Potomac.

War returned to the same farmland thirteen months ater—three days in late August 1862 that cost more than our thousand lives.

"It was more a battle," Leslie said, "but it's not as well nown. It gets lost in a series of battles, even though Lee, ackson and Longstreet were here for the South."

"You must have been here a hundred times to know it so well," he said, not sure how he felt about being indulged by her when he'd meant to indulge her with this trip.

"I've never been here before," she said, her face so intent as she looked out at the view that he knew his surprise had succeeded even beyond his greatest hopes. And he experienced the most incredible pleasure.

"But you know all about it."

"I've been reading about it since I could read, and hearing about it even before that. It's family lore, how Grandma Beatrice's grandfather lost an arm at the second battle. And whatever I didn't know before I've learned in the past few years."

He looked the question.

"The battlefield's been under pressure from developers who've wanted to put shopping centers here. The foundation's involved in fighting them off, plus I volunteered on my own. We thought it was safe once, but there are rumblings a new group is set for a second round."

He looked around at the peaceful, undulating land that had carved a spot in history. "Shopping centers!"

She grinned. "My sentiments exactly. C'mon, let's walk it before the fast food and video stores move in."

And walk they did. Following the battles, lingering at spots of human drama they'd learned from the guidebook or ranger. Those were the times it was hardest to resist the temptation to touch her, to push back a strand of hair, to put his arm around her, to hold her hand.

But he pushed temptation aside, and listened instead.

So when they returned to her apartment, he felt both noble for his restraint, and at least partially compensated because she seemed visibly more relaxed around him. Plus, he knew Leslie Craig better than he had when the day started.

"Thank you, Grady, this was a wonderful day."

"Don't thank me yet, this is just the beginning."

"What do you mean?"

"This trip was the first in a continuing series. I told you before—Gunston Hall, Mount Vernon, Leesburg, Fredericksburg, Harpers Ferry—you tell me where you want to go, and we'll go there."

"I didn't know you were such a history fan."

"I'm not. At least, I haven't been before, but today was really interesting." His surprise must have seeped through because Leslie gave him a wry grin. He hadn't expected to enjoy that aspect of the day. "Besides, I figure I should take advantage of the area's history, and you're a great guide," he added honestly. "So it benefits both of us. Isn't that what friendship's supposed to do?"

"I suppose that's one way of seeing it."

Leslie went into the building without succumbing to the urge to check if the sensation skittering down her backbone was because Grady was watching her.

*But let's face it, that's about the only thing you didn't succumb to.*

In the end she'd agreed to another outing the next weekend. He hadn't balked when she'd first said she wasn't sure if she had other plans. He simply offered to call during the week to find out when she'd be free. They'd work around her schedule, he'd said.

Which had made her feel ungracious—to quote Grandma Beatrice's most dire criticism, and yucky—to quote April's all-purpose description.

She grimaced at her pink face in the mirror as she prepared to shower. She was going to look like a scoop of raspberry sherbet for her date with Barry tonight.

If you could call it a date.

Barry Kerken had been a regular escort following his bitter and stressful divorce. About a year ago, nearly healed, he'd indicated he was ready to intensify their relationship.

When he accepted her firmly, gently repeated declarations that that would never happen, they settled into a comfortable friendship of sporadic dinners, lunches and telephone conversations. Several months ago, he'd started talking about a woman he was seeing.

When he'd called and asked Leslie to the theater for tonight, she'd learned Susan was out of town. Leslie expected a lot of tonight's talk would be about Susan.

With the right nudge, Leslie suspected Barry Kerken would propose to his Susan. Standing in her slip, applying light foundation in hopes of toning down her skin, Leslie decided this was a night for nudging.

Her deep sigh as she slipped her silk dress over her head surprised her. She was beginning to sound like April Gareaux, martyred inflection and all.

And there was absolutely no reason. She didn't begrudge Barry to Susan. Barry was one of her successes.

Though others might not understand or approve, her relationships with men like Barry filled a need in her. The need to help, to nurture. To watch someone grow, then to let them go.

"Lapdog," Grandma Beatrice had pronounced on the few Leslie let her meet. "He seems nice enough," her more tactful friends would say. Tris was not among the tactful. "You've got to change your outlook," she'd say. "If a guy's safe enough for you to agree to see him regularly, Leslie, he's too safe to be interesting."

Grady wasn't likely to draw any of those responses. But it did look now as if he was safe enough for her to see. By his own promise, he'd removed himself as a danger.

She was the one who'd recognized Grady needed tutoring in the art of being friends with someone of the opposite sex. She had the experience, and now, after clearing away the confusion of physical attraction between them, she had a willing pupil.

How could she possibly feel anything but pleased?

Some habits form quickly.

By the end of the next weekend, Leslie was in the habit of mapping out trips with Grady and planning her weekend around them. She was also in the habit of relaxing her guard around him. She had no need of a guard because he stuck to his promise faithfully.

That next weekend, they couldn't decide whether to go to Fredericksburg, which offered both Colonial and Civil War history an hour's drive south, or to Gunston Hall. They compromised by going to both—Fredericksburg on Saturday and Gunston Hall on Sunday.

She insisted on being home by six on Saturday, still wary he might try to extend the day into dinner. He didn't, and she felt rather foolish, especially since her deadline meant she had to cut short her exploration of James Monroe's law office. She'd gotten into conversation with a guide who'd been perfectly happy to show her several items too fragile for general display. Because of her deadline, though, they had to leave before she'd gotten to see all there was to see. Talk about hoist on her own petard!

Then she spent the evening at home, restlessly alone.

So Sunday, after they'd toured the spare loveliness of George Mason's home, with an on-site expert showing them renovation research, then enjoyed the peace of sitting above the Potomac amid two-hundred-year-old boxwoods and a resurrected flower garden, she suggested they stop for dinner in Old Town Alexandria.

If it was a test, he passed with flying colors. They ate in a casual seafood restaurant near the water in an area that predated the capital across the river, as easy in conversation or silence as two friends could be.

Still, she'd felt a disinclination earlier that day to have him come up to her apartment, so she'd met him at the street door.

But this Saturday morning, that wasn't to be.

The phone rang as she was stowing a guidebook to Harpers Ferry, West Virginia, into her bag. She considered letting the machine take it, but it might be Grady saying something had come up and the trip was off.

Instead, it was Grandma Beatrice—not a woman to be cut short when she had something to say. And she had a good deal to say.

She buzzed the door open when she heard Grady's voice. By grace of a long cord, she opened the door to his knock and waved him in. She gestured to the phone, shrugged and signaled an invitation to sit.

"I agree," she said into the phone. "It's a bad situation all 'round. And I hate to see it. I had hoped that visit would help, but there wasn't a sign that it—"

Grady straddled a chair, his arms rested on the back, his chin on top of his arms and his eyes on her.

Leslie listened to her grandmother describe signs of improvement in April after her trip to D.C.—faint, perhaps, and not long lasting, but there nonetheless—but every other sense was attuned to Grady. His gaze never wandered.

"In that case, I'll invite her back.... I know I don't have to do it. I want to." She heard the familiar lecture about having her own life to attend to and sidestepped it with the ease of practice. "I know that, too. But I want to do it. I'll check on dates, and call Melly—no, I think I'll call April directly. It should be her decision."

She wrapped up the conversation then, promising to keep her grandmother updated on the possible visit.

"Sorry to keep you waiting, Grady." She gathered her tote bag and sweater, adding, by way of explanation, "My grandmother."

"The one you talk about? Grandma Beatrice?"

"Yes."

"I'd like to meet her."

Looking up from locking the door, she surveyed him, but his expression remained bland. "Not right now you wouldn't. She's on the warpath."

"With you?"

Had she imagined he sounded as if he'd take issue with anyone on the warpath with her? "No, not with me. With my cousin, Melly, and her daughter, April."

"What's their problem?"

She sketched Melly and April's history as they walked down to the street door. "So I'd say April's problem is a case of teenitis drastically compounded by her father's death and the fact that her mother doesn't stay put for more than three weeks at a time."

"That can be tough on a kid."

His voice was almost too bland. As he opened the car door for her, she got a better look at his face, but it told her nothing, except his eyes had that protective veneer.

"Yes, it can."

"Nice of you to try to help out." He paused before closing the door. "Letting the kid decide if she wants to come or not is smart. Shows you understand she's a person."

She wondered if he'd seen only one side of the issue. But he'd shut the door, so she waited until he was in the driver's seat to address the other side.

"I do see that April's a person, and that she has some cause to be unhappy. But I can understand Melly, too. She's always craved adventure and excitement. And April is so sullen. She's not very easy to be around. All she wants to do is sit around all day and watch television." Grady swung his head away from her, as if checking for oncoming traffic, but he didn't pull out of the parking spot. "It's like she tries to be a black cloud, blocking out the sun. And it's such a waste. She's really bright—"

"Maybe that's the problem."

"What do you mean?"

"Sometimes adults don't want kids around who see too much."

Leslie thought about her reaction to April's uncomfortably acute observations when the gourmet basket arrived. The teenager had recognized—and voiced—some issues Leslie hadn't wanted to hear, or to see for herself. Yes, Grady definitely had a point.

"And that kind of kid would be bright enough to pick up on the adults' reactions," she said, thinking out loud.

"Stands to reason."

"So where does that leave them?"

"It probably leaves them two choices. Either the kid stops seeing, or at least stops letting the adults know about it. Or else the kid does let the adults know, and that probably makes the adults real uncomfortable."

Leslie shifted the conversation then by saying how much she was looking forward to seeing Harpers Ferry. It didn't seem fair to take up the whole afternoon with her family's problems.

Grady cooperated, teasing, "You might not have seen it before, but I bet you know all about it."

"As a matter of fact," she answered deadpan, "did you know that Harpers Ferry is where the Potomac and Shenandoah rivers come together, and where the states of West Virginia, Maryland and Virginia come together."

He laughed, and April, Melly and their problems were mentioned no more.

But Leslie wondered about that insight to April, and about the man who'd provided it.

* * *

After a sumptuous lunch the next afternoon at the Red Fox Inn in Middleburg, Virginia, renowned as the heart of hunt country, Grady went along with Leslie's demand to walk through an area that retained vestiges of an eighteenth century village. It was the "brisk" part he objected to.

"Too hot."

"It's not that hot. It's not even out of the mid-nineties."

"That's plenty hot enough to melt this boy from the shores of Lake Michigan, my dear Southern belle."

She kept her mouth straight, but her eyes glinted. It was a very appealing expression, especially with a faint breeze ruffling the wisps that had escaped from the loose way she'd pinned her hair up. The reactions he'd kept a firm clamp on for longer than he cared to think about stirred stubbornly.

"In that case, you can set your own pace," she allowed, "but I intend to leave you in the dust."

"No dust." He shook his head. "If I try to move fast, wherever I go there'll be mud from all the sweat."

Laughing, she walked ahead, leaving him to his more leisurely pace. And to a very lovely view as the pale green skirt of her sundress gently swayed with her movements. The stirring deepened, and he grimly turned away.

He caught a glimpse of something that made him stop, then back up.

There, perfectly framed between not-quite-straight brick exterior walls of two shops, was a building of the same vintage, on the next street. But this building had a split personality—the left side painted in sparkling yellow with every speck of trim highlighted in bright blue, the right side in staid tan with white shutters.

Leslie would love it.

He opened his mouth to call to her and raised his arm to wave her back.

But his arm dropped to his side unwaved and his mouth closed without speaking her name.

He'd made it his business, or at least his pleasure, to know what women would love. Women loved flowers, perfume, jewelry and other indulgent gifts.

Oh, yes, he knew what women, in general, loved. But a specific woman's specific tastes? Never.

Until now.

But he did know Leslie's. He knew exactly what her reaction would be if he showed her this vignette. He knew the expression of her pleasure, in detail and color.

He knew what made her happy. He knew what made her sad. He knew she liked to eat the inside of cake first, saving the frosting for last. He knew she fingered the links of her bracelet watch when she was worried. He knew she sipped her coffee until it was nearly cool, then drank it down. He knew she was loyal and caring. He knew she listened and counseled, but didn't unburden herself to others. He knew how much she gave to others, and how little she allowed them to give back.

He knew she was like no other woman he'd ever known before. No, not "known," because he hadn't really known those women. He'd merely encountered them in brief and intense explosions of interest that left only a rubble of memories. But Leslie he truly knew.

That certainly brought a reaction as varied as the colors that made up her hazel eyes. Besides many he couldn't identify, he recognized a few. A kind of satisfaction—he'd set out to get to know Leslie Craig, and he was succeeding. A warmth he'd always reserved for the small circle that included Paul, his parents and sister, Michael, Tris and more recently Bette. And a restless kind of confusion he didn't like at all.

Because what he didn't know was what to do with his knowledge of Leslie Craig.

He couldn't use it to—what? His mind boggled at filling in a word. Seduce, Tris's term, held a sharpness he didn't like. Woo? An old-fashioned word, and bottom-line, what he meant was as old-fashioned as humanity. But woo included a tangle of implications. Win? That made Leslie sound like a trophy, and at his worst he'd never felt that way about any woman, much less her.

There wasn't a word; there was just a feeling. But even if he could describe it, he couldn't pursue it because he'd promised Leslie.

Use his knowledge of her to deepen their friendship. Sure, but what about the sensations when he looked at her? The recurrent urge to touch her? The dreams he woke from knowing she had visited them—and not as a friend?

He suddenly realized he'd stared at the half-and-half building long enough to draw the attention of passersby. He headed after Leslie, walking fast.

But not fast enough to outstrip the persistent, edgy question in his head: So where was this going? Or the answer: He didn't have a damn clue.

## Chapter Seven

Grady grew uncharacteristically quiet as the afternoon waned. Now, sitting in Sunday-evening returning-to-the-city traffic stopped dead by an accident, Leslie watched him rub a palm across his eyes, then his mouth, as if to wipe away the lines that bracketed them.

The pang she felt should have been guilt; she'd known he was working grueling hours, yet she'd blithely accepted the time he'd devoted to her these past few weeks. But the feeling was softer than guilt, and more disturbing.

"Tired?" She couldn't keep concern from her voice.

He turned to her, and she held her breath.

"I've never worked so hard at making a friend in my life." He leveled a look at her and added evenly, "Or worked so hard at trying to charm a woman."

Honest words that deserved an honest answer.

"I've never been subjected to so much charm in my life." That was honest. Though perhaps not the whole answer.

She'd caught herself wondering now and then if he really had given up any thought of being more than friends. And had thoroughly chastised herself.

She'd said friends, and she meant it. That was all she could be to him. It would be too unfair to let him become more than that to her.

He studied her a long time. When he did speak it was slowly and seriously. "Maybe you haven't let anybody try."

There it was again, that disconcerting perceptiveness of his. That slanting look that seemed to slice to her soul, that seemed to say he saw things hidden even from her. It made her uneasy to be reminded so sharply how much he hid under the surface of his charm, looks and success.

She couldn't pretend that she wasn't sidestepping the implications of what he'd said, but she did it, anyhow.

She tried for wry humor with, "Think you're going to show off your great powers of perception with me as the case study, huh, Roberts?" and got much more of a response than she'd expected.

"Perception? Me?" Grady laughed. "I think you've got the wrong guy in mind. Maybe you're mixing me up with Michael Dickinson. Dark-haired guy, shorter than me, remember him? That must be who you're thinking of."

"No. I mean you."

"I'm not perceptive, ask my friends. Nuances slide right by me. I don't pick up on moods or signals. The only way I catch undercurrents is if they start to drown me."

She looked at him, at his good-natured grin, at his loose-jointed posture, at his open blue eyes, and she realized he truly believed that about himself.

But she didn't.

She'd seen too many examples of his snagging nuances, moods, signals and undercurrents. Not just with her, but with Michael and Tris and Paul and Bette. Even the first time they met seven months ago. Tris had roped Leslie into having dinner with her and Grady, to act as a buffer to keep the conversation from getting too close to her break with Michael. Tris had done an excellent job of hiding her unhappiness, but she hadn't fooled Grady. That had been clear to Leslie, even as a stranger to him.

Now she knew him, but she had no idea why he might deny his ability to sense other people's feelings.

*Sometimes adults don't want kids around who see too much.*

His own words provided the clue.

"What about your parents?"

"What about them?"

If she'd had any doubt, it ended with those terse words. His insight to April came from firsthand experience.

"Are they perceptive people?"

"No." He turned his head to look out the side window, so his next words were muffled. "But then we're not close, so maybe I don't know them well enough to say."

She waited for him to explain, but when he shifted in the seat before facing her again, she knew it wouldn't be that easy.

He grinned, his eyes veiled. "Besides, how would I know, since I'm not perceptive myself."

"You say you're not close, do you see them often?"

"Now? Hardly ever."

It seemed incredible to her, but his words invited the question. "And when you were growing up?"

"Before I started school, they'd take me along most trips."

She remembered snuggling in blankets in the back seat with her older brother while her parents drove through the night to family vacation destinations; she didn't think Grady was talking about the same thing.

"What sort of places?"

"London, Paris, Rome, Hong Kong, Honolulu, the Riviera. The Riviera a lot. They liked it there."

He hadn't. "Do they travel for business or pleasure?"

"Both, I guess. My father's an international business consultant. But I don't know how seriously he takes it. He and my mother have always liked the travel and glitter. He doesn't need to take it seriously. My great-grandfather made enough on the patent for a tool prototype they're still using so none of us have to work."

But he did work, and he did take it seriously. And she knew without a doubt it wasn't the travel or the glitter that made him do both.

"What happened when you started school?" She kept her voice quiet, the questions not too interested, aware how close he was to answering no more.

He shrugged. "I stayed home."

*I,* not *we.* "It must have been an adjustment."

Another shrug. "Not really. Staying with a nanny in a hotel or staying with a nanny at the house—it wasn't that different."

Leslie's hands clenched at her side, in pain and anger. Pain for the little boy Grady had been. And anger for his parents. What was wrong with these people? They'd been given the greatest gift possible, a child to love and cherish. And they hadn't seen beyond their own selfish pleasures. Not seeing, or not caring, that they were starving their child of love. Not seeing, or not caring, that behind the good looks, easy charm and business success, the man he'd become was lonely and vulnerable.

Carefully she stripped emotion from her voice. "So was that when you met Paul, when you started school?"

"Not right off. Let's see." He narrowed his eyes to look into the past, clearly more comfortable with these memories. "I remember Judi being born and Paul's eleven years older, so we must have been right around eleven."

"So you've known all the Monroes a long time."

"Yeah. I spent most summers with them, and a lot of vacations." She heard a lot of things he didn't say—that his parents came and went in his life, but the Monroes stayed. That what he knew of family life and a family's love came from the Monroes. His fond smile grew wry, and anger and pain surged through her again. "I used to hope my parents would be away for Christmas so I could be with the Monroes. At that age I preferred Mrs. M.'s cookies to any four-star restaurants at Kitzbühel or St. Moritz."

She saw his discomfort with the conversation's seriousness, heard it in his lighter tone.

"Lousy skier, huh?" she tried teasing.

"Damn good, actually—"

"Modest, too—"

"But they frown on night skiing, the parties weren't for kids and old TV shows dubbed in German weren't too entertaining."

With no inclination to tease now, Leslie remembered from their first Smithsonian outing how Grady had spoken of old movies as if they were old friends. Perhaps his first friends. His reaction to her remark about April watching TV also made sense. Was it another area where he'd had special insight into the girl, because he, too, had escaped an unhappy situation as a youngster through that medium?

"About time." Grady's mutter pulled Leslie's thoughts back. At the crest of the hill in the distance, the brake lights of the cars flickered off, on, then off again. "It's finally opening up. Probably will be slow going, but I should have you home before too long."

Grady's discomfort was almost palpable. She'd seen the phenomenon before—people who'd confided more than they'd meant to want nothing more than to be away from their confidante. He was probably regretting that they'd arranged to spend Tuesday afternoon together on a visit to Mount Vernon, just down the Potomac from Washington.

At first, seeing Grady, so confident and at ease in social situations, reacting this way seemed incongruous.

The incongruity disappeared when she considered his life.

Not only didn't he know how to be friends with a woman, he didn't know a lot about being close with people, period. Because he hadn't been taught by the people who should have been closest to him.

Most people he'd encountered had been so dazzled by his exterior, they never bothered to look inside. She'd seen that for herself—at the wedding, at the Smithsonian reception, at the boardwalk. So he'd come to believe that what he thought, felt—what he *was*—didn't have value.

Grady needed more than a few lessons in being friends with the opposite sex. He needed to learn his tremendous value. More than anything, Leslie wanted to help Grady Roberts see the good in himself.

For the first time, Grady had been almost glad to drop off Leslie.

He'd talked too damn much.

Maybe he needed a break.

He left the car with the hotel valet and picked up his written messages from the front desk with an automatic smile for the young woman before taking the elevator to his room.

Maybe he'd just gotten stale. Working long hours every day, then seeing only Leslie. Not even Tris and Michael. Under the circumstances he hadn't wanted to invite any lectures from Tris or questions from Michael.

But that didn't mean he couldn't see someone else.

He knew other women in Washington. A woman with the commercial real estate firm he'd hired to locate an office had made it clear she'd enjoy his company, no strings attached.

Probably just what he needed. Time with someone new. He wouldn't have a clue how she ate her cake and she wouldn't get solemn over his childhood. She'd seemed perfectly content to take him at face value—making it clear she enjoyed both the face and the net asset value.

He'd know exactly where he was with her. No different approach required. No uneasy feeling, no uncomfortable questions.

He pulled out his appointment book, looking for the slip of paper she'd given him.

What was her name? Suzi Boyd, that was it.

Grady grimaced. Paul was always teasing him that all the women he dated had names that ended in *i*. The joke had gone flat lately.

A fluke, but his past of Randis, Melodis, Kerris, Tammis and Barbis symbolized dating women who had more in common than the way they spelled their names. *No strings.*

He looked at the name and number on the piece of paper, but he didn't reach for the phone.

All right, maybe he wasn't in the mood to see Suzi Boyd. There were other women.

But he didn't look through his book. He sat in the chair and stared out the window at the same flag of the same embassy he'd looked at while he left a message on Leslie's machine that first weekend. He should find out what country that was.

He could ask Leslie. She'd love the tiny challenge. She'd probably march right over there, knock on the door and ask. And in under a minute she'd be invited in and made an honorary citizen.

When he realized he was smiling, he didn't try to erase it with a frown, but accepted it.

Maybe he hadn't talked too much. Maybe he'd just talked about the wrong things this afternoon. He didn't usually talk about those things to women. To anybody. But as she'd pointed out, he was tired. And he'd spent so much time around her, it had been easy to let things slip.

He did need a break. He looked at his book next to the pile of messages, then away. He wasn't in the mood to see other women right now. But there were other ways to get a break.

He could go to Chicago. His assistant said the Burroughs deal seemed to be coming to a boil. And he'd promised Jasper Burroughs he'd see the sale of the Burroughs candy company through its final stages in person.

He looked at his appointment book, thinking about calling for a plane reservation, without much enthusiasm, and the top message slip on his stack caught his eye. Carol Drew had called.

Before he could think about it—lately he'd been thinking too much, along with talking too much—he dialed the number. He was put through to Carol Drew's car phone, got an update and made an appointment with her for Tuesday afternoon. He hung up grinning.

Perfect. He'd cancel the plans with Leslie, get the breathing space he needed and do some serious house hunting. And nobody could lump Carol Drew with his past women— she had a wallet full of grandchildren photos, a tendency to call him "dear" and wonder if he'd eat right living alone, and no *i*.

He immediately dialed Leslie's number.

"Something's come up, Leslie. I won't be able to take you to Mount Vernon Tuesday."

"Okay."

"I'm sorry."

"It's all right, Grady, I understand."

He wished he did. Why'd he feel as if he was depriving himself of what he wanted when he was just giving himself room?

"It's just I know you got the afternoon off work and—"

"Grady, it's all right. Really. I know how hard you've been working. And with everything you need to do in expanding your business I'm surprised you've had any time to chauffeur me around the countryside. I should be apologizing to you for taking advantage of your generosity—" He made an inarticulate sound of protest, but she kept going. "And don't worry about my taking the afternoon off work. They've been after me to whittle down my vacation time."

"Good, then you can take Wednesday afternoon off, and we'll go to Mount Vernon then," he heard himself say. "And don't make any other plans for the weekend. I have something special planned."

"The whole weekend? I don't—"

"The whole weekend," he repeated firmly. "And no, I won't tell you more because it would ruin the surprise. You'll just have to trust me."

At the end he could tell she wasn't entirely convinced, but she agreed. And he'd been so busy getting her that far that it wasn't until after he'd hung up that he realized that for someone who'd wanted a break, he'd not only traded one afternoon together for the next afternoon, but had put a lot of effort into making sure they'd be together for the weekend.

He knew they both knew the trust he'd asked for involved more than having a fun weekend.

He talked too damn much.


Through her open office door, Leslie could see Grady leaning against the doorjamb of the waiting room. Considering it was nearly half an hour after the time she'd said she'd be ready to leave, he looked remarkably patient. Still she felt a sense of urgency as she finished reading over the draft of a program announcement the education director had brought in for her to review.

From the corner of her eye, she saw Grady stiffening.

"Grady? What are you—?" Tris's voice cut off abruptly. From the hallway outside Leslie's office, she looked from Grady to Leslie, and back.

"Tris." Grady's nod was nearly as stiff as the one-word greeting.

"How are you, Grady?" Tris didn't sound too limber herself.

"Fine. You and Michael?"

"Fine, thank you. Uh, well, I better get going."

"Okay. See you later."

"Yeah. See you later."

Leslie waited until they were in Grady's car, crossing Memorial Bridge to pick up the George Washington Parkway on the way to Mount Vernon before she asked the question.

"What was that all about?"

"Hmm?"

"Don't give me that vague noise. I want to know what that was about with you and Tris."

"Tris?"

"Yes, Tris. Tris Donlin Dickinson, the woman you've known for more than a dozen years. Remember her? She married one of your best friends. You were in their wedding. Two months ago. Though you two sounded like people who weren't real sure you knew each other well enough to say hello. So, I repeat, what was that all about?"

He slanted a look at her, and his eyes were guarded. She stared at him insistently. He sighed.

"It's no big deal, Leslie." His tone was very good, but she didn't believe him. "Tris doesn't approve of my, uh, spending so much time with you. She seems to think I'll be a bad influence on you."

"I see." And she did, and it made her want to wrap her arms around the strong, golden-haired man next to her, and never let anyone hurt him ever again, including a woman who was a dear friend of his and hers.

Teaching Grady Roberts lessons in friendships was becoming a dangerous proposition.

Shortly before noon Saturday, Grady stepped from Washington's hazy heat, already intense enough to grill the unsuspecting, into the protection of the air-conditioned vestibule of Leslie's apartment building and pressed the button above her name.

The answering buzz mildly surprised him. Only that once when she'd been on the telephone with her grandmother had he been up to her apartment.

Upstairs, she met him at the door.

"You had a phone call from your office. They asked you to call back as soon as possible. Said it was the Burroughs account."

She gestured him toward the phone.

"Damn. It's been brewing for a while, but I thought... Well, this could take a while. I can go back to the hotel and come back when I've cleared it up."

"No need. But if you use the bedroom phone, I can run the dishwasher and do some other things in here. Okay?"

More than okay. Being in her bedroom might trigger reactions that were less than comfortable to ignore, but he'd trade that for the potential information to be gained.

While he punched in the numbers of his calling card, he looked from the rocking chair with the sweater draped on the back to the peach, green and white quilt-covered bed to the slice of the moderately neat walk-in closet visible through the partly opened door.

On the mellow wooden surface of a long bureau, he saw a grove of framed photographs. More pictures were sprinkled in front of volumes that packed a ceiling-high bookcase. He scanned the titles, noting a heavy leaning toward history, plus classics, romantic suspense and mystery. On an eye-level shelf, the teddy bear he'd given her at the beach listed against the *Man in the Iron Mask*. As his call went through, he picked up one picture showing a strong-featured woman with gray hair and eyes that promised both humor and strength. Grandma Beatrice, he thought.

Before he could examine other individual faces, or try to match the children of yesterday with the adults of today, much less separate friends from family, his assistant in Chicago answered and delivered the news that the Burroughs deal had hit a snag. The potential buyers were bickering among themselves, threatening the whole deal.

Grady's attention zeroed in on the problem. He'd worked too hard and too long on selling Jasper Burroughs's business not to try his damnedest to untangle the snag. It took nearly an hour, but he was satisfied when he hung up that if the potential buyers could be brought around, they would be satisfied.

Tempted to continue exploring Leslie's room, he heard her coming down the hall. So, instead, he hurried her out the door, into the car and on the road to his surprise.

"Have any plans for the Fourth of July?" he asked.

She gave him a mock-suspicious look. "You're planning on taking me to Philadelphia to view the Liberty Bell?"

He laughed. "I thought something closer to home. I hear there's quite a celebration on the Mall. People picnicking, then a concert, then watching the fireworks."

He knew it was a gamble. All their other outings had carried the excuse that he was providing transportation she didn't have. That didn't apply here, and her silence made that uncomfortably clear.

"On one condition," she finally said, and his shoulders eased. Conditions he could deal with. "You let me treat you to the picnic on the Mall."

"But—"

"That's the condition, Grady," she said sternly. "It's small thanks for all this. Take it or leave it."

He sighed as if she'd backed him into a corner. "I'll take it."

"Good. Then it's settled. Now isn't it time you told me where we're going?" she asked as they headed west along I-66.

"Nope."

She grumbled good-naturedly, and he was certain she was intrigued.

That changed abruptly when they turned south on Route 29. It was as if her mood also changed direction.

She sat straighter, looking intently at the road signs. Her feet were flat on the car floor, her knees together and her shoulders rigid when she faced him.

"Where are we going?"

"It's a surprise."

"Grady..." The word packed a load of wariness. He glanced at her, and she smiled, probably hoping he'd believe she was kidding. He didn't. The smile was as stiff as her posture. "Some people don't like surprises."

But she wasn't one of them. That was something else he knew about her. She'd liked the idea of a surprise just fine until they turned toward Charlottesville. She clearly was familiar with the road, and just as clearly she didn't like being on it. Was there something in the seventy miles between here and Charlottesville that made her react that way? Or was it her hometown itself? But why on earth would she be so reluctant to go there? It wasn't as if she was estranged from her family.

"All right, here's a hint. First we're going to the home of a man famous for what he wrote and the offices he held, but whose favorite role was gentleman farmer."

"Monticello." His heart sank at her hollow tone.

"You don't like Thomas Jefferson's house?"

"Oh, I do like it," she said quickly. "It's a beautiful spot. And it's fascinating. Really gives you a sense of the man, and the times."

"Good," he said, pretending he had no cause for disappointment at her reaction to his surprise. "Then I thought we could look around the University of Virginia at the part Jefferson designed. We have dinner reservations at a historic inn and rooms for overnight so tomorrow we can get an early start on seeing Ash Lawn, because I read Jefferson's supposed to have helped design that for Monroe. Then we'll finish with Madison's Montpelier."

She was silent.

"Unless you have a dislike of Jefferson and everything associated with him that you haven't confided in me."

"Oh, no," she said. He believed that.

Grady let her words about Jefferson's wide-ranging interests and ingenuity slide past and tried to interpret the tone. She meant what she was saying, but it was a smokescreen. A cover-up for her inexplicable discomfort.

It wasn't with him, because she'd been fine when they started the trip. It wasn't because she had no interest in Jefferson. *Charlottesville.* He kept coming back to that.

"You know," she started with studied casualness that made him instantly alert. "As long as we're this close it would be a shame not to give you a better view of the Blue Ridge Mountains. Skyline Drive's not far west of here."

And Charlottesville wasn't far south. He recognized delaying tactics. He could confront her, and risk her clamming up. Or he could go along, and hope that if she didn't open up, she at least let inadvertent clues slip.

"Sounds good. There's a map in the glove compartment. You can navigate."

It wasn't her fault the sky's floodgates had opened to dump an ocean's worth of water on them.

It probably would have happened even if they'd kept on the main road to Charlottesville. But the fact that she'd directed them on to roads that couldn't be considered "main" by any stretch of the imagination didn't help.

With the wipers going full speed and the car barely going at all, they still only got glimpses of the road ahead. Everything was so waterlogged it was difficult to distinguish where the narrow roadway ended and the dark vegetation lining it started.

She'd had them twisting and turning on back roads for a couple of hours. They had seen some pretty country. And she'd bought herself more time with impulsive requests that he pull over so she could explore first a country store, then a display of handmade quilts.

Time was what she needed. Time to adjust to the idea of visiting her hometown, with all its associations and memories. The idea of returning to UVA's campus, where she'd received Frank's marriage proposal. Returning to Monticello, where she'd told him they were expecting a baby. Of almost certainly passing the main intersection where the car accident had taken her unborn baby—and so much else— from her. Of running the risk that the inn Grady had chosen was the one where Frank and his second wife had celebrated the christening of two children since then.

She'd faced these ghosts before. It wasn't as though she hadn't been back at all since she'd moved to Washington— fled, her grandmother accused her—a decade ago. She had been back. Twice. Each trip carefully planned and emotionally prepared for.

But this time there's been no time, because of Grady. Grady....

She looked over at him, concentrated and intense, but his driving as confident as ever.

It was just the unexpected prospect of going back to her hometown that had her on edge. It had nothing to do with revisiting those scenes with this particular man.

From his speculative looks and a few leading questions she hadn't answered, she suspected he'd sensed her reactions. But he hadn't protested when she directed him into time-consuming byways under the guise of "exploring."

He hadn't even complained that she had them on a road the map didn't show when, after a preliminary rumble of thunder, the rain gushed down. But she felt responsible.

"Maybe we should pull over."

"Nervous?" Under the neutral word, she thought his question had an edge that applied to more than the weather.

"It's getting pretty bad, Grady."

He said nothing, but his brows drew tighter. From displeasure or concentration?

Nerves and humidity condensed into a chill down her back as they crept along. The dashboard clock said twenty minutes passed, but it felt so much longer she wondered if the storm had affected that, too.

A dip in the road gathered standing water into a mini-lake. Grady slowed to a steady crawl to ford it. That was the only reason Leslie saw the sign, a flash in the instant's clarity after each swipe of the wiper blades.

She waited until they'd reached relatively firmer ground— here the water sheeted across the road instead of swirling like a tidal pool—before saying, "There's an inn up ahead. The sign says a mile, on the right."

He said nothing, but when they reached the turnoff indicated by a sign that probably was white with bright blue lettering when it wasn't seen through a gray gauze of driving rain, he eased even slower and turned the wheel.

He swore, not with full volume but with plenty of feeling.

The car seemed to slip sideways, as if determined to keep going straight.

"What is it?"

"Power steering's gone," he muttered. The muscle in his forearms tightened as he wrestled the wheel around, steering from another kind of power.

A drive, blessedly straight, ended in a paved rectangle with a half dozen or so cars. Beyond stood a solid two-story farmhouse, built to accommodate an era when families and furniture were big. It wouldn't be as posh as the accommodations Grady'd arranged in Charlottesville, but Leslie found it much more appealing at the moment.

Grady brought the car to a stop, flipped off the lights, wipers and engine and clasped the top of the wheel with both hands as he turned to her.

He looked tired, but his eyes glittered a little. Perhaps with the challenge of battling the elements.

"Ready for a bath, or you want to sit it out here?"

"We might end up floating it out if we stay here, so I'll take my chances on a bath."

"Okay." He twisted to lean over the seat to reach their bags. The rolled-back sleeve of his shirt brushed along her arm, leaving goose bumps in its wake. "You want to try to protect yourself from the rain?"

She shook her head, her voice momentarily unreliable. Taking her bag from him so he could grab his own, she swallowed and said in a moderately normal tone, "There's no way to avoid getting soaked in a gully washer like this, so it's best to save the dry clothes for when we get inside and can change."

"Shoes, too?" He nodded to where she was unstrapping her sandals.

"Definitely shoes, too."

She put hers inside the bag, slipped her bracelet watch off her arm and inside a pocket.

He grinned, and she grinned back, exhilaration replacing the tension of those final minutes on the road, and a warm glow of affection covering feelings less comfortable to consider.

"Ready?"

"Ready."

The doors sprung open, slamming closed behind them as they sprinted through the dousing rain. The water was chilled, but couldn't defeat the accumulated heat of the past few weeks, so the air steamed around them. They zigzagged around parked cars, meeting where a curved path of paving stones led from the parking to the front steps.

"C'mon!"

Grady grabbed her hand and kept her sprinting through rain so thick it seemed like solid matter instead of liquid. Panting and laughing, they splashed barefoot up the wooden steps and skidded to a halt in the relative protection of the two-story porch's deep overhang.

"More towels, Marty!" The screened door opened to a woman whose short brown-and-gray hair curled tightly all around her face. She shook her head at them, but smiled warmly. "Two more drowned rats on the doorstep. Towels'll be here in a shake."

Thanks and exclamations on the weather were interrupted by the arrival of a thin, middle-aged man with a fringe of straight black hair around a balding dome and an armful of fluffy green towels. The woman's introductions were hurried.

"I'm Karen Tanner, and this is my husband, Marty. Welcome to Tanner's Inn. I see you were smart enough to bring a change of clothes. Soon as you dry off enough so you don't leave a river on the wood floors, you can take turns in the powder room down the hall. We'll be serving dinner in an hour or so. We usually have menu choices, but we've got such a full house, it's family style tonight."

"It sounds wonderful," Leslie said gratefully.

Grady flashed her a look, but said nothing. Surely he couldn't mean for them to go on now, she thought as Karen Tanner, talking all the while, led her through two antique-filled parlors and a hallway to the powder room.

Before too long, she was sitting on a cushioned glider watching the power of the storm from the protection of the deeply recessed porch and contemplating the wonder of being dry, off the road and in possession of a glass of fine Virginia chardonnay wine. That's how Grady found her.

He stood a moment, looking out through the porch's screen at the rain lashing the ground in a straight torrent, and Leslie found herself studying him.

His skin showed bronze against the white of his shirt at the collar and rolled-back sleeves. His legs looked long and lean in trim jeans. Light from the room behind them streamed through the window, making his hair, still sleeked to his skull, gleam like something collectors would covet. Lamplight carved his profile as perfect angles and curves against the deepening dark of the storm blending into night.

"It has to let up some time," he said, then looked at her as if gauging if she were prepared for that eventuality.

She wasn't. Why was he so all-fired set on getting to Charlottesville?

"But you said the steering . . ."

She couldn't see his face well in the shadow, but he was shaking his head. "Temporary. Must have gotten wet from going through all that standing water."

"It's not likely to dry out in this."

"It's not the rain coming down that messes it up, it's the water coming up from underneath."

She tried a different tack. "I'm hungry."

She had the impression he smiled. "Me, too. We'll see how it's steering after dinner."

"Mmm." She made a noncommittal noise. "Want some wine?"

"Sure." He accepted the glass Karen Tanner had left for him, and sat down beside Leslie.

They didn't touch, not the slightest brush of fabric on fabric, but she could feel the warmth of his body next to her. Without any need for conversation, they sat in the growing dark, watching the storm, gently rocking the glider and sipping their wine.

And for no reason at all, Leslie was reminded of what a dangerous man Grady Roberts could be.

Along with dessert, Karen Tanner brought the news that flash flooding had hit the district, with rain-glutted streams washing out two bridges and covering several stretches of road.

The family-style meal she'd promised was delicious, though not quite as family style as Leslie expected. Besides a large table in the middle of the room, there were three tables for two set around the corners. Marty Tanner had seated a young couple whose abstracted manner screamed honeymooners at one of those tables, a silver-haired couple who held hands across the table at another and escorted Grady and Leslie to the third.

She cast a quick glance at the jumble of people at the main table but, meeting Grady's look of blended amusement and challenge, didn't say anything.

Instead, she'd devoted herself to making their conversation lively, interesting, humorous . . . and as far from her reaction to the prospects of going to Charlottesville as humanly possible until Karen Tanner's news.

"So we can't go on," Leslie said to Grady. No relief, no triumph, leaked through in her voice. "It would be foolhardy."

He raised one eyebrow at her. "Equally foolhardy to go back, then."

What an idiot! She'd been so focused on not wanting to go to Charlottesville, she hadn't thought this out. Worse, she had the sudden impression geography wasn't the only issue in this conversation of going on and going back.

She broke the look, mildly surprised to find chocolate cake blanketed with raspberry sauce sitting in front of her. She'd forgotten about dessert, and she'd forgotten about the woman who'd brought it. But Karen still stood next to the table, watching them with unabashed interest.

"Guess we'll have to stay," Grady said evenly. "If you can put us up for the night, Karen."

"Well, we can, but... It's a shame the small cottage by the stream's already taken by that couple." She gestured to the honeymooners, and Leslie shifted uneasily that this sharp-eyed woman put her and Grady in that category. "It's lovely, if I do say so myself. And it's very private. But with the weather, we've only got one room left, and it's a single. It's got a private bath, but just the one bed—a twin."

"Oh."

Leslie was aware of the woman looking from her to Grady, and wondered what she read in their faces—but not enough to meet the woman's eyes or look at Grady herself.

"There's a couch in the room," the woman added. "Good sized, too. It was our son's room before he went in the air force. We only use it for emergencies like this."

"Thank you. We'll take the room."

Grady sounded as unflappable as he had on the phone with his office this morning. She hadn't listened, and she'd tried not to hear, yet she couldn't miss the calm tenor of his response to a situation that clearly had rattled the man who'd called.

It was a timely reminder of another facet of Grady. He'd shown her the lighthearted charmer from the first. Lately he'd been a relaxed friend, the person she suspected not many beyond the Paul-Bette-Michael-Tris group saw. And she'd caught glimpses of another layer beneath that, carrying vestiges of a lonely child.

In all of this, though, she mustn't forget that Grady had made himself a very successful businessman, accustomed to complex negotiations that transferred whole businesses and were worth thousands—*millions* of dollars. That did not happen by accident; it derived from strength, intelligence and determination.

He'd be a valuable ally. Or a formidable opponent.

"Good. I'd really hate to think of anybody trying to get around out there tonight." Karen Tanner moved off, leaving a silence unfilled by the drumming of the rain.

"Grady—"

"I said we'd take the room, Leslie. I didn't say we'd share it. I can sleep down here somewhere. But it would be stupid to risk driving strange roads on a night like this. It would—"

"It *would* be stupid to risk driving unfamiliar roads on a night like this," she interrupted, surprising him, judging by the way his head jerked up. "I was going to say I thought it was a good idea to take the room. As for your sleeping down here," she continued briskly, with a thought to the antique furniture's deficiencies in both padding and length, "it's silly to waste a perfectly comfortable couch."

His blue eyes studied her a long moment, stretching her ability to return the look with total blandness.

"Okay." She released a breath at his acceptance, her lips curving as he continued, "If the couch is under six feet, you get it. If it's over, we'll toss for it."

## Chapter Eight

"It looks comfortable enough." Leslie bounced the sofa cushions with her hand.

"Safe for you to say, it's over six feet long."

She grinned at his morose tone. This would work out fine. The room was long and narrow, with the single bed in one corner and the sofa at the opposite end, facing French doors that opened to a small deck and with its back to the bed. For being in the same room, they were as private and as far apart as possible.

On top of that, Grady had been casual almost to the point of offhandedness about the situation.

And best of all, they weren't in Charlottesville.

"Have a seat," he invited. "Unless you're tired and want to go right to bed."

She groaned. "If I went to bed after that huge meal, I think I'd sink through the mattress to the floor."

They'd lingered over their coffee so long that they'd been the only ones left in the dining room. To make amends for keeping Karen and Marty so late, they'd insisted on helping with the dishes and ended up hearing all about the inn's history. Two hours later the four of them had been sitting around the kitchen table, enjoying a nightcap poured by Marty and a "sliver" of cake insisted on by Karen.

For an instant after Karen used the word, Leslie met Grady's eyes and allowed herself to recall that moment on the back steps of the beach house, the sensations of his strong hands holding hers, his teeth and lips, his touch.

Then Marty started an anecdote about the great-aunt who'd willed him the inn, and Leslie escaped the memory.

That had been the only lapse, and it had been hers, not his. So there could be no harm in talking for a little longer. Besides, there were things she wanted to know.

"Unless you're too tired," she offered out of fairness. "You were the one doing all that driving."

"Tired, yes. Sleepy, no." He sat, slipping off his shoes, then stretching his long legs across the scarred coffee table. "So have a seat." She complied. "It sounds like Marty's aunt has a thing or two in common with your Grandma Beatrice."

"They do sound like sisters beneath the skin, don't they? Growing up, I thought every family was required to have at least one member like that. The grande dame requirement." He said nothing, so she made it more direct. "Doesn't your family have anyone like that?"

"Not really."

Not direct enough, apparently. "What's your family like?"

He shrugged. "I told you, we're not real close." She waited, and was rewarded when he finally added, "I don't think they really wanted a kid. Maybe I was an experiment that convinced them they weren't cut out to be parents.

Maybe I was a mistake. Either way, they sure didn't know what to do with me."

"What do you mean?"

He frowned, quick, impatient. "Sometimes my mother would come into my room, at the house or some hotel, and look at me like a piece of modern sculpture she couldn't quite fathom. The nanny'd make some fatuous remark about how nice that Mommy came to tuck me in, and then she'd get this hunted look. She'd come to the bed and fiddle with the covers, air kiss my pillow and get the hell out of there."

Grady Roberts wouldn't know what to do with sympathy. His parents had never gotten close enough to give it; he didn't let the world close enough to see when it was needed. Curbing her instincts, she asked lightly, "So nannies cared for you."

"Mostly. I got pretty good at taking care of myself. Sometimes I'd watch old movies and pretend Greer Garson from *Mrs. Miniver* or Donna Reed from *It's a Wonderful Life* was my mother." He gave her a look she couldn't decipher. "But never Katharine Hepburn."

"And your father?"

"He never came in."

The anger and pain she'd felt when he first talked about his parents surged back, but she held it in check. To help him, she had to first understand. "And when you got older?"

Another shrug. "I guess they would have been willing enough to have me around, although—" His grin grew sardonic. "Having a thirty-three-year-old son makes it difficult to maintain the fiction that they're in their early forties. But by the time I was old enough to join in their pursuits, I had different tastes." A more genuine smile reached his lips. "I still prefer Mrs. M.'s cookies to four-star restaurants."

Ideas tumbled through her head. How could she make him see that his parents' rejection was their fault, not his? That the surface of good looks, charm and success he showed to the world was not the sum of his value, wasn't even half. How could she get through to him? How could she help him the way she'd helped others, like Barry, see the good in themselves? And why did it seem so much more important to succeed with Grady?

"How about equal time here, Leslie. You don't talk about your parents much."

He said it matter-of-factly, but she wondered if he regretted his revelations.

"They both died while I was in high school." A mist in her eyes made her blink hard. "Twenty years, and it still hurts."

He moved closer, a reassuring presence, but touched her only briefly, fingertips to her arm. "I'm sorry. I didn't mean to bring up something that gives you pain—"

Pain? What about his pain?

"No, it's okay. I guess it wouldn't hurt so much if I hadn't loved them so much. I had a wonderful childhood. Lots of love, lots of laughter. And I was very lucky to have Grandma Beatrice, too, after the accident."

He looked the question. She drew a deep breath; she intended to ask more questions so it was only fair.

"Mom and Dad were coming home from dinner with another couple. The driver of an oncoming car fell asleep, it crossed the center line and hit them head-on. Mom and Mr. Reynolds were killed instantly. Mrs. Reynolds died two days later. Dad recovered enough to be home for about two months. But his heart just wasn't strong enough. I was finishing my freshman year in high school when he died."

"So you lived with Grandma Beatrice."

She nodded. "From the day of the accident. My brother, Harry, was a freshman out at Stanford. He couldn't have taken on a young teenager, and nobody wanted him to." A slight smile lifted her lips. "Least of all me. I love him dearly now, but he was the bane of my existence growing up. Besides, he had his life, his future, to get on with. There was never any question but that I'd go to Grandma Beatrice."

"That must have been rough on you. I can't imagine..."

He couldn't imagine the pain, or he couldn't imagine loving someone enough to feel the pain?

"I can't deny I wish my parents were here, traveling out to California to see Harry's kids, debating retirement and clucking about how times have changed. But I know they loved me." Impulsively she put her hand to his cheek. The slight prickle sensitized her palm and fingers. "I had that love for fourteen years and nothing can take it away."

Grady looked into her eyes and saw the strength that her family's love had given her. Enough strength to have compassion even while she was hurting.

He wanted to pull away.

Instead he covered her hand with his, binding the touch of her long slender palm and fingers to his skin. He didn't need compassion from her; he needed passion.

Without taking his eyes from her face, he shifted her hand until his mouth found her palm. Using tongue and lips, he explored the taste and sensation of the gentle mounds beneath each finger, the delicate hollow at the center of her palm, the rise to her wrist.

And he watched her eyes change, watched the haze of desire blur the distinct colors.

Still holding her hand against his face, he bent his head to hers. He could cover her mouth in a swift raid she wasn't anticipating. He could rely on the potent chemistry between them to carry her beyond her doubts.

But somewhere in those final two inches before his lips touched hers, he discovered he didn't want that.

He wanted more. Yes, he wanted the chemistry, the desire he'd suspected in that first kiss by the Smithsonian rose garden, then tasted for an instant at the reception and more fully that night on the beach. But he also wanted the friendship and trust he'd had these past weeks.

So he paused, even knowing she might withdraw. She might stiffen; she might end this kiss he so desperately wanted before it even began.

From the scant distance he'd preserved, he met her eyes, then let his gaze drop to her mouth before raising it once more to her eyes. It was as blunt a declaration as he could give—he wanted to kiss her, he was going to kiss her, unless she did something to stop it.

What she did was tilt her head, slicing a fraction off those separating inches and presenting a most enticing angle. He mirrored her movement without conscious thought, and their lips brushed, lingered and separated.

Her eyes were clouded, but the wariness he'd worked so hard to erase had edged back in, though not as strongly as the desire. Not nearly as strong as the desire.

Her mouth softened. Slightly wet, the lips parted.

With deliberate slowness he slid his fingertips along the line of her jaw, up the sharp angle to her ear, where they traced so lightly he wasn't sure himself if he still touched her, or only imagined the smooth, graceful curve. His fingers slid into her hair, disappearing in the soft thickness as they spread wide to cup her head.

He wanted her to see the kiss coming and accept or reject. He wouldn't take her by surprise.

Their lips didn't brush this time, but met fully.

When he released her mouth disappointment joined the other emotions in her eyes. He tilted her head between his two big hands in order to change the way their mouths meshed and a flash wiped the disappointment from her eyes.

She changed the angle the third time, a brief touching that fired off a chain reaction in him. The kisses blended into one another and he lost count. Though the sensations were distinct, sharp memories.

From cupping the back of her neck, his hand came around to trail down her throat, then grasp the collar of her shirt, to draw her closer. They were half lying on the couch, her leg between his, her hip brushing against his hardness. His shirt was opened, gone. He didn't remember the mechanics of opening her blouse and bra, but he would never forget the sensation of stroking her soft breast.

She arched, filling his hand more completely, the perfect curve molded in his palm, the nipple's sweet hardness becoming the catalyst to a chemical reaction that produced a shortage of oxygen, a tightening of muscles and a high-octane explosion in his blood.

But it produced a different reaction in her.

He felt her drawing away and heard her murmur the word "stupid," a protest at herself not him.

He overruled her with a hard, swooping kiss, letting her body carry much of his weight, riding the reaction that always flared between them. And when she put her arms around him once more, he knew she wouldn't pull away, so he gentled the kiss. But not right away.

The momentary desperation he'd felt before the first kiss was banked down by their marathon of kisses. Long, deep, deliberate kisses. Languid caresses that trailed off into simply touching one another. Then began again with slow-moving magic.

He knew by her breathing that she had slipped into a light sleep at one point while he held her. An unconscious movement brushed her hand against his chest. He hoped to heaven she was awake after that, because the exploration of his ribs and breastbone and collarbone that her hands em-

barked on just about killed him. He hated to think she could
do that to him in her sleep.

But eventually the touches grew slow once more, and
Leslie slept in his arms, while he pushed every thought away
except how good this felt.

Leslie jolted awake.

"What's wrong? Something's wrong."

"Shh, it's all right." Grady's whisper didn't soothe her
because she was aware simultaneously of the warmth of his
arms around her, his legs tangled with hers and the heat
gathered deep inside her from his touch, his nearness.

Dear Lord, how she wanted him.

"It's the rain," he said softly against her hair. "It
stopped. That's what woke you."

She knew he was right, but she couldn't relax. Not while
he held her like this and she wanted him so desperately.

He recognized her stiffness; she could tell that in the way
his hold eased, as if she might shatter if he moved the wrong
way. He loosened his arms, shifted his legs.

Resisting the urge to bolt or give in to the false modesty
of hurriedly adjusting her clothes, she sat up. Moving away
from him, she turned her bracelet watch to see the face.

"It's late."

"Depends on how you look at it. Could be early. Very,
very early."

She shot him a look, then decided against fully meeting
his eyes. This way she couldn't know for sure that he wasn't
talking strictly about the hour of the day.

"But either way," he went on, "we should get a little
sleep. We have a full day of sight-seeing ahead of us."

Suddenly she was too tired to worry about that. Too tired
to worry about anything except changing into her paja-
mas—she'd brought her most modest, least enticing night-
wear—brushing her teeth and slipping into bed.

She must have fallen asleep, because the next thing she knew, she heard rain. Lifting her eyelids, she also saw watery daylight misting into the room. It took a moment to realize the light was from the sun, but the "rain" was the sound of the shower.

Getting up, she eyed the rumpled blanket and dented pillow on the couch.

The pillow, the blanket and the indentations on the couch's cushions gave an impression of the body that had rested there. She could almost see it; for a second she was disappointed she'd fallen asleep too soon and stayed asleep too long to see it in reality.

*Foolish, Leslie. Very, very foolish.*

Almost as foolish as she'd been last night, actually earlier this morning.

She'd come very close to making love with Grady. Much too close.

Now she had to concentrate on getting them back on track for a friendship, to reclaim the territory she'd lost—no, that she'd freely given. She couldn't put the blame on him; she'd been an equal partner in those kisses and touches. But she could put blame on herself, because she knew she couldn't ever be anything more than friends with Grady. She couldn't...

Her head jerked up. Grady leaned against the bathroom doorjamb, wearing only jeans and watching her. She hadn't heard the shower shut off or the door open.

His feet were bare. The snug jeans were zipped but not snapped at the top. A glimmer of water showed here and there in the narrow line of golden hair in the center of his chest. His jaw bore a glinting stubble. His mouth was solemn and his eyes bored into her with an intensity that made her dread his next words.

But all he said was a mild, "Next."

She scooped up her clothes and toiletries bag and headed past him.

His hand on her forearm stopped her as abruptly as a brick wall would have.

"Grady—"

"No." The single harsh word stopped her warning; they weren't necessary anyhow because his tone clearly said he knew what she'd meant to say. And that he rejected it. "If you say it would be foolhardy to go on, I'll just answer that it would be just as foolhardy to try to go back."

His hand dropped from her arm, and she let out a pent-up breath.

He sounded almost normal when he added, "We'll start with the easy stuff. You take your shower. I've got to check the situation in Chicago. I'll see you downstairs."

He was still on the phone in the guest parlor when she came down. She'd had the first cup of coffee before he joined her in the dining room.

"I have to go back, Leslie," he said without preamble. "I'm sorry. We'll have to head back to D.C. right after breakfast. I can catch a noon flight from Dallas if you wouldn't mind dropping me off and taking the car back to the city for me."

"Of course."

"I'll be back on the Fourth. I'm holding you to that picnic."

"Well, if it works out.... But don't worry if you can't because—"

"I'll be back." He glanced out the window at the brightening sky. "Damn."

"It's all right. I understand."

He studied her, from her hair to her chin, from her mouth to her eyes. "We will take this trip eventually, Leslie. Foolhardy or not, we will go on. I promise you that."

* * *

A promise or a threat?

Which had he intended it as? Which did she take it as?

Lord, she wished she knew the answers.

Returning to Washington after dropping Grady at the airport, Leslie found a message on her answering machine from a former co-worker who'd broken up with her husband of eight years. When she called back, the woman almost begged her to have dinner together that night. Listening to Janey's problems would keep her from thinking about her own.

That left the afternoon.

Her apartment didn't offer enough puttering opportunities. She considered writing letters, but couldn't dredge up anything to say that didn't involve Grady, and that was too dangerous. Phoning would be worse, especially since the only two people she had any inclination to talk to were Grandma Beatrice and Tris, neither one shy about asking questions. Not a good idea.

Finally she changed into her coolest shorts and top and walked to the zoo. The hot, humid weather, unbroken by yesterday's rain, kept the crowds down. Those who were there moved as slowly as the languid animals.

She bought an ice cream, found a shaded bench and stopped trying to hold off her thoughts.

Had she done him a disservice by letting their relationship go on this way? Had she given him signals he misinterpreted? Had she given him signals he interpreted correctly, but she hadn't intended to let out?

How could she help him learn about friendship if that's not what she's feeling for him?

She absolutely wouldn't fall in love again, especially with someone like Grady. It could only hurt her, and it wouldn't be fair to him, especially if he had come to truly care for her.

But maybe he'd pursued her simply because she said no. Maybe he'd confused her efforts to play mother hen to him as she had to so many friends—this time vastly complicated by physical attraction—with something else. Maybe the best thing would be to go ahead and have a fling with him so he could get past her and go on with his life as he had with every other woman.

Sensations rippled through her. The remembered sensations of Grady's touch on her skin, his lips on her mouth. The imagined sensations of a more complete union. The anticipated sensations of his moving on.

Maybe she should cut the relationship entirely, right now. Even at the cost of strain among their mutual friends. Even at the cost of missing him dreadfully.

She had the questions down pat.

Now all she needed were answers.


"If we work right through, we can get it all done. A few more hours and we could have this wrapped up for good."

Grady's words didn't slow the silver-haired man's straightening and gathering of papers.

"I told you at the start, Grady. I lost one wife and missed two kids growing up while I was building Burroughs Candy. I'm going to make damn sure I don't risk doing that with my second family while I'm selling it," said Jasper Burroughs. "I'm going home to give my son a bath and help put him to bed and to have dinner with my wife. The offer will still be here in the morning. We'll finish then."

Grady knew better than to argue. He calmly said good-night, dismissed the secretary, made notes for the next day, read over a memo and wondered what he was going to do with himself.

He'd immersed himself in the Burroughs deal the past three days. By necessity at first, getting up-to-date, researching changes Burroughs wanted in the counteroffer to the buyers, then presenting the counteroffer. In between, he'd caught up on the other Chicago accounts, consulted with his assistant and kept his Washington contacts active by telephone.

Leaving no time to think about Leslie Craig.

But, at barely seven o'clock of a summer's evening with his desk cleared, that wouldn't be the case tonight.

He looked at the telephone, and decided against it. He wasn't sure what he'd say to her, but whatever it was, the telephone didn't seem the way to do it.

For the first time he could remember, he wasn't sure what he wanted.

His body had strong opinions on the issue. All he had to do was get near Leslie—hell, just thinking about her did it— and his body made its opinion clear.

And even though she persistently pulled back from the wanting, she wanted him, too. But if he broke through her resistance and they did make love, what then?

He hadn't worried about the morning after with other women, much less the days and weeks after. He'd wanted, and he'd gone after.

*Because he hadn't known those other women.*

Not as friends, not as people. So he hadn't had anything to lose. With Leslie he did. A friendship he didn't want to lose, maybe couldn't afford to lose.

A clatter in the hallway of an early arriving cleaning crew startled him. He was getting jumpy.

Three solid days in the office was too much for anybody. What he needed was a quiet evening at his condo and an early night. He got his car from the office garage and headed north.

When he passed the turnoff to his condo, he was only mildly surprised. He wasn't surprised at all when he pulled into the driveway of the Monroes' Lake Forest home.

"Oh, how lucky," Nancy Monroe said, "I grilled two extra lamb chops. You must stay for dinner."

"Nothing lucky about it," said James Monroe, slipping an arm around his wife's waist. "You always cook extra, but you're right, he's got to stay for dinner. We haven't seen you since Tris and Michael's wedding."

"Thanks, but I really can't stay," he insisted in turn. "I just stopped by to say hello."

The Monroes out-insisted him.

Conversation was wide-ranging and unfocused—his business, the Monroes' impending grandparenthood, the Cubs' season, the lakeshore's erosion, Paul and Bette's new house, Chicago's politics, James Monroe's easing toward retirement, Judi Monroe's summer job as a waitress in Yellowstone Park. He drove away well fed and oddly comforted.

He swung by Paul and Bette's house on his way through Evanston. The last vestiges of twilight showed the shapes of new evergreens and flower beds. Lights at the back of the house indicated someone was home. Still, he used his car phone to call first. Mrs. M. had said Paul was in Dallas for a couple days consulting on a major appraisal; Grady didn't want to startle Bette with a knock after nine o'clock.

"We haven't seen you in ages, Grady. Are you in Chicago?" Bette demanded after the first greetings.

"Not exactly."

"You're not calling from D.C., are you? This doesn't sound like long-distance."

"No."

"All right, Grady, where are you?"

"In front of your house."

Before the clunk of the phone fully registered, he saw Bette at the front door, calling out with an undercurrent of laughter. "You get in here right now, Grady Roberts."

He hung up and did as he was told.

Stopping at the kitchen, Bette brought out a pitcher of iced tea, two glasses and a plate of cookies, then led Grady to the big screened-in porch at the back of the house.

"The iced tea's great, Bette." He took a glass and sat at the round table where she was working on a project. Neatly stacked magazines flanked a yellow legal pad filled with notes. A pile of cutout magazine pictures sat to one side, with three cumbersome albums opposite him. "But the cookies . . . I just came from the Monroes', so . . ."

She smiled; they both knew her mother-in-law's penchant for feeding anyone who walked in her door. "So you couldn't possibly eat another thing."

"What're you working on?"

"Garden—" She pointed to one magazine stack, then gestured more broadly at the other stack, plus the pictures and albums. "And nursery. I'm getting that organized so I can show the workmen coming tomorrow exactly what we want for the colors and wallpaper."

A smile pulled at his lips. "Leslie said you'd redecorate the room for the baby."

Bette gave him a searching look. "She was right."

Getting up got him away from her look. Pretending a great interest in the pottery candle holders and oil lamps gathered on the windowsills that opened into the house provided an excuse to keep moving.

"We were going to do it ourselves, but organizing's about all I'm good for these days," she said with a grimace at her cumbersome body. "Let me give you a word of advice, Grady. If they ever figure out a way for men to be pregnant, don't plan to be eight months' pregnant in July, not unless you can spend the time in Alaska. Anyway, Paul wanted to do the nursery by himself, but as many things as he's good at, wallpapering isn't one of them."

Grady picked up an oil lamp, the pottery cool and smooth in his palm, his mind hundreds of miles to the east.

"We tried the powder room, and it was a disaster. He blames Michael. He says if Michael's renovation on his Victorian down in Springfield had included wallpapering, he would have learned that along with paint stripping, plastering and painting... Grady? Grady."

He snapped his attention back to the screened porch in Evanston, Illinois, and to Bette.

"Sorry. My mind wandered. I've got this big deal going. It's been a long, complicated sale and the commission can make the financial year for us." A slight exaggeration but a comfortable explanation of his inattention.

Not to Bette.

"You've had big deals before. You love them."

"Yeah." He grinned sheepishly. "Don't know what's the matter with me."

"Offhand, I'd say you're lonely."

Caught off guard, his grin faltered and he tried to retrieve it. "Hard to be lonely in my life-style." He let the grin go. "Remember the first time Paul brought you to meet Michael and me?" She nodded, a wealth of memories in her eyes. "I told him then that he was proving he was smarter than me because he saw the value of quality over quantity. And in you he'd definitely found quality."

Her eyes misted. "Thank you, Grady."

"Don't cry on me, Bette." His panic was mostly kidding, but not all. What did you do with an eight months' pregnant, crying woman? "If Paul finds out I made you cry he'll have my hide. Besides, you know how I feel about you."

"I know. But it's nice to hear it. Everybody needs to hear the words," she said with an emphasis that made him slightly uncomfortable. In contrast, the gentle tone of her next few words initially lulled him. "But tell me the truth,

Grady, you stopped being satisfied with quantity quite some time ago, didn't you?''

He tried to slough it off with a puzzled shake of his head. "I don't understand what you're getting at, Bette."

"Oh, I think you do." Her bland response didn't leave much room for denial. "Just remember, Grady, changing takes a lot of patience. Not just with yourself, but patience with your friends. It might take a while for everybody to catch up with you."

"Now I'm sure I don't understand."

She tipped her head consideringly. "I remember that first night I met you and Michael, too. And I remember thinking that you have a knack for accepting people, Grady. As they are, right this moment. Not as they were, not as you'd like them to be. Not everyone is as good at that as you are. It takes them a while to catch up with a friend's changes. But they will catch up. That's all.''

"If you say so."

"I say so."

He left soon after. In the short drive home, he realized he didn't dread the night in his solitary condo quite as much as he had when he'd left the office.

Monday she wasn't ready. Tuesday and Wednesday Tris was out of town. Thursday Leslie went to Tris's office.

"Busy?"

"Not too busy to talk."

"Good." She closed the door, ignoring Tris's questioning look, and sat on the low bookcase by the window, twisting her watch so she could see the time. If this did not go the way she wanted, she was not above creating an appointment to cut it short. But she would start by assuming it would go the way she wanted, which required being direct. Very direct.

"I don't suppose for an instant that you're not aware that Grady's been taking me to some historic sites around the area." Tris opened her mouth, but Leslie held up a forestalling hand, and she shut it. "If you didn't know it through Grady, I am absolutely positive the grapevine would tell you since he called here once or twice."

So far, so good. Tone light; Tris listening.

"I told you from the first, Tris, that I am not one to fall for the Grady Roberts charm, even if he plied it. And I'll tell you again. But—" She leaned forward and spoke each word with uncustomary precision. "If I did decide to fall, it would be my decision and my concern alone."

Even as she relaxed her pose, she stopped another imminent protest by talking on. "But that's not an issue. The issue is that I saw you and Grady when you ran into each other here last week, Tris. It made me want to cry. And then it made me want to knock your heads together. First you for being so cool to him, then him for pretending it didn't hurt him and then both of you together." She looked at her friend. "Don't do that to him, Tris."

"I'm just looking out for you," Tris said stiffly.

"I know, but I can look out for myself."

"I've known Grady a long time and I know—"

"Yes, which is exactly the problem." Tris looked skeptical, but she let Leslie continue. "I've been thinking about this for a while. Before you all got together again last summer for Paul and Bette's wedding, you didn't see Michael for who he really was, but only as a buddy. When you did open your eyes to him last August, you fell in love with him. I think you've been nearly as blind about Grady. For a long time you saw him as a hero. You long ago outgrew that, and last summer you had a chance to accept him for who he really is, flaws and all—the flaws you'd never allowed yourself to see in your hero."

"You see flaws in him?" Tris asked slowly, as if not quite believing it.

"Of course I do." She also saw strengths that no one else—including Grady himself—gave him credit for. "But it seems like that's *all* you're seeing in him. Grady is your friend. Don't judge him so harshly. Don't cut him out of your life. He needs your friendship."

The regret and a bit of guilt in Tris's eyes both relieved her and made her sad. Without her, neither Grady nor Tris would have anything to feel bad about.

"I just don't want you to be hurt."

"I know you don't and..." She couldn't quite get out the words to assure Tris that she wouldn't be hurt. "But in the process, you're hurting Grady. Nobody wants that."

Leslie sat utterly still, letting Tris study her for signs of unhappiness. She wasn't unhappy, not really, because she'd accepted her life a long time ago. So there could be no signs to see. Could there?

Tris hesitated so long that when she finally spoke, Leslie let out a silent sigh of relief.

"Leslie, you've always been there for me. Right from the start, when you let me—no, you *made* me—talk my way through the aftermath of that foolish marriage I made right out of school. And with Michael... Well, I don't know what would have happened if you hadn't thrown us together during that snowstorm. I don't know if I would have had the nerve to confront him otherwise—"

"You wouldn't have."

Tris made a face, but kept on. "And I don't know if I would have recognized some of the things you spotted about our relationship."

"Now, that you would have done—eventually."

"But you've never let me help you. You're my friend. I love you. I want to be here for you, too. Won't you let me?"

Fighting the urge to lean on that offered shoulder, Leslie dredged up a humorous drawl, though she didn't feel the least amused. "But that's just the point. There's no need. Besides, that's not the way it works. You can't reverse the roles. Bless your heart, I'm the older-woman confidante. I'm supposed to provide the comforting shoulder and the guiding word. I'm way past the point of needing them myself."

She exited before Tris could make the protest Leslie saw forming on her lips.

Reaching her own office, she softly closed the door, then leaned against the wall, eyes closed, trying to hold on to the reality of what she had to give to the world, the only role left to her.

*Please don't take that away, too.*

## Chapter Nine

"I'd hoped Tris and Michael could join us, but they're in Illinois," Leslie said for the third time.

Grady looked at the woman sitting on the far side of the quilt, repacking leftovers into a hamper for the second time. Of the thousands of people blanketing the Capitol's west lawn, she had to be the most uncomfortable, and the most determinedly cheerful.

Ever since he'd arrived at her apartment this afternoon, she'd talked almost nonstop. Not once—as they took the metro to the Capitol, joined the stream of holiday-making humanity, found an open spot in the grass and consumed their picnic of fried chicken, potato salad and fruit—did she let the topic slip any closer to the intimacy they'd experienced at Tanner's Inn and where it might lead them than Kansas was to a mountain.

"I know. They're in Springfield."

"How do you know that?"

"Tris called. Said she and Michael were going to be in Springfield for the Fourth and asked if I'd like to join them."

"She did?" Leslie smiled, and for the first time he thought she really meant it. "That's great."

"I told her I was spending the Fourth with you."

"Oh." Now she looked concerned and tried to hide it.

"It's all right, Leslie. She didn't break my sword over her knee or anything. No firing squad at dawn. She just said okay, and they'd see me next time we were both in the same place. It seems we're back to buddies as usual."

"That's good."

He waited for her to look up, but straightening a corner of the quilt took a lot of attention.

What the hell, he might as well bring it out in the open. He knew she must've talked to Tris, but he'd like to hear it from her. "In fact, I was going to ask you about—"

"Oh, look, the concert's going to start."

The orchestra was merely beginning its warm-up, but Leslie seemed determined to hear every note. Around them talk and laughter hummed, but she turned her face to the stage in rapt attention, and turned her shoulder on him.

He lounged on his side, propping his head in one hand. Beyond the hamper she'd placed between them, she sat very straight. Either she'd received a recent lecture on posture or she was tense about something. Or someone.

Bits and pieces of this afternoon came together with what he knew of her, and congealed in a lump in his gut.

Music flowed around him as the day's light and heat faded. Familiar, upbeat songs. A famous conductor and well-known singers invited everyone to join in, a national sing-along on the front porch of the nation's Capitol.

Leslie sang, he didn't.

Even the stirring marches that had an elderly couple to their left tapping the arms of their lawn chairs and the trio of kids in front of them marching in place didn't lift his spirits.

By the time the concert reached its rousing finale with Tchaikovsky's *1812 Overture*—complete with cannon shots as a fitting segue into the fireworks—he'd resolved to get this out in the open. Whatever "this" might be.

"Lesl—" The first rocket tore through the air with an anticipatory crackle. Boom! Color exploded with the sound, followed by a wave of "ooohs." He tried again. "Leslie—"

"Oh, isn't that beautiful." Since the color had faded, she had to be enthusing about the residue of the first firecracker or a faint track of the next one's ascent.

"Leslie—" Another explosion swallowed his words.

"I love the ones that go from green to red like that," she said before he could try again.

He waited for the next one to go off, then spoke quickly, trying to avoid interruption from a firecracker or her enthusiasm. "I thought we'd try a trip to Charlottesville again next weekend. I could meet—"

Bang! A rocket exploded in a circle of dazzling white. As it began to evaporate, it let off more blasts of light and noise. Bammedy—bam!—bam!—bam!

She winced, but he couldn't tell if it was from the sound or his proposal.

"I hear Monticello's beautiful, Leslie. I'd like to see it with you."

"Next weekend? I'm afraid that's not a good time for me." She spoke around another eruption of noise that presaged a shower of blue and yellow.

The polite distance of her tone iced his heart.

"The weekend after, then."

"I'm afraid—"

He fought down the words that would accuse her of being exactly that—afraid. Instead he rapped out, "The one after that."

"I don't want to make plans for any out-of-town trips right now." She sounded so damned reasonable he wanted to shake her. Why was she doing this?

Well, he could fight reason with reason. He hardly noticed the red, white and blue streams across the sky.

"Fine. We'll try closer-in places. I hear Annapolis,—"

"No." The word had an edge; at least he'd rattled her. But she must have heard the edge, too, and he could see her retreating from its revelation. She gave a little laugh. "Let's just enjoy the fireworks for now."

With the timing of a perfect accomplice, another flare went out, trailing colored sparks before it burst into a rainbowed chrysanthemum against the inky blue sky.

"Oh, look at that, isn't that beautiful?"

He said nothing, following the smoke of a spent firework drifting into a forgotten part of the sky while people anticipated the next explosion.

Up in smoke.

He didn't like the sound of that. He wasn't accustomed to it, and he didn't intend to *get* accustomed to it, damn it.

He was unaware of speaking the last two words aloud until Leslie flicked him a look before raising her face to the sky again.

The look couldn't have lasted more than a couple of seconds, but it was amazing how much you could absorb in a snap of the fingers. He'd seen her determination. But he'd also seen concern for him, and a true and real fear. Leslie Craig was scared. Of being hurt, of getting involved, of caring too much? Maybe one, maybe all. But he knew for certain she feared him—being hurt by him, getting involved with him, caring too much for him.

In Chicago he'd been undecided how to proceed. Whether to pursue the chemistry between them when doing that might put their friendship at risk. But she'd left him no choice. She intended to withdraw from his life entirely. For fear of the chemistry, she wouldn't even leave him the friendship. So he had nothing to lose.

And the possible gains? He couldn't afford to think of that right now.

The deep breath she took to say good-night, to take the next step in sending him away forever, left a silence he filled forcefully.

"I'm coming up, and I'm coming in."

His hand under her elbow started her up the stairs.

Maybe it was just as well. In the privacy of her apartment she could make it a clean break tonight, finish it right now, instead of drawing it out.

Inside, she dropped her quilt and sweater on the bench and started past him to add lights to the dim lamp she'd left burning. He gripped her wrist, stopping her cold.

"Quit stalling, Leslie."

"I'm not stalling. I'm just—"

"Yeah, I know what you're just, and I know what you've been working up to all night. But before you say it, I want to know why. And not all that crap about being older or having nothing in common or wanting to be only friends. Because we've been friends these past weeks, and that doesn't change this."

Still gripping only her wrist, he angled his head to take her mouth. Adjusting to meet his lips more fully was the most natural thing in the world. As natural as it was to collaborate when he changed the angle. As natural as it was to part her lips when his tongue tested them. As natural as it was to meet and match the rhythm of his tongue's thrust and retreat.

He released her mouth and her wrist without moving back. She didn't move away; she couldn't. Not with those blue eyes declaring the same message as the harsh, uneven sounds of their breathing.

"You can't deny this, Leslie. You might want to, but you can't. You're too honest."

His eyes remained on hers as he drew nearer, and nearer still, until she couldn't possibly deny the message in his eyes. She could back away from it or she could accept it, but she couldn't pretend it didn't exist.

Slowly, as if against a great force, she lifted her hands to his arms. Then, gaining strength from the contact, she slid her hands to his shoulders, across their breadth to his neck.

Her eyes drifted closed. The sound of his breathing, the feel of his pulse under her palm were her anchors in the dark world.

He muttered something against her mouth; she didn't try to decipher it. She opened her lips, and took him back inside.

He took a step closer, and she encircled his neck, drawing him to her. Only then did he put his hands on her.

He skimmed one palm along her arm slowly, following the line from her shoulder to the back of her hand to where her fingers disappeared into his hair. As if to reassure himself that she really was holding him, her arms really were around his neck. His palms rubbed circles on her shoulders as the kiss grew hotter and deeper. Cupping her shoulders, he drew her tight against him. So it didn't matter when her knees felt as if they would give way; he was there to support her.

Maybe that was how it happened that she never quite recalled covering the distance down the hall, into her bedroom and to the bed. But she remembered the surge of satisfaction when she started to lie back, and Grady's hands were there to ease her descent. Even better, Grady's body was there next to hers, partly covering hers.

It was the way it had been at Tanner's Inn. The wanting, the drumming of *more* in her head, the craving for what she'd told herself she couldn't have, didn't really want. Oh, but she *did* want it. . . .

He started unbuttoning her blouse, the motions seeming so easy to his practiced fingers, while his other hand stroked her from waist to hip to knee and his mouth dazzled hers. Then the second-to-the-bottom button stubbornly refused to budge, and she felt the slight shake of his hand against her skin. Not as easy as she'd thought.

Tugging until she could reach his shirt, she started unbuttoning. She felt and heard his sharp intake of air. He gave her recalcitrant button a yank and it came free. One more button and he was pushing open her blouse, sliding the straps of her camisole down her arms, following its retreat with his hands and mouth. And she was drowning. Slipping into a sea of sensation where the only elements were his touch and her skin.

He dampened her nipple with a circle of his tongue, then slowly drew it into his mouth. Sensation swamped over her, and she clutched at his arms, but that was no way to save herself from this drowning, it only sank her deeper into the wanting.

She gasped a little as she shifted. He moved so his weight didn't pin her. She sat up and he followed.

"No, wait, Grady." She couldn't control her breathing. "We need to talk about this. We need—"

"Need? You want to talk about need, Leslie?"

From the first word, his voice, raw and smoky, held her immobile. She moved only her eyes. Watching as he jerked open the remaining buttons of his shirt. He took one of her hands in each of his, opening them with his thumbs when she clenched reflexive fists. "I'll tell you about need. I'll tell you about needing you, Leslie. Are you going to deny this?"

He pressed one of her palms to his bare chest and the other to the hard ridge below his waist. She felt the pulse of his blood through her palms, up her arms and into her own heart.

"This is need, Leslie."

He muttered the words almost into her mouth as he held her against him. She felt the jolt of his need under her hands when their lips met, and the surge of her own need.

"Grady..."

He lifted his head just enough to meet her eyes. Under the heat, his eyes were wary, his body tense. He expected her to say no, to pull away, and he would make himself accept it.

But she couldn't. She couldn't accept not giving this man what he needed. She couldn't accept not having what he offered. This one night...one night...she would give and she would have. In the morning... well, there was the night before the morning, and she would think only of the night.

Stretching her neck, she brought her mouth to his as she caressed him with long, deliberate strokes.

His response leaped under her hands, but he didn't move other than that. She ended the kiss. For an instant he stared at her, but only long enough for her to think that the blue of his eyes had burned clear of all protection. Before she could look into those eyes and see the man behind them, he locked his arms around her and brought them both back down to the bed.

His lips and teeth feasted on the tender skin where her neck met her shoulder. When he soothed it with his tongue, she arched in response.

That was the last clear moment she remembered. The rest was impressions, echoes of emotion. The hoarse, almost guttural sound of his words of need and praise and desire. The strained, taut clenching of his muscles under her hands. The clutch of sadness and regret when he opened a small foil packet. The prod of conscience to tell him... and the welcomed weakness when his kiss drove away all thought. The film of sweat that made her hand glide down his bare side when she grasped his hip. The scent of soap and man as their legs and arms tangled and clasped. The sensation of cloth against her skin as clothes that proved too intricate to remove were shoved aside in haste.

Oh, yes, she knew need.

And she knew the incredible, joyous sensation of having it met, and of meeting his.

She told him of the joy in small, soft sounds and glorious shudders of pleasure. He answered in a strained, hoarse explosion of completion.

Holding him, absorbing the heaving of his chest into hers, feeling the beating of his heart against hers, she knew she would always remember the honesty of his need, and hers.

She might have drifted, into sleep or simply out of conscious thought.

They lay tangled together, arms wrapped tightly around each other as if fearing that bodies this close could somehow slip apart.

But their breathing eased and their heartbeats steadied. At some point Grady shifted most of his weight to one side. Maybe that woke her. Or feeling the rub of her camisole twisted around her waist.

She eased from Grady's hold, gaining just enough room to sit up. With her hands on the camisole, preparing to pull it off, she looked over her shoulder and found Grady awake, and watching her.

A look. That's all, and she could feel her breasts tightening, her blood stirring.

Then he touched her, light fingers low on her back, just below the gathered material.

Still caught by his eyes, she let out a breath, slowly, audibly. In a smooth motion, he sat up, his hands replacing hers on the bottom of the camisole, his mouth touching her shoulder. She had only to raise her arms, and that's what she did. He slid the camisole leisurely up, letting his fingertips trail over her waist, her ribs, her breasts—oh, so slowly there—before a touch to her shoulders. Then he drew the filmy material over her head and sent it arcing gently into the room's shadows.

His hands returned to cup her breasts, drawing her back against the sleek strength of his chest, which she'd seen gilded by noontime sun or silvered by moon. Those beach memories now melded with the sensation of the warmth and solidity of skin and muscle covered by a fine prickling of hair.

The urgency of their lovemaking hadn't allowed for exploration. She didn't—couldn't—regret that, but this, oh, this was another introduction to pleasure.

His head next to hers, he gently stroked her breasts with fingers and palm but without touching the sensitive centers. He was so blond, yet his hands looked dark and strong against the glowing paleness of her skin. Watching, and knowing he was watching the same play of hard and soft, dark and pale, was a pleasure that rose from inside. Against her back, his chest moved with harsher breaths as he finally took each peaking nipple between thumb and finger.

A moan escaped, and she dropped her head back to his shoulder, while his hands continued their pleasurable torment. She could feel his body changing, tightening. Turning, she kissed his neck, tasting the faint saltiness and taking more of it with her tongue. He shifted until he could meet her mouth, opening her lips, kissing her deeply. She was panting at the end, drawing oxygen in thirstily at the same time she tried to return to the kisses.

But he was more urgent, his strong hands shifting her, steadying her when she hardly kept her sense of balance. He seemed to understand her balance better than she did, bringing her to equilibrium astride his thighs at the same time he dizzied her with his mouth and hands.

She waited for him to complete their joining, but he didn't, drawing her down to him, but no farther. He slid his hands up her belly, across her ribs and around her breasts, his thumbs brushing the tips with a feathering touch so she wanted to cry out for more. She needed more.

And he gave it to her.

He lifted up to take one nipple in his mouth, tugging gently, then more deeply to suckle strongly.

Still she needed more, and she reached for it in the only way she could, by seeking to take him inside her, just as his hips surged to meet her.

She did cry out then. A cry of completion, and of a beginning toward another kind of completion.

What had started slow and dreamy, ended in need nearly as frantic as the first time. Replaced by the necessity of meeting each other as fully, as strongly, as possible. And left her sated and exhausted.

She fell asleep marveling at that.

Grady knew by the rhythm of her breathing against his arm that she was asleep. It was his first realization when he came back to rational thought.

The second was a kind of self-horror. What had he done? He wished he didn't know the answer, but he did: He'd lost a precious level of control. Not all of it, thank God, not enough to hurt her in his driving desire—he never wanted to hurt her. Still, too much. Much too much.

He'd always prided himself on being a considerate, patient lover. No woman had ever faulted him there. Smooth, that's how he liked to think of himself.

But there had been nothing smooth about this lovemaking. Nothing considerate, nothing patient. It had been as raw as the need he'd expressed in words and actions.

His feelings for Leslie had been stripped to a primitive base he'd never recognized in himself, much less expressed.

And now he didn't know how to reclothe those feelings in polite trappings.

He prided himself on comfortable mornings-after. He worked hard to make them that way, by never doing anything that could be regretted in the light of day. No declarations, no impulses, no revelations.

But hadn't their lovemaking been all those?

A glance toward Leslie ended almost before it began. He swore viciously at himself. He couldn't even look at her when she was asleep. How could he when she woke? He tried to imagine enacting the casual, urbane behavior of his customary mornings-after. He couldn't.

Carefully he eased out of the bed. He stilled when Leslie stirred, but she didn't wake as he silently dressed. He found a piece of paper and pen by the telephone. He stared at it a long time, finally wrote a few words, signed it and propped it against the phone.

He opened the door but before he crossed the threshold, he turned and looked back.

The shadows seemed to shift, break up and reform, like clouds in a restless sky. But he could make out Leslie's face, the strength and beauty of the bone structure highlighted like a pen-and-ink drawing. Her right hand, pale and elegant in the faint light, rested on the sheet. It would have rested on his chest if he had stayed where he was, a gentle weight against his skin.

He walked out without closing the door behind him.


"So you wrap up the Burroughs deal this afternoon?" Paul asked before taking a healthy hunk out of his hamburger with the works. Since Bette had developed an aversion to onions and pickles, he indulged those tastes at lunch.

"Two-thirty, so we have to keep this get-together short." Grady would have preferred not to have it at all. But when Paul asked him to lunch, he could think of no excuse except the truth—he didn't want someone who knew him so well examining him. Bad enough that his housekeeper, Harriet, his employees and the man at the newsstand looked at him as if he were a bomb about to go off. At least they didn't say anything. Paul wouldn't be that reticent.

"Bette said you stopped by the house last week."

"Yes."

"She said you planned to spend the Fourth in D.C."

"Yes."

"Suppose you planned to see Leslie Craig?"

"Yes."

"Must have been a short trip."

"Yes."

"Things didn't go the way you planned?"

"Back off, Monroe."

"Boy, you're in a foul mood." Paul placidly chewed another hefty bite without taking his eyes off Grady. "Here I am, trying to catch up on what's going on in a friend's life and he jumps on me. Something bothering you?"

"I said back off, and I meant it. The last thing I want right now is some lecture from you on not hurting people. Unless I do it from—what was it you called it?—honest thoughtlessness. Good to know I'm an honest jerk."

Paul studied him with narrowed eyes, then put down the burger. His brows slowly rose as his expression changed. "How the mighty are fallen."

Grady swore, but Paul leaned back comfortably and grinned. "You know one of the things I noticed when I was first seeing Bette was a tendency to snap at my best friends. First I made some crack to Michael, then I ripped your hide a bit. Strange thing, huh?"

Grady glared at him.

"Looking back I figure it was because I was fighting myself, but it was easier to take it out on you guys."

Paul was full of it. He wasn't falling for Leslie, not the way Paul had fallen for Bette. He just ... cared about her. And he didn't have experience at dealing with anyone as a friend and lover. He needed time to adjust.

"On the other hand, maybe it's simpler in your case. Maybe it's the Burroughs deal, having something you thought was wrapped up only to have it unravel again, when you'd rather be in Washington getting that operation going. And you'd rather be spending time with someone nice."

Grady knew Paul Monroe too well not to realize his words, placating as they might sound, carried a strong element of teasing, if not downright glee. But he wasn't in the mood to battle this one out.

"Maybe."

"Sure, that's probably it," Paul said cheerfully. "You're overworked and you miss—" Their eyes met, Paul's dancing, Grady's warning. "Uh, Washington. Pretty city, Washington. Exciting, too. Center of power and all that. And of course there's your business there."

That conclusion allowed Grady to relax enough to get through the rest of the meal on good terms with Paul. But all that afternoon and throughout a celebratory business dinner with Burroughs and the other principals, a persistent thought jangled in his head.

He did miss Washington. But it had nothing to do with the city or business. He missed Leslie.

The next day he flew to D.C.

She'd expected it. Though never, even in her most pessimistic moments, quite that quickly.

*I will call you. Grady.*

That's what the note on her nightstand said. Should she contact the *Guinness Book of World Records?* This had to be a record for fastest, shortest brush-off.

She'd gone to bed with a man with a long-standing reputation for being all pursuit, and she'd woken up to a four-word note—five counting signature. Did signatures count? Why should she be surprised? Or hurt.

This man she'd set out to get to know so she could help him had, instead, come to know her too well. He knew how to short-circuit her resolve to break off with him for good. And he knew, God help her, how to make her happy. She wouldn't—couldn't—let that become the ability to make her unhappy. She'd learned a hard lesson when her marriage ended: never look to anyone else for happiness.

But she knew him, too.

She'd known what was likely to happen and it had; knowing what to expect, she'd still done it. Craigs learned early to accept the consequences of their actions; she'd handle this. Not even the best mother hen succeeds every time. She'd salvage what she could of her pride and poise, and smooth it over so Tris, Michael, Paul and Bette wouldn't feel forced to choose one or the other of them.

So when her buzzer sounded early Saturday afternoon and the voice over the intercom announced it was Grady, she knew what she had to do.

She had a bad moment when he walked in. Echoes of his touches still sang in her body, and it was hard not to reach for him. Harder still to take the necessary step back when he stretched out a hand that would have caressed her hair.

He dropped his hand to his side and went past her. She didn't offer him a seat, but he didn't seem to notice. He paced to the far end of the couch, turned around and came back to her, before repeating the pattern.

"I guess I should have called, let you know when I was coming back to town instead of showing up at your door, but...I wasn't sure how...I mean, what to say to you."

"That's all right. I didn't expect to hear from you."

He spun around and stared at her. He looked irate. "Why not? I said I'll call you." He sounded irate.

"Yes."

"But you didn't believe me?"

He sounded chagrined, yet somehow challenging her for an unspecified weakness. Stifling the questions that surged to her lips—Should I believe you? Do you want me to believe you?—she marshaled the approach she'd planned.

She shrugged, as if his calling didn't matter.

He winced, the beautiful blue eyes masked a moment.

"I meant it, Leslie. I may be a lot of things not all that admirable, but I am not a liar. I meant it." He looked at her, then out the window, then at the wall before zeroing in on the back of the sofa. "And I mean it when I say that the other night... It— Being with you...making love with you..."

His voice trailed off, and she could feel the prickle of awareness shimmer along her skin. No, no, she couldn't let herself think....

"Making love with you was—" He'd started off well, but came to a stop. "Was good—I mean, it was so good, it was...special."

She could safely look at him because he was looking everywhere but at her. He'd sounded miserable at the end. The misery of sincerity, the frustration of trying to express unaccustomed emotions and feeling you failed? Could it...

No! How could she let herself think that way? It was awkwardness. The awkwardness of a decent human being in an uncomfortable situation he didn't know how to extricate himself from without inflicting pain. That's where she came in—Make-It-All-Better Leslie.

She forced a brightness into her voice she didn't feel. "That's nice of you, but not necessary."

His eyes snapped to her face and she wished he'd kept studying the couch.

"What do you mean, not necessary?"

"You don't have to say those things."

"I know I don't *have* to. I want to."

"I just don't want you to make a bigger deal of it than it really is, Grady."

He went ominously still.

"So it wasn't a big deal to you?"

His intensity was making her uncomfortable. "I don't mean it the way you're making it sound, like I do that sort of thing lightly."

"I know you don't do it lightly." Under the heat of his long look that seemed to recall each moment and touch of their Fourth of July night, her resolve began to evaporate. "That's why I don't understand what you're saying."

She tightened her grip on her reactions and shrugged.

"I'm saying it's not the end of the world. We can go on being friends. In fact, I think it'll be easier. You were right, there was that chemistry between us. Probably curiosity more than anything else. But after, uh, after the other night, we've gotten that out of the way. So now we can get back to being friends like before."

He stared at her, but she could read nothing in his face. How could eyes be so unrevealing?

"*Gotten it out of the way?* That's how you feel about making love with me? That's how you felt when I touched you and your skin seemed to hum with the pleasure of it? When you touched me and I thought I would explode? When I was deep inside you? You were *getting it out of the way?*"

She was too stunned by the raw pain and anger beneath his controlled voice to react.

"Well, we'll just get all of this out of the way for good, Leslie. You can kiss me goodbye and have it out of the way for damned good."

He gripped her above the elbows and hauled her against him. Stiff with shock, she felt the hardness of his body against hers, the harshness of his mouth on hers. But before she could gentle either the kiss or the touch, he released her sharply and backed away.

She thought he was going to say something more, but instead, he walked out of the apartment.

"Grady."

Her own whisper finally broke the spell of immobility. She went after him, starting down the stairs. They had to talk. What would they say? She didn't know. But she couldn't have him thinking what he thought now.

"Grady!"

The only answer was the echoing slam of the outside door three flights below.

The drive to the airport was a blur of monuments, green vegetation along the parkway and snatches of muddy Potomac waters. Turning in the rental car and buying his ticket moments ago were a vague memory. But each of Leslie's words was as clear as when she spoke it.

*I just don't want you to make a bigger deal of it than it really is, Grady.... Curiosity more than anything else. But after... the other night, we've gotten that out of the way.*

As clear, and as sharp as arrows. She'd taken aim at him and she'd scored a bull's-eye.

That's when it hit him. *She'd done it deliberately.*

He stopped dead two feet from the gate check-in.

This was another of Leslie's barriers. Not all that different from the thousand-miles-apart, age-gap, different-life-styles obstacles she'd raised and he'd disposed of. But there had to be something else, something more basic that caused her to put these blockades in their path.

"Do you mind?" The voice behind him made it clear its owner did mind. Grady came back to the present, and the realization he'd blocked someone's path to the counter.

Stepping to one side, he looked at the ticket in his hand. He hadn't made a success of himself in business by giving up. And this was a damn sight more important than business—a damn sight harder to figure out, too.

Figuring out the core reason for this barrier building by Leslie would be his task. Whatever it was, he'd fix it. In the meantime, he'd storm past her latest barricade.

He slapped the ticket into his other hand and headed to the main counter to turn it in.


"So I popped the question, and she said yes."

"Oh, Barry, I'm so pleased for you." Leslie hugged the man she'd first known when he was in such pain and now looked so happy. Her eyes teared up, partly for him, partly for herself. Selfish it might be, but in the face of Barry's joy, she couldn't help but feel the contrast with her situation.

But she *could* hide it. "That is absolutely wonderful news," she said.

Barry squeezed her tight, right where they stood, in the narrow aisle of the Wisconsin Avenue deli.

When she'd realized she couldn't catch Grady, she'd gone back to the apartment. She'd stared at familiar walls and furniture and paintings and pillows. She had to do something, something to keep from mindlessly chasing off to his hotel or the airport or Chicago until she'd thought this through, which she couldn't do with Grady's reaction too fresh to allow for dispassionate reason.

Laundry? No, the cyclical whirring heightened thoughts.

Clean. With difficulty she wrestled down a heavy, framed landscape that collected cobwebs from the wall by the bookcase. She wiped off the wall, then scooched down and started on the glass front with cleaner and rags. But her eyes kept traveling to the patch of carpet behind the couch where Grady had paced this morning. She jerked her head the other way—and looked straight at the bed where they'd made love. The word she said would have drawn a severe reprimand from Grandma Beatrice.

She stood. Her apartment held too many moments filled with Grady. She had to get out.

So she'd walked to the deli. She bought two packages of chocolate licorice and was heading out when she ran into Barry. Bursting with his news, he poured it right out there between the anchovy olives and the marinated onions.

"And it's all because of you, Leslie," Barry said. "If I hadn't met you after the divorce—"

"You would have been just fine."

He shook his head. "I know you don't want to hear it, you never do, but I'm going to say it, anyhow. You're one terrific woman, Leslie. I love you."

He kissed her on the lips then, a kiss whose only passion was in its affection.

It ended abruptly, as if Barry had been jerked away from her.

"Let go of her."

Barry *had* been jerked away from her. He looked as if he wouldn't have minded that so much if the large hand on his shoulder hadn't then jerked him into nose-to-nose proximity with the very angry face of Grady Roberts.

"Grady, what are you doing—"

"What am I doing? What are *you* doing?"

She had no idea where the calm came from, but it enveloped her. Maybe it was the cool blood of that ancestress who had faced off soldiers on both sides of the Civil War. Or maybe it was born of an overwhelming joy that Grady had come back.

"I wasn't going to ask that. I can see what you're doing. You're hurting Barry's shoulder—oh, Barry, I'd like you to meet Grady Roberts, the business broker I suggested you have your cousin talk to. Grady, this is Barry Kerken, someone I thought would be a good contact for potential clients. Although now he's probably a former good contact for potential clients."

Grady didn't look distressed at the idea of losing a contact. He didn't even look sheepish. But he did ease his hold on Barry. Enough for the other man to take a step back against the shelf of anchovy olives and flex his shoulder.

"What I was going to ask," Leslie continued, "was what you are doing back here?"

"We have to talk."

He said it so grimly her calm faltered.

Barry sidled another foot away from Grady. "Well, I'll just leave you two to talk, then."

Grady didn't look at him, but Leslie forced a smile.

Barry cleared his throat and gained another few inches of breathing room. "Yes...well, I'll be going..." He stopped and, looking more miserable than heroic, added, "Unless you don't want me to go, Leslie. I mean if you're not comfortable."

Grady looked at him then. To his credit, Barry didn't cringe.

"No, no, I'll be fine, Barry. Thank you. It was wonderful seeing you and hearing your great news." She pushed down an inappropriate burble of laughter. "Congratulations again."

The instant Barry disappeared around the end of the aisle she wondered if she should have kept him around. Now it was only the two of them. But she pushed aside that instant of weakness and met Grady's eyes.

"You wanted to talk?"

"We *are* going to talk. But not here. In private."

Any remaining inclination to laugh did not survive the silent walk back to her apartment.

## Chapter Ten

Inside the apartment, she faced Grady and waited.

And waited.

He appeared disconcertingly willing to stand there and stare at her. For someone who'd insisted they talk, he was noticeably silent. Worse, she had the impression a good deal was happening behind those devastatingly blue eyes.

Maybe another topic would defuse the tension.

"Did I mention that my Cousin Melly's daughter, April, is going to visit me for the month of August? I'll take some vacation time, so I can really show her the city."

He remained silent, and intent. So much for her Southern social manner coaxing a defused response from him.

"Melly's not going to be around in August and we, that is Grandma Beatrice and I, thought a month in one spot would do April good before Melly takes her off again in the fall."

No response.

"Remember me talking about April?" she asked brightly.

"I remember."

His tone also said he wasn't interested in an April detour. Leslie could open the main topic herself, of course, but not face-to-face with him looking that way.

She turned away and spotted the painting on the floor by the hallway. She scooched down and grabbed the cloth.

"I tried to catch you when you left before, Grady." She polished the glass with all the power of nervous energy. "But you were already out the door. I wanted to tell you . . ." The impact of his eyes on her back felt as if it would leave an impression on her skin. "I didn't mean . . . uh, I mean, some of the things I said probably came out the wrong way. I wasn't saying that when we—that the other night didn't mean anything to me. It meant . . . a lot."

There. That was about as good as she could do. Both with the picture and by way of explanation.

She stood, hoisting the heavy frame. Placing her left foot on the magazine rack to make a platform of her thigh, she balanced the frame there. Another instant to gather her energy, then she'd slide the picture back into place—

The movement was smooth and unexpected. One second she was preparing for the final stage of hoisting the picture. The next second the weight was gone, Grady had stepped into the V of her legs, had one hand around her waist and was hanging the picture with the other.

"One-handed!" More disgusted than impressed with the unjust distribution of physical strength in this world, she focused on that over the sensations his nearness created.

"I know."

Before she tried to untangle what he knew, she needed a less combustible position. But before she could lower her foot from the magazine rack, he closed in, opening her more fully, bringing himself flush against her. And flush was exactly how it felt, complete with heat and color pulsing through her. She couldn't back away even if she'd had command of her muscles for that complicated maneuver because her fanny was wedged where bookshelf and wall met.

"I know," he repeated, low. "I know our making love meant a lot to you because it couldn't have meant what it did to me if you hadn't given so much of yourself."

He kissed her, slow and deep. When it ended, he sucked in a long breath, but his voice and his smile were the same. "That's probably what had both of us off balance. I know your talk about making love to *get it over with* was another effort to keep me at a distance, like the other excuses—the geography and age and life-style stuff—"

"That's not—"

"Only this time you almost succeeded because you went for my most vulnerable spot—the ego."

His wry honesty silenced her. Whatever his faults, self-delusion wasn't among them.

He shifted, trailing his fingers from her knee, up her thigh and under the edge of her shorts. Breathing with more difficulty, she remembered that night on the beach, and exactly where this caress might end.

"I like these shorts." A gentle tug on her earlobe with his teeth accompanied the low words. "I wanted you so badly that night." He was remembering, too.

Her turn now. "I know."

"Wasn't much of a test of your perception."

Yes, they had to talk, but not now. Later would be plenty soon enough.

He was unbuttoning her shirt one-handed, while the other continued to stroke and conquer her thigh. She assisted by shrugging one shoulder out of the shirt and he pulled it the rest of the way off.

She unbuttoned his shirt, spreading it wide to trail her hands down his chest, reveling in the groan that she drew.

Leaving him to dispose of the shirt, she continued her journey, opening his belt and sliding her fingers inside his
waistband to get the best angle on the button there.

"Not so fast," he mumbled.

But then he dipped his fingers under the edge of her
panties—and that was no way to slow things down.

Still, she took her time easing down his zipper, letting her
fingertips caress the expanding territory.

"Shorts... Damn."

If she'd worn a skirt... but she hadn't. Unhooking the
shorts and sliding them down allowed him the space to
gather the control she'd been so near to stripping from him.

"Any more of this—" Uneven breathing betrayed him,
but that he was talking at all was a victory of discipline over
desire. "And I'll take you right here."

"Uh-huh," she murmured.

A flash of intensified desire, almost pagan, crossed his
face, then eased. "Another time, another time. But I wasn't
very smooth the other night—" He sounded gruff, almost
embarrassed. "And I want to show you I can be."

She allowed him to lead her to the bedroom, absorbing
this lesson in Grady Roberts. He was uncomfortable with
the raw honesty of their lovemaking. It wasn't what he was
used to. It wasn't the familiar, practiced territory he knew.

And she was glad. With a fierce, triumphant joy.

Until that moment, she hadn't realized how much she'd
wanted what they'd experienced to be as unique for him as
it had been for her. Yet if he'd said those words, she would
have discounted them. His discomfort, though, was unmis-
takable, and endearing. It belonged to her alone.

But he showed no discomfort now. Sliding the clothes
from her body so skillfully she hardly felt them go. Caress-
ing her skin so patiently she hardly remembered to breathe.
Their bodies, both naked, slipped along each other, here
rubbing, here sliding, everywhere enticing. His lips discov-

ered her where she hadn't known she existed, drawing sensation from inside her to the surface to quiver and glow like tears. Drawing emotions from where she'd hidden them so long ago. Too many emotions, too near the surface. She couldn't let this go on.

She slid free, pushed him to his back, then restored the connection of body to body with her mouth on his chest.

"Leslie." The word was stern, but his breathing convulsed and the muscles under her mouth clenched.

"I don't want smooth." She spoke against his skin, the prickle of fine hairs guiding her to his navel. She circled, then dipped her tongue. "Not this time."

He jolted up, intending, she was sure, to take control, to ease them back to something smooth and civilized. She didn't want that. Or to continue his exploration of her secrets, body and soul. She couldn't afford that.

Eluding his hands, she continued her quest, until he dropped back to the bed with a groan that rewarded her.

It was a brief surrender.

"No more, Leslie." He reversed their positions with dizzying ease. His face intent, his voice hoarse, he promised her, "You win this time. But next time..."

"Next time," she agreed.

Oh, but first there was this time, and the rightness of having him inside her, meeting, retreating, returning, stroking, until the straining to attain the impossible burst into an impossible pleasure.

She watched him, his intent face drawn tight as the shudders wracked him, and she cushioned him when he collapsed with a guttural groan of completion.

Someday she would have to let him go, but for now she held him. She would wait, just a little longer, before telling him the truth that would push him away. She would give Grady time to know his value, to know a true relationship.

While she gave herself the pleasure of loving him, not as a mother hen, but as a woman, purely as a woman.

"I don't want you to see that guy anymore."

It was almost as if her own conscience had spoken, warning her away from Grady. Except the voice was Grady's.

"What?"

"That guy at the deli who was hanging all over you."

"Barry? That's ridiculous, Barry's a friend. Besides, he's engaged. He'd just told me the news and I was congratulating him."

"Yeah? He didn't act engaged when he had you wrapped up."

She started to say something, and stopped.

Grady propped up his head to watch her. He hadn't known where her thoughts had gone a little while ago, though he'd suspected he wouldn't have liked it. But this time at least he could follow her progress.

Her expression shifted from amazement to resolve; from reacting to what he said, to his right to say it. He didn't think he was going to like this, either.

"Grady, you can't tell me who to see or who not to see. You have no claim on me. I have no claim on you."

"Well, maybe that can change. In time." This was uncharted territory for him, stepping into it left him feeling uncertain, a little scared, but dogged.

"You don't understand. It won't change. It can't change. Because we can't have a claim on each other."

A thread of desperation wove into her words. He could understand that, he felt a little that way himself. Maybe even a shade deserted. Why would she pull away from him now? How could she deny this closeness, built up of friendship, expressed through passion?

"Why?"

The demand rocked her, he saw that, but she gathered herself. "We're not headed for the same kind of life."

He swore to himself and at himself. She was still seeing his damned playboy image. And the worst of it was he'd deserved it. But he thought she'd seen how he'd changed; more importantly, he thought she'd seen what he'd always been beneath the image.

"That's not true. I'm not saying I'm ready. I'm not saying I'm any prize in the relationship sweepstakes, but don't dismiss me as just Good-Time Grady. That's not what I want from my life, that's—"

"Grady, you don't have to tell me—"

"No, listen." He gripped her hands, then consciously softened his hold. "Hear me out. Will you do that?"

She closed her eyes, and he had the uneasy impression it was to prevent his seeing pain in them.

"Yes, I'll do that."

She sounded so calm; he must have been mistaken. Still, for some reason, this wasn't easy for her. That made him all the more determined to be honest. Not only so she would know about him, but in the hope she might reveal whatever barrier she'd erected all the others to obscure.

He took a breath and let it out slowly. This wouldn't be easy. He hadn't said these words to anyone before. He'd figured the people who mattered in his life knew at some level, and no one else was important. But Leslie was important, so he searched for words.

"I already told you enough about my parents, so you know my home life wasn't the best." He waited for her nod and to give himself another second. "And I guess I mentioned about fantasizing my family was like the ones I saw in old movies. I suppose you could say the fantasizing didn't stop there... I mean, uh, I've always dreamed about having a family. Having a wife and kids and a real home, not

just some designer condo or a hotel room. The whole suburban dream—cookouts and playing catch with the kids and
cuddling with my wife in a hammock after mowing the
lawn—''

He stopped abruptly, fearing he'd gotten too earnest, but
saw only understanding in Leslie's eyes.

He managed a grin. ''Would you believe I've never
mowed a lawn in my life? But I'd learn how, just so I could
teach my kids. And play catch and help them with homework. We could take family trips and...''

Leslie listened to Grady's dream for a family.

At first with an awkwardness that broke her heart, then
with more assurance and fervor, he talked about how he
imagined raising his children. How he'd spend time with
them, how he'd love them.

How they would have the happy childhood he'd never
had. How they would know the love and security every child
should have, every child needs. And that he'd never had. He
didn't say those things, but she heard them, anyhow.

''So we *do* want the same things from life. I might need
some tutoring in this like I did with gift buying—'' His
crooked grin tore at her. ''But I think with time—and help—
I'll get the hang of it. I won't make you any promises and
I'm not asking any because I'm not sure where this is heading with us. But I am asking one thing: Will you give me
time, Leslie?''

Every word confirmed the heartache she'd seen coming
all along. It waited there for her as surely as an oak's leaves
died come fall. Backing away now might cushion some of
the chill.... But how could she pull away from him now?

''Yes, I'll give you time.''

She would love him with every bit of her soul, until he
could not possibly doubt the value of the heart he had to

offer. And she would treasure the time for herself, before she accepted the permanency of winter.

Then she would tell him a future for them was impossible, because she couldn't give him the one thing he wanted. She couldn't give him children.

## Chapter Eleven

Three weeks. Three weeks wasn't long enough to love Grady Roberts the way he needed to be loved.

But three weeks was all she'd had between that day he'd followed her to the Wisconsin Avenue deli—and the night that followed—and April's arrival.

Three weeks of laughter and loving. Out in public it really wasn't so different from the weeks when he'd been taking her to the historic sites, except he touched her more often—his leg against hers, his arm around her shoulders, his hand holding hers—which in a way was a very big difference. In private the touching expanded, reaching the most satisfactory of conclusions.

In their free time, he wanted to continue the historic trips, but she suggested saving those for entertaining April; the topic of Charlottesville she avoided altogether. Instead, they sampled nearby activities: an outdoor concert at Wolf Trap, a men's professional tennis tournament at Rock Creek Park, a free Shakespeare play at Carter Barron, a military band at the Jefferson Memorial.

Mostly they did things alone. But Grady did arrange one dinner with Tris and Michael. It went better than Leslie had anxiously anticipated. She wondered how much of that had to do with the soothing hand Michael kept on Tris most of the evening. From the activity she sensed under the table she wouldn't have been surprised if he supplemented it with some leg, knee and foot touches, too. Gratitude aside, however, she would have been blind not to recognize that touching his wife was no hardship for Michael Dickinson.

Grady stayed at her apartment, in her bed, every night except two, when he had to return to Chicago, and she'd missed him much too much for comfort.

Leslie offered her knowledge of the area to help him assess office possibilities. He not only took her up on that, but soon had her looking at houses with him, too. He said nothing overt, but some of his comments...well, if that had gone on much longer, she would have had to pull away even sooner than she'd planned.

In some ways, April's arrival was a relief.

It slowed her growing intimacy with Grady without her having to apply the brake herself.

In some ways it was pure hell.

As much as she loved her family, and felt that April had been dealt a less than satisfactory hand when it came to parents, the girl's monosyllabic, sullen answers challenged even Leslie's patience.

Surprisingly Grady dealt well with April. He made no effort to cajole or please April, treating her as matter-of-factly as he might a business associate. And she responded in kind—which was the friendliest Leslie had seen her.

It was the physical frustration Grady didn't deal well with.

Leaving her apartment, he tugged her after him into the shadowed stairwell and kissed her thoroughly.

"I'm too old for this stuff, Leslie."

"I thought you were doing just fine," she said dryly, still breathless.

He grinned, but shook his head. "Holding hands, having my arm around you at the movies and snatching kisses in the kitchen is for teenagers. Don't get me wrong, I like it, but I want more. Lots more. Can't we send April to daycare for a day?"

"Talk about being too old. Besides—"

He dropped his forehead against hers. "I know, I know. The kid's gotten shunted aside enough as it is." When he raised his head she caught a gleam in his eyes. "But how about if we showed her how much we trust her by leaving her alone in your apartment—"

"I do leave her alone—mornings—while I'm at work at the foundation."

"Then how about leaving her alone for a night while you're at play in my hotel room."

"Grady—"

He cut off her protest with a hard, deep kiss that pressed her flush against the wall. The kiss gentled, but picked up a rhythm that quickly had her body responding. She wrapped her arms around his shoulders, pressed her breasts against his hard chest and opened her legs slightly for him to nestle against her.

Lord, did anything else in the world feel as good?

Yes, one thing.

He slid his hand down her side, past her hip, along the back of her thigh, to behind her knee, then lifted, shifting so her thigh hooked over his, and bringing them a little closer.

And she remembered what he'd said three weeks before, about taking her right there, right then.

He wouldn't . . . would he?

"God, Leslie, I do need you." His hips took up the rhythm as his lips touched her cheekbone, her eyebrow, her chin. "This way, yes, but also—"

A door closing below them and footsteps on the stairs broke them apart like a shot. By the time Mr. Weidelman reached their landing, they both had their clothes in order and their breathing somewhat under control. Though Grady stuck close to the shadows.

Leslie considered it very fortunate that Mr. Weidelman took time climbing stairs and that his eyesight wasn't as sharp as his wife's. He merely gave them a curious look, wished them a good-night and continued on to his apartment.

Grady started to reach for her; Leslie stepped back.

"No. Talk about acting like teenagers. We can't do this out here. We might not be this lucky next time."

"And we can't do it in there." He jerked his head toward her apartment door. "We've got to think of a way to be alone together, Leslie. It's been twenty-two days." He studied her face for a moment, then seemed to relent. "Look, we're both tired tonight and we both have to be up early for work. But tomorrow we figure something out. I can't take another week of this, and I hope to God you can't, either." He kissed her hard and quick. "I'll call you tomorrow."

The knock on her office door and the buzz on her phone arrived simultaneously.

"Come in— Hello?"

"Hi, Leslie." Grady's voice came across the phone line, enough to make her heart beat faster. "Have I got news for you. Guess—"

"Leslie!" Tris came around the opening door already talking. "Guess—"

"—what!" The word came in stereo.

"What?"

"The baby!"

"Bette had the baby—"

"This morning—"

"A little girl—"

"Everybody's fine—"

"Paul just called—"

"Bette went into labor last night, right after dinner—"

"He started off calm, then he got so excited, Mrs. M. had to take the phone and give me the details. They're not sure on the name—"

"Seven pounds, two ounces. Born at 8:02 this morning and—"

"Wait a minute, wait a minute both of you," Leslie finally had a chance to order.

"Both of us?"

"Who's on the phone?"

"Grady's on the phone and," she added into that instrument, "Tris is here in the office and you're both talking at the same time, and I can only hear one at a time."

"Well, if you've got Grady filling you in, I'm going to go try Michael again. He was out of the office, but Sharon thought she could track him down." Tris raised her voice to be sure it would carry through the phone. "And nobody else better tell him the news before I get a chance to, do you hear that, Grady Roberts?"

He laughed.

"He heard," Leslie said. Tris gave her a suspicious look, but waved goodbye and closed the door behind her.

"I wonder if I could get to him first...."

"Don't you dare even try."

He chuckled. "Okay. I'd rather talk to you, anyhow."

"Grady, isn't this early for the baby to come? I thought Bette's due date was later."

"It was. But you know, Mrs. M. has said all along that she thought the baby would be earlier than that. And from what Bette said the past couple times I talked to her, I don't suppose she minds cutting a week off this pregnancy, not as long as the baby's fine, and from all reports she is. In fact," he said indulgently, "the report from Illinois is that she's perfect."

"I'm glad," she said sincerely, though she couldn't stop sad memories from joining her happiness for Bette and Paul.

"Leslie?"

"Hmm?"

"You know, I'll need help buying a baby gift."

Laughter broke through her memories. "But you're a graduate of the Leslie Craig Gift-Buying Course. You shouldn't need any help."

"That was for housewarming gifts. This is for a *baby*. How am I supposed to figure out what would make a baby happy or make it think about me every time it used the gift? Especially a girl! Now a boy I could have gotten a baseball outfit or enrolled him in the Michael Jordan basketball camp for the year 2005, but a girl..."

"All right, I'll help."

"Good. I thought we could shop in Chicago, say the end of next week."

"Chicago? But—"

"We'll take April with us."

"Grady, I can't—"

"And since you'll be helping me shop, it'll be my treat."

"But where—"

"The Monroes invited us all to stay with them in Lake Forest for a long weekend, so we can all see the baby but Paul and Bette will still have peace and quiet at home."

"But I don't—"

"They specifically asked if you'd come, too. Mr. and Mrs. M. remember you from the wedding, of course, and they've heard all about the beach weekend from Paul and Bette. You're part of the gang now. They know about April, and believe me, nobody could be nicer to her than they'll be. Besides, Paul and Bette would wonder why you didn't come to see the baby. Don't you want to see the baby?"

"Of course I do, but—"

"Great. And you know there'll be lots of people to keep an eye on April, so who knows, we might even manage some time alone together."

Was that the problem, that they hadn't had time alone together? Or was there something more going on behind that Katharine Hepburn bone structure that he'd come to know so well, that he'd come to need to see and feel and kiss daily.

Grady held down the disconnect button, not quite ready to make his next call.

Was Leslie backing away or was it his imagination? He didn't have experience with this sort of situation, so he had a lot of questions and nobody he could ask.

Especially the biggest question—what would his reaction be if Leslie stopped pulling away, if she started toward him? Would he have the emotional gumption to meet her with open arms, to give whatever he had to give and hope it would be enough? Or would he turn tail and run?

Nobody could answer that, not even himself.

He released the button and dialed his travel agent to book three airline tickets to Chicago.

* * *

"So Sharon Karik tracked Michael down at a Senate committee hearing with Senator Bradon and passed him a note. Joan wanted to see it, too, and of course she knows Paul and Bette through Michael, so she was really pleased, and she announced to the whole hearing that the state of Illinois just got a new constituent, and everybody applauded. Can you imagine? Baby Monroe's not even a day old and she's already been mentioned in the U.S. Senate!"

Leslie smiled. "Maybe someday she'll be there as a senator herself."

"Or as president! With Paul's gift of gab and Bette's organization and discipline there'll be no stopping that child."

"And we can brag that we're responsible for her first taste of crab cakes—in utero."

They laughed together.

"Did Grady tell you we're all going next weekend to see the baby? I hope they have a name by then. It's hard to keep calling her 'the baby.' Anyhow, he did tell you, didn't he?"

"Yes."

"You're not worrying about staying with the Monroes, are you? Aunt Nancy insisted you and April come, and she'll skin both me and Grady if you don't."

"That's very nice of her," Leslie said absently.

"I don't know if I'd call skinning me and Grady *nice*, exactly, but I get your drift." Tris's wry tone turned a little anxious. "You and April are coming, aren't you?"

"Yes, we're coming."

"Good." Leslie didn't respond and she didn't notice the silence had extended until Tris leaned across her desk and put a hand over hers. "Leslie, do you want to talk?"

"No. I'm fine."

Talking only brought the wound to the surface.

Only reminded her that other people still found the kind of love to build a life on—Tris and Michael, Paul and Bette. Only showed her that couples building a life on love had babies—Paul and Bette now, Tris and Michael someday soon. She'd probably be Aunt Leslie to those babies. And he'd be Uncle Grady, but by then he'd be with Aunt Sweet Young Thing, and they'd be building a life, a family.

No, talking wouldn't help.

"I'd like you all to meet Anne Elizabeth Monroe," Paul announced from the doorway onto the porch. He had one arm around his wife, and his eyes on the baby daughter she held. "Anna, these are our friends."

The bright blue eyes under a bit of reddish fluff acknowledged the formal introduction with a blink.

"The birth certificate says Anne, but Anna seems to fit her better," explained Bette.

Everyone was busy oohing and aahing over the form wrapped in a delicate white blanket.

After arriving in Chicago in the afternoon, they'd settled in at the Monroes', then drove down to Evanston for a tour of Paul and Bette's house and newly landscaped yard. But this was Anne Elizabeth's first appearance.

"Look at those eyes!"

"She's beautiful."

"She has Paul's hair."

"And Bette's top lip," Paul added with a significant look at his wife, which she returned warmly.

The phone rang, and Paul went to answer it. None of the rest of them budged from around the baby. James and Nancy Monroe, having been exercising their grandparently rights for the past ten days, were content to let the newcomers have front-row positions. Even April looked curiously at the tiny person.

"Bette, it's Judi on the phone from Yellowstone," Paul announced from the doorway. "She wants to talk to you."

"Oh, good. It seems like I've been napping every time Judi's called," she explained. She turned to Leslie, sitting next to her. "Will you hold Anna?"

Grady saw something flash across Leslie's eyes, but her voice was perfectly calm. "Of course."

With an emotion he couldn't define, Grady watched her open her arms, and the baby settle there as if she understood their security. Restless, he moved to the far side of the porch; couldn't have everybody crowding the baby.

"April, why don't you come sit beside me," Leslie invited.

Her expression mixing reluctance and fascination, April sat on the edge of the settee.

"I don't think I've ever seen a baby this young," said Tris. "Have you, April?"

"No."

Leslie said something more to her in a low voice that Grady didn't pick up, but he saw its effect as April relaxed enough to comment on Anna's squirming. She even gauged the strength of those baby kicks against her hand, and smiled at the sensation.

From across the room he studied Leslie. A woman who could make a baby feel secure, who could make a troubled girl smile, who could make a man . . . feel loved.

Loved.

With this woman perhaps he could build the loving family he wanted, but hadn't trusted himself to try for.

He'd always known he wasn't much good at loving—genes or environment, what did it matter, the result was the same. But Leslie . . . Leslie was loving enough for both of them, loving enough to make up for his lack. Maybe even loving enough to teach him.

Watching Leslie hold the baby, he let himself dream for the first time of a future with her.

Grady, Tris and Michael took Leslie and April sightseeing Saturday with an agenda unlike any tour company's. They drove past the schoolyard where Grady first met Paul over a bloody nose. They saw the harbor where the friends learned to sail. In Evanston, they visited Northwestern's campus, where Grady and Paul had met up with Michael, and later Tris. They stopped for midday sustenance at a little place Grady knew ... which just happened to be across the street from Wrigley Field.

Once in the city, they saw more traditional sights—the Water Tower, the Wrigley Building, the Art Institute, Grant Park, Buckingham Fountain and Sears Tower. But even the thrilling view struck Leslie as anticlimactic after the emotional landmarks of the morning.

Grady hadn't taken them to the house he grew up in and still his parents' official residence. She'd asked, and he'd shrugged it off.

Returning to the Monroes' in Lake Forest, they found Paul, Bette and Anna already there for the evening's cookout. When Anna grew sleepy, that was no problem, since her grandparents had designated one bedroom as hers, and it was nearly as well equipped as her nursery at home.

Paul and Bette didn't stay very late, but the rest sat on the Monroes' patio, talking while lightning bugs came and went. Leslie noticed that April seemed strangely content to stay with the grown-ups. But then maybe this was one of the few times she'd been included in the conversation naturally, rather than being ignored or spotlighted with questions.

Relaxed in a way she'd seldom seen him, Grady's fondness for the Monroes showed clearly. It made his estrangement from his parents all the sadder to her.

When the evening broke up, Grady caught her in the hall around the corner from the room she was sharing with April for a kiss that a half hour later left her lying in bed feeling dissatisfied and worried. If stopping with a kiss made her feel this bad, how was it going to be when there were no kisses?

She had to get used to it, that's all. Starting tomorrow, she would avoid being alone with Grady, avoid opportunities for the kisses and touches that made her want more. She would start getting used to not having him.

After Sunday brunch on the Monroes' patio, her new resolve received its first test—and flunked.

"Leslie and I are going for a drive," Grady announced, taking her hand and leading her toward the driveway. "We'll meet you at Paul and Bette's about two."

"Wait a minute—"

"It's all right. I promise we'll be back in time for me to help move that furniture Paul and Bette need upstairs, and then we can all get to the Monroes' before Mrs. M. tries to fix a meal suitable for feeding the entire roster of the Chicago Bears," he said, reassuring her about the wrong thing. "I have something I want to show you. Something I hope you'll want to see."

Her protest died right there. His family's home, that's where he was taking her. He'd thought about it since yesterday and decided . . . to go the opposite direction.

They were headed south, but Mrs. M. had definitely pointed to the north when she'd mentioned where Grady's family lived.

"Where are we going?"

"It's a surprise." He grinned.

"We're not going to see where you grew up?"

Stupid question, Leslie. And the wrong question; she knew that even before his grin faded.

"No."

She didn't have the heart to ask about their destination after that, so they drove in silence, past Evanston into the city. Short of downtown, though, he left Lake Shore Drive and made a couple turns before pulling into a driveway that dipped dramatically under a tall building and opened into a forest of parking spots. He pulled into one and stopped the car.

"I told you I had something to show you."

The grin was trying to return, so she played to his humor. Anything to erase the bleakness her mention of his family home had spawned.

"An underground garage? Not too thrilling, Grady."

"It's what's above the ground that's thrilling. About eighteen floors above the ground, to be exact."

"Oh? What's that?"

"My apartment. That's what I brought you to see." He leaned across the seat and kissed her. "More specifically, my bedroom." And kissed her again. "More specifically still, my bed." He ran the back of his fingers down her throat and just under the collar of her blouse. "Want to see my engravings?"

She laughed a little shakily. "You don't really have engravings, do you?"

"No, but I've always wanted to use that line. I've been saving it for the right woman."

"I'm flattered." Flattered and a little stunned by the heat in his eyes, which told a much stronger message than any words he said. "But I shouldn't stay. I thought this was going to be a short trip." She hurried on, avoiding the reminder of where she'd thought they were going. "I shouldn't leave April on her own with the Monroes. It's not fair to them—"

"They love having her around."

"Or to April."

"They'll look after her."

"I know that, that's not the point."

"What is the point, then?"

"We already dragged her off on this trip, to see a lot of people she didn't know, and then we go off and leave her. April hates getting shunted around like so much excess baggage."

He looked at her curiously. "She told you that?"

"No. But it stands to reason, doesn't it? It's what her mother does to her all the time. And I think it's part of why she's so wary of staying with me. She's not sure if I want her around or if she's been foisted off on me."

"I can guarantee that Mrs. M. won't treat April as if she's been foisted off on her. Mrs. M. loves kids. And you know Tris and Michael will be nice to her."

"I know, but—"

"We haven't been alone in a long time, Leslie. Who knows when the next time might come. If you don't want to make love . . . well, I just want to be with you."

It had been a long time, and the next time might never come. She had to tell him the truth, and she had to do it soon. Resolve be damned. She was human; she wanted this time with him. Perhaps this one last time.

"I want to be with you, too, Grady. And I want to make love with you. I want it very much."

Grady held her hand for most of the drive back to Paul and Bette's house. The first time the steering wheel required both of his hands, she'd started to pull hers away, but he'd snatched it back and pressed it against his thigh, where it remained until he could fold it in his hand again. After that she hadn't tried to withdraw.

Maybe she'd needed the continued connection, too.

He wished he knew why he needed it so badly.

He thought about that as he helped Paul and Michael maneuver four cumbersome bookcases up two flights of stairs to the third-floor room being outfitted as a home office. The cases weren't unbearably heavy, but avoiding banging up walls, railings or shelves took teamwork.

The women were indulging in teamwork, too—shopping. He'd watched Leslie go off with Tris, Bette and April to find Bette postpregnancy clothes, and he'd wanted to call her back.

What was the matter with him?

Their lovemaking had been as hot, strong and satisfying as ever. Only he couldn't shake this feeling that there'd been an undercurrent of sadness to it, too. He couldn't pin it down to anything Leslie said or did, not even a look in her eyes. But it left him wanting to hold on to her hand as long as he could.

He wondered what she'd say if she knew how he felt about her hands. How he loved to watch them, especially on him. How their touch drove him crazier than the rub of skin against skin could possibly explain. How he imagined sometimes that they were strong enough and gentle enough to hold someone's heart.

Laugh at him—no, she wouldn't laugh at someone else's emotion. Though she might raise that one brow of hers in slow-motion surprise. He wouldn't mind that so much, because there'd also be understanding in her eyes.

Those hands of hers . . .

Why did he fear that if he let her hand go for a moment, the next time he reached for it, it would be gone?

"Where did they go?" Tris, the first one through the door, looked around the empty porch. "I heard Michael."

Right behind her, Leslie gave the three partly empty beer bottles on the table a quick look. "Looks to me as if they're celebrating a job well done."

Bette joined them, surveying the scene. "Or commiserating on a disaster," she said, glancing up as if she might be able to see through ceilings and floors to any disasters awaiting her upstairs.

"I considered that," said Leslie, doggedly keeping the humor in her voice. It hadn't been easy. Whatever progress she'd thought April had made over the past weeks seemed an illusion now, as the girl lapsed into limp indifference to everything around her. On top of that she'd caught both Tris and Bette eyeing her with concern. "But I think there'd be a few broken bodies strewn around in that case."

"You're probably right."

"I could have sworn I heard Michael's voice out here," Tris insisted. "Though it was awfully soft."

"You think she's cracking up?" Leslie asked the increasingly silent April, the reluctant tail of their group now, as she had been all during the shopping trip.

"Dunno," was the only response.

"I heard him."

"You probably did," said Bette. She held up a plastic gadget about the size of her hand. "Through this. It's the baby monitor. We can hear any sounds in her room, but noise where we are won't disturb her— Listen."

She turned a tiny knob and they all heard the rhythmic creak of a rocking chair, then Michael's voice.

"Hey, this isn't all that hard."

"Yeah?" Grady teased. "Then how come you turned stark white and had to wipe your hands on your pants before Paul handed her to you."

"Sounds like you want to be next," said Paul.

"Oh, no, wait a minute, I didn't say—" The women grinned at one another at the change in Grady's voice. Beneath her grin, though, Leslie felt a strong pull of sadness.

"Sure sounded to me like somebody itching to hold a baby. Here, Paul, you take the baby so I can get up, and Roberts can have his turn."

Tris giggled softly. "He's got the hang of it, but he won't try to stand up holding her!"

Muffled sounds of movement mingled with Grady's protests.

"I have got to see this," said Bette. "C'mon. Just watch out for the second step from the top. It squeaks."

"I'll be right behind you," promised Tris. "I wish I'd seen Michael holding her, but you're right, this will be too good to be missed."

Leslie followed Bette and Tris, needing to see and wishing she didn't.

Upstairs, they silently made their way to the open nursery door. April hadn't followed, and her conscience pushed at her to find the girl. But across the room, Grady was seated in the rocking chair, his total attention focused on the bit of humanity Paul held out to him, and she couldn't make herself leave.

"Not yet. I'm not ready yet."

Michael chuckled wickedly, and Grady cursed under his breath, then added a hurried apology to Anna, which made both Paul and Michael laugh.

Michael spotted the added spectators but heeded their fingers-to-lips signal, and the lesson went on.

"Just open your right hand and put it in your lap, and open your left hand and put it up a little bit," instructed Paul. "Good. Okay, now . . . Relax your hands, Roberts— I'm not going to drive spikes through them. Okay . . There!"

"Omigod." Grady seemed to barely breathe the word, but Leslie thought it sliced right to her heart.

"You are now officially holding a baby," announced Michael.

"And doing very well," said Bette, stepping into the room.

"Bravo!" Tris called softly. She went directly to Michael, slipping an arm around his waist as he looped his around her shoulders. "And it sounded as if you're well on your way to becoming a baby-holding virtuoso yourself, Michael."

Amid explanations of how they'd heard part one of the lesson and merciless teasing of both Michael and Grady, led by Paul, Grady started to gently rock, looking down at the baby in his arms. The tension had disappeared; he looked like a natural holding a baby, and Leslie wanted to find a refuge where she could let the tears slide down her cheeks. Instead she smiled at the jokes, and tried not to openly stare at Grady and Anna.

"All right, I think we've taken enough abuse here," Michael finally declared. "Let's talk about what happened when the first sound came over that baby squawk box."

"Oh, no, that's not necessary. Not necessary at—"

"Sure it is, Paul. I think the ladies would be very interested to hear how you leaped out of your chair—"

"Probably have a dent in the porch ceiling from his head," Grady interposed without looking up.

"—hurdled the chaise longue and ran down the hall so fast that when he tried to make the turn for the stairs he almost slid right out the front door, then thundered up the stairs like an elephant stampeding. Then he screeches to a halt outside the nursery and tiptoes in—as if Anna might not have heard him!"

When the laughter died down enough that he could be heard, Paul retorted, "Let me point out that these two clowns wouldn't have known what I did if they hadn't been right on my heels doing the exact same thing."

"Maybe so," conceded Grady. "But we weren't the ones who tried to change her diaper."

Michael took up the tale then, drawing more laughs, though Paul staunchly maintained he'd progressed a lot in a skill that obviously couldn't be mastered overnight. Capturing a squirming bottom in a diaper fiendishly disposed to slipperiness took a lot of practice.

With the teasing continuing around them, Leslie met Grady's eyes.

"She's asleep. She fell asleep while I was holding her," Grady said in quiet awe, and he smiled.

Leslie looked away.

Nancy Monroe's dinner was so delicious and so plentiful, they all ended up lazing on the patio. But this time, April excused herself almost immediately. Leslie supposed the girl could have simply had her fill of grown-ups. Still, she'd better check on her—though not right away or April would feel nagged. In a little while.

A little while turned into an hour. The fading light, soft breeze and easy conversation left her relaxed almost to the state of limpness. Though the interlude at Grady's apartment might have had something to do with that, too.

She turned her head to look at the man next to her, and felt a start of surprise. She forgot what a good-looking man he was. Which was silly, considering the amount of time she spent with him. Or maybe it wasn't silly. He'd let her see beyond his surface. And she was repaying him with secrets and dishonesty.

She stood, blinking against fullness in her eyes.

"Do you need something, dear?" Mrs. Monroe asked.

"No. Thank you. I'm going to check on April."

"Want me to come with?"

"No. Thank you, Grady. It'll be better if I go alone." Better for herself, if not April, she thought as she climbed the stairs.

But every other thought disappeared as she stepped into the spacious room they shared.

The closet doors stood open, one half of it gaping empty. Two drawers were only partly closed and the nightstand was cleared of April's Walkman and cassettes.

She didn't remember getting down the stairs, but she was standing at the doorway to the patio.

"April's gone. She's run away."

## Chapter Twelve

Bette had pointed out it made more sense for Leslie to stay in the house, by the telephone, since she didn't know the area and would be the logical one to get the most information if April called. Bette also stayed, in case the baby woke.

Leslie and Bette checked the house in futile hope, then sat in silence while Mr. and Mrs. Monroe, Grady, Michael, Tris and Paul fanned out for a quick look around the neighborhood. They turned up nothing.

"I'm going to call the police." Leslie's voice was calm, and her answers succinct as she gave the police dispatcher a brief description of April, but her hand shook.

The searchers went out again even before the police car arrived. The police officer was polite and reassuring, suggesting that a girl who didn't know the area probably hadn't gotten far. But Leslie didn't feel reassured, even after he left with as many of his questions answered as she could, even with April's description broadcast to other patrol cars, even with everyone else out looking.

Time became her enemy. Creeping by as she waited, while each minute added horrible possibilities to what had happened to April.

When Anna's hungry cry demanded Bette's attendance upstairs, she gave Leslie a hard hug before leaving.

The back door opened to Grady, and Leslie stopped her pacing and spun to face him.

"You found her?"

"No. I wanted to—"

"Then what are you doing here?"

"I wanted to see how you're doing."

He reached for her, but she moved away and kept on pacing. "Don't worry about me. Worry about April."

"We'll find her," he said with an utter certainty that slashed her nerves. How could he be so certain? How could he be so certain everything would always work for him?

"Leslie," he went on soothingly, "you need to—"

"I can tell you what I don't need, Grady. I don't need you." He winced. She ignored it, turning away to keep on pacing. "Somebody to find April, that's what I need."

"Look, I know you're upset. Scared about April, but it'll be all right, Leslie, everything will be all right."

"Why?" She spun on him and repeated it. "Why? Because you want it to be? Because you're accustomed to having things the way you want them? Well, let me tell you something, Grady, things don't always turn out the way you want them to. Things—"

"I know that." But he said it too softly to penetrate her fear and frustration and sorrow.

"—don't always go the way you want them to or the way you plan them or the way you pray they will. Things don't always…" A shuddering breath stopped her words, but her eyes were dry.

"Leslie…let me hold you. Let me make it better. Just for a moment, I know, but—"

"No! Don't you understand? There are things you can't make better. But you *don't* know that, do you? You think having children of your own and bringing them up the way you think you should have been brought up is going to make everything better. It isn't. It's not going to make your parents into loving people, it's not going to erase your lonely childhood. And it's a horrible reason to want to have a child…horrible and selfish. And even if I could give you a baby, I don't know if I'd want to because that's not the reason to want a baby. But I can't…God, I can't."

A sob overtook the words.

Grady stood, frozen. His arms, which had been reaching for her now looked as if they would hold her off.

Over the urge to let the tears come, she drove home the words he might try to tell himself he hadn't heard: "I can't have a baby and that's something you can't make better, not ever."

In her heart, Grady's stunned silence translated to the rejection she'd always known was waiting. But it didn't change that she owed him an explanation. Bearing an infinite weariness, she tried to pay what she owed.

"I shouldn't have let this go on so long. I didn't intend to, but…well, you are used to getting what you go after." The ironic tone faded to sadness. "The trouble is, this time what you went after wasn't what you thought it was. I'm not what you thought I was."

She sighed—tired, so tired—then spoke carefully. "I was married before, Grady. His family and mine have been friends forever. I knew Frank all through school. We went to UVA together and were married right after graduation.

We had exactly the life we'd planned. I had everything I wanted. We decided to start our family after a couple years. We wanted two boys and two girls, and I got pregnant almost right away. Frank teased me about being right on schedule, then he gave me this watch to celebrate." She fingered the bracelet watch she always wore. "Everything was perfect . . . perfect."

She wrapped one hand around the opposite elbow, a futile instinct to protect her innermost self.

"I was driving back from the obstetrician. He'd just told me—he'd promised me—everything was perfect. It was sleeting. The road was slick. It started with one car barely bumping another, but nobody could stop behind them. It was a chain reaction. I was in the middle, where the impact was worst. That's what they told me. I don't remember it. I just remember saying goodbye to the doctor's receptionist, then waking up in the hospital four days later. They'd tried to save the baby but there'd been too much trauma from the accident. He didn't have a chance. And I was hemorrhaging... The doctors were very good, I know that. They saved my life. I know they did everything they could... But I can't ever have another baby."

Memories spilled in then: the grim words, Frank's shock, Grandma Beatrice's strength. The numbing grief.

"Frank never said anything. Never reproached me, never said an unkind word, but I knew how he'd wanted children. And it was there between us. All the time between us. Like a wedge. And once a wedge is in place it opens up spots for more things to come between you. And pretty soon, you've drifted apart. That's what happened to us, we drifted. I asked him if he wanted a divorce, and he said yes. I took my maiden name and left Charlottesville the day my son should have been six months old."

He said nothing.

She started to walk past him. He put out an arm and she had to stop to avoid having him touch her.

"Leslie—" His voice sounded rusty, ragged. "Leslie, give me a chance. Give me a chance to think, to come up with something to say to you, to—"

"No, Grady." She held out her arm as if to ward off a blow. "Even if you say all the right things, it won't work. I walked away from my marriage with only this engraved watch, but with you I don't think I could bear to keep even that much. I can't afford to strip myself clean again. I won't risk it."

The door opening was like a shot in the silence.

"Grady! Oh, there you are." Michael looked from Grady to Leslie and back.

"What do you want, Michael?" Grady stepped forward, blocking any view of Leslie.

"A couple of neighbors who'd been out bicycling just told Mrs. M. they saw a girl who looked like April heading to town about an hour ago. I was going to drive in and check it out. Thought you'd want to come."

"Yes. I'll be right there."

Michael took his cue. Grady waited until the door closed behind him. "Leslie—"

"Don't, Grady. Just find April. Please."

He hesitated a moment, the walked out.

"Nothing—damn it."

"Make another circuit, Michael."

"Okay." He turned a corner. "Grady, if talking would help . . ."

"If I knew what the hell to say it might. But thanks."

Silently, both intently squinting beyond the streetlights into shadows, they circled Lake Forest's business square for the fourth time.

Grady leaned forward, peering across the tracks at the train station. "Let's check over there."

Before Michael stopped the car in the parking lot, Grady was out of it, making for the darkest corner of the platform where he'd spotted an even darker shadow.

After Bette took Michael's call from the train station, Leslie let herself be shepherded with the rest of the returned hunters into the family room by Mrs. Monroe, who was busy dispensing heavily sugared iced tea.

The door opened, and April walked in, flanked by Michael and Grady.

"April!"

"She's all right," Grady reassured.

"Where were you? What did you do? Why did you... Oh, God, the things that could have happened—" Leslie swallowed a sob.

April looked at her in surprise, then hung her head.

"Leslie, I'd like to talk to you." Grady's voice, pitched low, was stiff, perhaps with nerves.

"No. There's nothing more to talk about." She turned to the others. "I want to thank you—all of you—for looking for April, for... and for finding her." Her eyes didn't quite reach Grady's. "I am so grateful for your help. I don't know what I would have done—" Blinking hard, she took her relative's arm. "But now I think April and I need to do some talking—"

"Ah, no. No talking. Not tonight," interrupted Mrs. Monroe, separating Leslie and April. "Most certainly not tonight. I am taking this child to tuck her into bed right this moment. And you stay where you are," she ordered Grady, who'd taken a step toward Leslie. "I said no talking tonight, and I meant it. Besides, you're needed down here to help that nice policeman fill out his report. They said he'd be over in a few minutes. Tris, why don't you take Leslie in hand and get her into a hot tub and get some of that tension out of her? And, Jim, I think a bit of brandy for everyone else wouldn't be amiss."

"Except Bette," Paul interposed.

"A swallow would be good for her and won't hurt the baby. I used it myself as a young mother. How do you think I survived having you?"

With that parting shot, she herded Leslie, Tris and April out of the room, secure everything had been arranged to her satisfaction.

Tris not only got Leslie into a hot, scented bath, she returned shortly with a generous snifter of brandy, and insisted Leslie drink it.

With fear for April seeping out of her blood and brandy seeping in, Leslie found herself telling her story for the second time that night.

The strange thing was that by the end she felt better. Would she have felt this way if she'd told Tris all those years ago when Tris had confided her past sorrows?

"And you told Grady all this tonight?"

"Yes."

"And?"

"And nothing."

"What did he say?" Tris demanded.

"It doesn't matter what he said. Because that won't change the facts."

Tris looked at her levelly. "You mean the fact that you can't have children."

Somehow it sounded different when Tris said it than when it echoed in her own heart. Not better; it would never sound better. But less . . . less defining. She wasn't sure that made sense, and she wasn't prepared now to examine it.

"Yes. That, and the facts about Grady."

Tris shook her head. "I'm not so sure about the facts about Grady anymore. I know I'm the one who warned you about him, but—"

"Not that. I'm talking about the fact that from the start Grady has pushed aside obstacles between us as if a relationship were a challenging game to be won. But this—" She patted the abdomen that would never again grow round with a child. "Is one obstacle that all his wealth and charm and power and good looks can't overcome, one situation he can't change. And when he realizes that, he'll know the game's lost and he'll be grateful I ended it now."

"What are you doing sitting here in the dark, Grady?"

Waiting for the light, he thought. But the light he hoped for wouldn't come with the morning.

"Are you all right?" added Nancy Monroe.

"I'm fine."

"You don't look it, dear." She softened the words with a hand on his shoulder. "At my age having trouble sleeping's to be expected, but you're too young."

He didn't feel young.

Leslie's refusal to talk to him wasn't all bad from Grady's viewpoint. He had a lot of sorting out to do. But sorting out was not conducive to sleep.

"I'll make some coffee."

"Thanks, Mrs. M., that would be great."

They drank coffee in silence as, through the French doors, the lake and sky gradually revealed themselves.

When he stood, Nancy Monroe said nothing, but looked at him inquiringly.

"Thought I'd go sailing this morning," he said.

"It looks like a nice morning for it." But she was looking at him rather than the weather. "Alone?"

"Not if I can help it."

"Do you think that's wise?"

"Maybe not, but I'm going to try."

"Be careful, Grady. Trying to help someone can be a dangerous business."

He thought of that as he stepped into the room Leslie and April shared. He absorbed the quiet as his eyes adjusted to the shadows. Leslie slept on her side, facing him. A frown stitched her brows as if pain squeezed them together even in sleep. Her hand was on her pillow, near her cheek. Two steps, and he'd be to the bed. He could hold her hand, stroke her hair and ease that frown.

Instead, he walked around the end of Leslie's bed and touched April's shoulder.

"C'mon, April, wake up. We're going sailing."

A wave pushed the boat sideways, and April's hold on the seat tightened.

"You sure you know how to run this thing?"

He didn't smile. "I'm sure. I've been sailing since I was about half your age."

He concentrated on the soothingly familiar actions, letting her adjust to the boat and to him. When they were out to where the open horizon carried equal weight with the shoreline behind them, he set the boat into an easy course.

"When I was about ten, I brought a boat out here and seriously considered never going back. I figured they'd never find me."

She gave him a quick look, clearly bracing for a lecture on her stunt the night before. "You would have hit Michigan."

"I'd turned north once I got out here. Since you know geography, you know there's a lot of lake between here and land heading that way."

"Somebody would have found you." She sneered.

"Depends how soon they started looking. Big lake, small boat."

"They would have missed you right away." The jerk of her head indicated the land they'd left. The sneer was slightly less pronounced. "They would have sent somebody after you."

"I didn't know the Monroes yet." He let that sink in. "I was out here nineteen and a half hours, from two-thirty in the afternoon until almost ten the next morning. And nobody came after me, because nobody missed me."

"Your mom and dad—"

"Were in Europe. And the nanny they'd hired enjoyed her bourbon. She didn't last long. But long enough."

April stared at him, and he saw the aching loneliness that went to her core, and he wanted to cry for her, and the child he'd been, who understood her too damn well.

She bent her head in an absorbed study of her hands clasped in her lap.

"Gets awfully dark out here on the lake at night," he said. "The water seems to swallow any light that makes it this far. It's dark above you, and even darker below, and you have no idea which way you're going—not only north or south, east or west, but up or down. There were times I thought for sure I was drowning even though I was still in the boat."

"Why'd you come back, when nobody'd missed you?" Her whisper told him what he'd feared—she'd considered it—and what he'd hoped—she was looking for a reason not to.

He remembered Mrs. M.'s words: *Be careful, Grady. Trying to help someone can be a dangerous business.* The danger was not only to him but to the fragile girl across from him. With an inarticulate prayer, he spoke slowly.

"I would have missed me."

Three tears splashed on the back of her folded hands. She hurriedly scrubbed them dry on her shorts.

"That night out here by myself, I realized that even if nobody else cared about my life, I did. I was pretty young, so the words weren't real clear, but I figured it was my life, and I was going to do something about it. I saw other kids who tried to do their best because it made their parents happy. I was going to do my best, even though I had to do it for myself. Had to do it alone."

He made a sound, not quite amusement. He hadn't thought about that night for a long time. "You know, though, about the time I decided all this, the wind kicked up and I had to fight like hell to stay afloat." Her surprised eyes came to his face. "It was almost as if the lake was telling me deciding's not enough. You've got to work at it. Sometimes it's harder than others."

A half-gulped sob escaped, but she didn't look away.

"And when I met the Monroes, I didn't have to do it all alone anymore. They're not my parents, but they are my family."

Eyes brimming and mouth trembling, she stared. Would she reach out or pull back into that self-protective shell? He wished with all his heart that Leslie were here, no matter how much being with her would hurt. It would be worth the cost because surely she could help this child better than he could.

"It's just..." At April's uncertain words, his spirits leaped. "It's just that I'm so lonely."

The wail of that last word was one of the loveliest sounds he'd ever heard.

"I know you are, April. I know you are."

Only a couple decades of sailing stopped him from going to her and risking overbalancing the boat. But when she stood, he tugged her onto the center seat alongside him, tucking her face against his shoulder and letting the boat rock them both.

"I don't want to go back to Charlottesville because as soon as I get there, Melly's going to drag me off on another of her trips." She snuffled and sat up straighter. "I get in her way. She doesn't want me around. She just thinks she has to and I hate it. I hate it!"

"What would you like to do?"

She looked startled that he hadn't tried to reassure her that her mother did want her around. Startled, and then thoughtful, as if she'd never gotten past the point of what she didn't want to do to consider what she did want to do.

"I'd like it to be different." The wistfulness in her voice had Grady swallowing hard. "I'd like my dad to still be alive, and for him and Mom to stay in one place together so we could be a real family."

He sighed. "I know, April. I used to wish the same thing. I wanted a little house with a white picket fence, instead of the hotels and grand houses. But it doesn't work that way. I couldn't change my parents, you can't change your mother. But you might be able to change other things. To do that, first you have to think about what you'd like to do. What do you want?"

"I want to stay in one place." The answer was heartfelt and immediate. "I want to go to one school all year long and never have to walk in as the new kid ever again in my whole life."

"Where would you like to stay?"

"Well..." Contemplating what she might like to do instead of resisting what other people had planned for her transformed April. "Charlottesville's not bad," she said judiciously. "There's a couple of kids I like to hang out with and the teachers weren't too prison guardish."

"Okay. What else?"

She looked at him a little shyly. "I kinda like Leslie. I mean, visiting her in Washington and everything."

Progress came slowly, he supposed. If she wanted to mask her feelings for Leslie under the guise that she liked the city, who was he to criticize?

"Have you told her that?"

"No." He said nothing. After a moment, she added, "You think I should?"

"You think Leslie's more likely or less likely to invite you back if she knows you enjoy visiting her? And if you were Leslie, would you like to hear somebody enjoyed visiting you or would you rather they kept it a secret?"

"All right, all right, I'll tell her."

Her mock surrender was the closest thing to humor he'd heard from April. It set the mood for their return trip. She even showed interest in sailing, and he was happy to teach her.

She grew quiet as they neared the dock.

"Guess you and Leslie won't be seeing each other any more after this trip, so I probably won't see you, either."

He forgave her the stab of pain her first words caused because he thought he understood how she might be feeling about the second part. April Gareaux had connected with so few people in her young life that she felt the impending loss of one keenly.

As Mrs. M. had said, this helping other people had its dangers.

"What happens with Leslie and me doesn't mean I can't keep in touch with you. I could write, if you'll promise to write back."

"Write?" Hope and wariness blended in the word.

"Sure. It's good for you." Her doleful look at that dreaded phrase drew a further offer. "And if you do that, I could call now and then, if that's all right with you."

"Okay." He raised an eyebrow, and she added more enthusiastically. "That would be great."

He would keep his promise to April no matter how much the reminder of Leslie hurt.


Grady insisted on driving them to the airport. He'd decided to stay on in Chicago a few days "to clear up business," and Leslie had suggested they take a taxi. But Grady wouldn't budge; he was driving them to the airport.

Paul, Bette and Anna had come up to the Monroes' for breakfast. The goodbyes and thank-yous masked the tension. But in the car it rose through the silence.

A block from the Monroes', Grady turned north instead of continuing west toward the airport. He gave no explanation, and no one asked, though Leslie caught the look Tris and Michael exchanged.

In less than five minutes, he stopped in front of a house just visible through an iron fence.

"You wanted to see it" was all he said.

But she'd already known.

Like the Monroes' it backed on Lake Michigan, but that was where the similarities ended. This was a solid, gray mass, designed to impose, not to welcome. The grounds were perfectly kept, but lacked imagination. The windows and doors gave the impression of seldom being opened. With no sign of neglect, it had an air of desertion.

Without another word, he pulled away, and the rest of the drive was accomplished in silence.

While Michael and Grady checked the baggage curbside, Tris took Leslie aside. "Look, we'll get April to the gate and get all the boarding passes."

"No, I—"

"Leslie. I've never known you to be a coward. You have to say something to each other. You *have* to."

Leslie didn't agree, but she didn't protest when Tris and Michael led April away after a round of hugs with Grady.

Inside the terminal, April said, "I have to use the rest room." Tris started to protest, but heard a snuffle the girl tried to hide and understood.

"I won't run away," April added with new dignity.

"I know you won't. We'll wait for you right here."

From their spot, they could see the back of Grady's blond head through the glass walls of the terminal.

"He was very sweet to me when he brought me to the airport last year," Tris said, fighting her own snuffle. "You'd said you were sorry after we'd made love for the first time, and I was so miserable."

His mouth twisted. "I remember. And it wasn't much fun on my end, either."

She touched his cheek, and he covered her hand. "I didn't think a drive to the airport could ever be more miserable than that one, but this came close." Grimly she added, "If he's really broken her heart, I will tear him limb from limb."

"What if she's really broken his heart?"

Tris looked up at Michael, totally secure in his love yet still able to remember the pain of thinking she'd never have it. "It would break my heart."

Michael put his arm around her and drew her close.


"Leslie—"

She wouldn't have turned if he hadn't put his hand on her arm. Even then, she didn't look at him.

"Leslie, give me some time. Give me a chance to—"

She was shaking her head. "That's just it, Grady. Time isn't going to change this. Nothing is. I want to thank you—

for this trip, for being so kind to April, for all those wonderful trips around Washington, for—'' Her voice faltered, and he took a step closer to her. But she backed away. ''For everything.''

Then she did look at him.

''Goodbye, Grady.''

And she was gone.

## Chapter Thirteen

The thing that kept hitting him in the face when he thought he was concentrating on something else was that he'd been certain he knew Leslie so well, and yet here was this aspect of her, this event, that had such an impact on her life, that turned it upside down and turned her inside out, and he'd had no inkling of it.

Did he know her? Had he been fooling himself? Was he capable of knowing someone well?

The thought, and the questions that invariably followed, became a constant itch.

Still, he surprised himself four days after Leslie left when he heard his voice saying, "The thing that keeps hitting me in the face..."

The Chicago office was running so well he didn't have much to do and he was too smart—at least in business—to interfere. So he'd taken to long walks. This afternoon's walk took him to Paul's office. Paul could be out consulting with a client ranging from the Smithsonian to a neighborhood collector, but it was as good a destination as anywhere else. When Grady walked in, Jan Robson, Paul's longtime secretary, waved him into the inner office.

He'd been sitting on the leather couch under the windows talking about nothing in particular for several minutes when the words came out. "The thing that keeps . . ."

"You're looking at it all wrong, Roberts."

Grady almost grinned for the first time in five days. It's a good thing he hadn't expected sympathy; Paul's words of wisdom ran more to bracing than nurturing.

"When you like someone, really care for them—" Grady absorbed Paul's sharp look, but didn't dispute or confirm that description. "Continuing to get to know them better all the time is one of the pleasures. If you're lucky, that never ends. Because the other person's changing and growing all the time, too. And that makes for some very interesting surprises." His smile grew distracted for a moment. "It's really the same thing with friends. Hey, look at the way you've surprised all of us in the past few months."

"I suppose I have. I've surprised myself some, too."

Paul nodded, at the same time studying him speculatively. "And I wouldn't be surprised if you keep on surprising us—and yourself—now that you've started. The first thing is, you've got to decide what you want."

Too bad it was the first thing, because that seemed to be where he got stuck. What *did* he want?

Abruptly Paul swiveled his chair and started digging in a desk drawer. "I know I had that business card here somewhere," he muttered. Then he shouted. "Jan! Have you seen Alicia Carpenter's business card around?"

The office door opened and Jan walked in with a slip of paper. "No, because you insisted you wanted to keep it in your, uh, file. But I did enter her information in my re-cords. Here."

"Thanks, Jan. What would I do without you?"

"Disintegrate," she said, deadpan.

Paul was already dialing the telephone. "I have some-body I want you to see, Grady. You go and talk to her and—Alicia? It's Paul Monroe. How soon can you arrange to talk to a friend of mine?"

Leslie smiled serenely through the rest of the week, though she thought her face might crack.

She listened to Janey's plans to pursue a long-delayed college degree. She bolstered Barry's confidence before his first visit to his in-laws-to-be. She untangled a dispute that had started with a hard slide into second in a softball game and had escalated into a wrangle over the flow of informa-tion from the foundation to a preservation magazine. She spent every possible moment with a subdued April. She avoided confidential talks with Tris. She wondered if the time would come when Grady's voice, touch, face and scent didn't accompany her every second.

Melly had been scheduled to pick April up that weekend, but to no one's surprise "something came up." Grandma Beatrice was coming instead. To avoid a grandmotherly third degree, Leslie planned to exploit the rule that Craigs did not discuss private matters in public.

They had lunch out. Went shopping. Had high tea at a hotel. Attended a Kennedy Center concert, then went out for a late supper.

"Well, Leslie Aurelia, you have succeeded," announced Grandma Beatrice upon their return to Leslie's apartment. "I am too exhausted to probe the reasons for the decidedly pinched look around your eyes. You do not look at all well, and I do expect an explanation. Though not tonight. I am going to bed. Good night, girls.''

Another time being classified with a thirteen-year-old as a ''girl'' would have amused Leslie. This night, she meekly said good-night, then sank down on the couch, where she would sleep.

April stood in front of her, eyes on the floor, hands pleating the sides of her skirt. "I, uh, I . . . thank you for having me stay with you."

She smiled, valuing the formal and stilted words for the effort it took to produce them. "You're very welcome, April. I've enjoyed having you here, and I hope you can come back."

April's head jerked up. "You want me back?"

"Of course."

"But I ran away and caused all that trouble . . ."

Leslie leveled a look at her. "Yes. You did. You also apologized to me and the Monroes and to the policeman, and you promised never to do that again."

"I won't." Leslie believed her. "But there's still . . ." April's voice trailed off, a tide of painful color swept up her cheeks and she looked away.

"There's still what?"

"The . . . the other trouble I caused."

"What other trouble?"

April glanced at her suspiciously, but seemed to accept Leslie's puzzlement as sincere. Paying her penance, she blurted out, "With you and Grady. Breaking you up."

"Oh, April." Leslie drew her down to the couch beside her. April didn't resist. "Bless your heart, you didn't break us up."

"But everything was fine until I left. I saw how you looked at each other, sort of like Melly looks at a guy when she's going to take off, when she doesn't want me around.

But when Grady brought me back, you two weren't—'' She gestured helplessly, lacking the words to express what she'd sensed. "You know, *together* anymore."

Leslie took her by the shoulders and looked directly into her eyes. "That wasn't your fault, April. I swear to you, it wasn't your fault."

"Really?"

"Really."

"But..." April accepted the reassurance but her brows knitted. "But you love him, don't you?"

Leslie started to brush off the question, then stopped. Meeting April's look, she said, "Yes. But my loving him isn't enough. My loving him isn't the problem."

"But I think he loves you..." April offered eagerly.

Leslie's lungs burned as if she'd breathed in fire. "Maybe he—" She started to say "does," but "did" was more honest. She couldn't bring herself to say that. "Maybe he started to, a little. But there were other things involved, other problems. So we have gone our separate ways."

"But—"

"That's all, April," she overrode the girl firmly. "It's time for bed. We've had a long day and we have a lot to do in the morning. We need some sleep."

She hoped April got more sleep than she did. Staring at the living room ceiling, she lay in the dark, missing Grady, wishing things could have been different and reminding herself they weren't.

At least, with all the things that needed doing in the morning, Grandma Beatrice couldn't focus her interrogation.

They packed April's belongings in the car, Grandma Beatrice promised a long telephone call to "get to the bottom of this," they hugged and Leslie stood on the curb waving them off. Alone.

* * *

A week after taking Leslie to the airport, Grady walked down granite steps in Evanston. At the bottom, he turned and surveyed the turn-of-the-century building, its limestone bulk softened by pots of flowers and an understated sign.

The sign might be oblique, but the activity inside wasn't. This was a haven for women who for many reasons would not keep the child they carried. It directed them to medical care, provided them counseling and companionship. And it promised good families for the babies.

So why had Paul sent him to an adoption agency?

Of course, Paul would say he hadn't; he'd simply sent him to talk to Alicia Carpenter. The fact that she worked as a counselor at this adoption agency was beside the point. Or was it?

Either way, Grady acknowledged that Alicia Carpenter was a good person to talk to. With no-nonsense compassion, she'd made him order the thoughts that had been flying around in his head like debris in a tornado.

He found himself quoting Leslie a lot, telling Alicia how Leslie had described him as a man accustomed to getting whatever he wanted. But that this time he had to face that he couldn't. This barrier he couldn't push aside. This situation he couldn't fix, or change. No matter how determined or how resourceful.

He could have the family he long envisioned. Or he could have a life with Leslie. But not both.

Under Alicia's guidance, the huge question of what did he want separated into smaller questions—no more easily answered, but at least comprehensible.

Could he accept never having a child he helped create? Could he accept not having his ideal family? Could he accept that the dream born of a lonely childhood to "change" history by raising his own child in a totally different way wouldn't ever happen?

Could Grady Roberts, after a lifetime successfully manipulating his world so he didn't have to accept things he didn't like, accept all this?

Could he imagine not having Leslie in his life?

Looking up at the building, he acknowledged that he didn't know the answers. He just didn't know.


Two days later and still not knowing, Grady watched a dark-curled girl in a ruffled yellow sundress and tiny white sandals meet her baby brother for the first time.

Alicia Carpenter had suggested he think about what they'd talked about and come back to see her in a couple days, after it had had time to settle.

Forty-eight hours had passed and he'd thought of virtually nothing else. But settling? No.

When he arrived for his appointment, the receptionist asked him to take a seat on the bench in the vestibule.

He watched a woman holding a baby and a man with his arm around her shoulders come down the stairs and cross to a living-room-like area off the vestibule.

"They're here!" an adult voice proclaimed from deeper in the room, then the couple and the baby were surrounded by a gray-haired couple, two younger women, another man and the little girl. The woman holding the baby crouched down to the little girl's level, and the babble quieted.

"Andrea, this is your new brother, Benjamin."

The little girl, dark eyes wide, nestled against her mother's side and ventured a tentative hand over the side of the blankets to improve her view.

"Did I look like that?" Her tone hinted at disapproval.

"Yes," said the woman. "When you first came to us, you looked very much like this."

"Oh." She digested that, then looked around at the faces above her. "This is my brother. His name is Benjamin. He's in our family now, too."

Not an eye remained dry, including Grady's.

He'd just seen a miracle. As amazing and magical in its way as childbirth. A miracle of love.

And Grady had found his answers.

How simple it all seemed now. Flesh and blood hadn't made a family of him and his parents. It wouldn't prevent him and Leslie from making a family, whether that family was the two of them or—through adoption—three or four. The only thing he couldn't accept would be not having Leslie in his life. He loved her, loved her in a way he never thought he'd be capable of.

Now he had to make her believe that and make her understand what they could be, together.

"Ms. Carpenter will see you now."

Grady came to with a start. Blankets, baby clothes, diapers and other belongings gathered, the family was preparing to leave, now one member stronger. He watched, smiling with their joy, until the front door closed behind them.

"Good. I want to see her, too." In Alicia Carpenter's office he didn't waste time on a preamble. "I've decided. I want to adopt."

Alicia looked both amused and annoyed. "And you think that's it? You've decided and now I'll walk out that door, find you a baby and hand it over? That's not how it works, Grady. Not from our end, not even from yours. It's not that simple. How about the woman you're involved with?"

"Leslie's great with kids. You should see her. Nobody could meet her and not know she'd be a great mother."

Alicia leaned across the desk toward him. "Grady, you don't even know if this woman wants a long-term relationship with you, much less marriage. Don't you think you should resolve all that first?''

He sat perfectly still as the possibilities her words evoked washed over him. What did he really know of Leslie's feelings? They hadn't talked about relationships or futures. He'd been too unaccustomed to the concepts; she'd been too protective of her secret. What if the image of them together hadn't ever occurred to her? What if...

Slowly he sat back. He sensed a light touch on his cheek, the soft stroke that an elegant, capable hand might make. It caressed his chin, his neck, his shoulder and settled over his heart. He saw Leslie's eyes when they had made love, so full of emotion, so giving.

"She loves me. She really loves me."

Wanting to whoop in exultation, he settled for a grin. The caress and the image remained, though he focused again on the woman across the desk. "She *does* love me."

Alicia sighed, but he didn't believe for an instant that she was really exasperated. "Okay, say she loves you. What if she doesn't want to adopt? Some people don't—women as well as men. They're not comfortable with it.'' She held up a hand, and he swallowed his automatic response. "Especially someone who's gone through what Leslie's gone through, the loss and the pain. From what you've said, she's made a life for herself that doesn't include children. She might not want the risk. Think about that, think about it all. More important, go back and *talk* to her about it. And listen to her, really listen."

He looked away, staring unfocused out the window to see Leslie's face as she held Paul and Bette's baby, Leslie's hands as she stroked April's hair, Leslie's tears when she told him she could never have a baby.

"I will. I will talk to her, and I will listen. But I know that this woman has too much love in her not to want to share it." He looked back at Alicia. He'd learned to read people and he thought that, despite herself, the counselor was impressed. Still, her nod was neutral.

"Okay, Grady, for the sake of discussion, we'll accept all that, too. We'll say Leslie wants to adopt and we'll say the two of you are approved—not a mere formality, let me assure you. There's still the question of babies."

He waited, but she didn't continue. "What do you mean, the question of babies?" What else had this whole discussion been about?

"That's what you have in mind, isn't it, Grady? A newborn you and Leslie can watch learn to smile, crawl, walk and talk, all the milestones? Yes, I can see that's exactly what you're thinking." She leaned forward across the desk. "But, Grady, that's everyone's dream, and there aren't as many babies as there are dreamers."

But those other dreamers couldn't give a child what he and Leslie would, he knew that. And knowing that, he believed to his core that nothing could stop them.

"Well, I can see I haven't convinced you." She sat back with a sigh, but kept her eyes on his face. "But there are other possibilities, Grady. There are other children—not babies, but children—who need families. Some have special needs. Physical or mental disabilities. Some are minorities, some are emotionally injured and some are simply past that cute, cuddly stage of babyhood. But every one of them needs love and security. Every one of them."

The sadness in her voice told of the children she saw who didn't get those basic needs met.

April's face came sharp and clear into Grady's mind. Not a baby, but a child. A child not battered or starved, thank God. A child with a parent, yet still adrift without the love and security she needed.

"Would that be something you would consider, Grady?"

"It might," he said very slowly, while the borders of his envisioned future broadened a little more. "I'd have to talk to Leslie about that. See how she feels about it."

Alicia laughed. "Now that's progress."

That Friday evening Leslie walked out of the office building and into the broiler of a Washington September heat wave with Tris at her side. Hovering at her side to be accurate.

Tris had done that this whole week, ever since April's departure. At least she didn't press Leslie to talk about Grady.

Today she'd stuck particularly close, popping into Leslie's office what seemed like every few minutes, except for an hour-long break when she said she had an errand to run at lunch. She'd also badgered Leslie into leaving work right on time, when Leslie had thought a few extra hours would be just the thing to put her ahead for the next week . . . and fill in a lonely Friday night.

So now they exited the glass doors with Tris debating, with no help from Leslie, the merits of stopping for a TGIF drink with co-workers or heading straight to her house for the dinner she'd insisted Leslie join. All the while, Tris's head whipped back and forth surveying the area.

Leslie wondered a little guiltily if Tris had said they'd be meeting Michael here and she'd forgotten, or never heard. She hadn't listened that closely to Tris; once she gave in to Tris's good-hearted bullying to spend the evening together, she figured it didn't much matter which option they chose. She'd follow wherever Tris led.

Where Tris led was down the block to a brand-new, bright red Suburban parked at the curb. Half expecting to see Michael, Leslie took in that a man was leaning against the passenger side of the vehicle. But Michael and Tris hadn't said anything about a new car, had they? And Michael wasn't that tall . . . or that blond.

"'Bout time you got here. I'm about two minutes from a ticket."

For an instant the evidence of her ears and her eyes didn't compute. And then it burst in her head with a roar that blocked out all other thought.

Grady . . . Grady!

"You brought the bag, Tris?"

Tris handed him an overnight bag that was a dead ringer for Leslie's.

"Wait a minute . . ."

Ignoring her order, which had all the firmness of Jell-O, he opened the passenger door, tossed the bag into the back seat and started around to the driver's side.

"C'mon, Leslie. Get in," urged Tris.

"That was my bag."

"Yes, and it has your clothes in it. That was my lunch-time errand. Now get in."

Tris's hands gave her a firm push in the direction of the open door, but Leslie stopped short.

"Wait a minute." This time the words had authority to them. "First I find out what's going on here, then I decide if I'm going anywhere."

"I'm doing for you what you would have done for me in the same circumstances," said Tris. "In fact, you did something very similar by sending Michael and me off alone together during a snowstorm so we could clear up misun-derstandings and figure out how we felt."

"This isn't the same thing at all. There's no misunder-standing here. There's nothing unclear about this. No amount of talking is going to change—"

Grady stopped in the act of opening the driver's door and looked across the top of the vehicle to where Leslie stood on the curb.

"I'm taking you to Charlottesville for the weekend. April's trying to work out a way she can stay there when Melly takes off, and she's getting caught in the middle between Melly and Grandma Beatrice. She needs you. They all need you."

It didn't occur to her until they were on the road to wonder how he knew her family's inner workings. He'd said they needed her, she'd believed him and she'd gotten in, closed the door and put her seat belt on without another word.

But when the question did occur to her, it also brought a niggling suspicion that he'd used those phrases—"She needs you. They all need you."—deliberately and with every expectation that she'd react exactly the way she had.

That was also when it occurred to her that the whole thing might be a blind, though she couldn't imagine why he'd go to such lengths. It wasn't as if she'd been refusing his phone calls; she hadn't heard from him since she'd left him at O'Hare Airport. Eleven days and seven hours ago.

But he continued on the most direct route to Charlottesville, and before long she felt the familiar discomfort of returning to the place that reminded her of what she'd once hoped for, had lost and would never have. Only this time it was worse because she was returning there with the man she would love for the rest of her life and with the knowledge that she couldn't have him, either.

"What's this all about?" she demanded when the silence became too clogged with unbearable thoughts.

"I told you," he said equably, but without enlightening her any.

That seemed to loosen his vocal cords, or perhaps it was because the traffic lightened away from Washington. Either way, he launched into an update on his business, including soliciting her opinion of the three finalists for his Washington office location.

After they'd discussed those, he added, "I'm pretty sure I've found the house I want, too. It's in Old Town Alexandria. It's one of the few places that hasn't had much modernizing so it'll take a lot of work, but then it would be just the way I want it. Of course I'd want you to give it your okay before I did anything."

Abruptly wary, she studied him. He kept his eyes virtuously on the road, which gave her only his profile to examine, and it showed little. He might mean he valued her opinion on a historic building. Or he might not.

"And as you can see, I got permanent transportation instead of renting all the time. I figured this would be great for hauling things, too, when I get a chance to try those auctions and sales in the country like you suggested."

"I suggested?"

"Remember, when you helped me shop for Paul and Bette's housewarming gift? You said the way to get bargains was to haunt the estate sales in the outlying counties. I thought it would be fun to furnish the house that way. I seemed to have developed a taste for antiques during all those trips we took."

As they methodically gobbled the miles to her hometown, he talked on, adroitly threading a fine line between excluding and including her in upcoming projects and trips and dreams.

What was he up to?

She couldn't figure Grady out. He didn't try to change her mind that they didn't have a future together. How could that bother her when she knew it was the truth? But neither did he say he'd accepted that they *didn't* have a future together. In fact, he acted as if nothing had happened.

As they reached the outskirts of Charlottesville, he pulled a paper from behind the visor and consulted it.

"This isn't the way to Grandma Beatrice's," she said after a few minutes.

"That's right. I thought we'd have a nice dinner at the club before we went back to the house."

The club . . . the summer she'd fallen in love with Frank . . . their wedding reception . . . then, after the accident, her one-time friends turned to pitying strangers.

"No." She barely got it out, but his expression told her he wouldn't be satisfied with that. "I don't want to go there. There are other places—"

"Grandma Beatrice and April are expecting us at the club." His quiet voice was implacable.


The first half hour was a blur to her, at the time and forever after. Then, gradually, she started to notice things.

The way Grady charmed her formidable grandmother. The tentative smile that hinted at the person April might yet become. The warm welcome by Charlie, the waiter who'd been the first man to hold out a chair for her.

Grady rarely addressed his comments to her, apparently content to keep the conversation flowing so her silence didn't stand out. But he'd positioned his chair close enough that under the tablecloth his thigh touched hers, and she was certain it was his way of offering support. She found herself drawn to the warmth of that touch, and shifted to increase the contact with its firm, muscled length.

His eyes met hers then, and what she saw rocked the certainties she'd clung to the past eleven days.

"Leslie Craig? Oh, my Lord, it is you!"

A whirlwind in blue clasped Leslie, then held her by the shoulders to get a better look at her. Brown eyes, sheened with moisture and marked by neophyte laugh lines, looked back at her.

"Cathy? Cathy Palmer?"

"Of course it's me. Though now it's Cathy McMahon. Kevin walked out on me three years ago—best thing that ever happened to me. Alan and I got married last fall. But this is no time to get into all that." She flashed a look at Grady that said she'd prefer a time when she could ask questions as well as give information.

Leslie performed the introductions, a little self-conscious, but also feeling a swell of pleasure at introducing Grady. "And you remember my grandmother..."

"Of course. It's wonderful to see you, Mrs. Craig."

"And my cousin Melly's daughter, Ap—"

"No, not April!" Cathy gave a groan of mock despair. "I won't tell you how little you were when I last saw you, but let me say that your looking so grown-up, makes me feel ancient." April looked both embarrassed and pleased. "It also reminds me, Leslie, just how long it's been since I've seen you."

"Too long," Leslie said, and realized she meant it. And the fault was mostly hers. Not only had she stayed away from Charlottesville, but the times Cathy and her then-husband, Kevin, had visited Washington, she'd shied away from seeing them, fearing it would trigger painful memories. Eventually Cathy had stopped trying.

"Entirely too long. So I won't take no for an answer—you have to come over tomorrow for the pool party we're having. All of you. My Uncle Talbert is coming, Mrs. Craig, and I know he'd love to see you, and there'll be lots of kids your age, April. And, Grady, I can promise you there'll be a number of us who've known Leslie forever and would be happy to tell you every deep, dark secret of her past at the drop of a hat."

"That sounds like an opportunity not to be missed." Grady unleashed a grin that made Cathy blink in appreciation.

A surge of panic struck Leslie. Not at Grady being told her dark secrets, but at being reminded of her own bright hopes. "Oh, I don't think we can. There are some family things that—"

"That can't be dealt with until Sunday," Grandma Beatrice interposed smoothly. "Melly won't be back until then, anyhow. We would love to come, Cathy. Just tell us the time and the address."

"Here, I'll write down the directions. Come any time after two, and plan to stay for dinner."

"That sounds great," said Grady. "That will give us time to visit Monticello in the morning like we've been wanting to, Leslie."

She stared into his eyes and saw absolute determination.

Was Grady out to make her face all her emotional ghosts in one ghastly weekend?

Yes.

Thirty-eight hours later she knew that's exactly what he'd set out to do.

With the able assistance of her grandmother and, Leslie suspected, the connivance of April, Grady had plunged them into her old social circle, making her face what she'd avoided because she thought it would be too painful.

It wasn't.

She felt like someone who'd braced for the flare and crash of a firecracker only to have it fizzle.

Oh, there were a few twinges. But it didn't take her long to realize that the wounds left by her failed marriage and its causes had healed for good.

If she'd had any doubts after the trips to Monticello and the campus, followed by the "remember-when" fest that lasted until midnight around Cathy McMahon's pool, they'd disappeared this morning when she saw Frank and his family.

Slightly suspicious when Grady insisted they go to church and Grandma Beatrice insisted on the ten o'clock service, she still hadn't expected to see Frank Reddy sitting three pews ahead of them. Even if she'd expected it, she wouldn't have been prepared for her feelings.

It was like seeing a ghost. She knew she'd once loved that man, had wanted to build a future with him. But she could not, for the life of her, remember why. She felt no pain, no regret, no envy. Only a mild affection.

After the service, Frank spotted her and, after a moment's hesitation, started toward her. Now Grady was the nervous one. She could feel it humming through his body, although they touched only where his hand cupped her elbow.

"It's all right," she said, and meant it.

It didn't allay the doubt in his eyes. Still, after introductions, he tersely announced he would wait for her at the car, giving her privacy to talk to her ex-husband, the father of the only baby she would ever conceive.

They didn't talk long and she never remembered the exact words, only the recognition that though they wished each other well they had little to say to each other.

Walking toward the car—and Grady—she found herself hurrying. She saw him before he saw her, and pain twisted through her at the lines of strain on his face. Especially when he wiped away all signs of the tension as soon as he

saw her. For all his nonchalance, this weekend was no easier on him than on her.

Sliding into her seat, she leaned over and kissed him on
the cheek.

"Thank you, Grady."

She couldn't have articulated what she was thanking him
for, so she was glad he didn't ask. She was also glad the
tightness around his mouth and eyes eased.

In silence, they drove to the house for the family conference on April's future. This wasn't going to be fun; Melly
had already shown a tendency to get defensive and April
regressed too easily to sullen silence. But Leslie found great
strength in Grady's presence next to her.

"The child's education is being neglected with this no-
mad's life you inflict on her," Grandma Beatrice declared
once they'd reached the meat of the issue.

"Most kids never get the chance to see the things April
sees. That's educational. And you like it, don't you,
honey?"

"I want to stay in Charlottesville," April said doggedly.

For the first time Melly paused long enough to look at her
daughter. "With your great-grandmother?"

Her tone left no doubt Melly wouldn't have taken that
option. And April's determination did seem to flicker after
a glance at Grandma Beatrice. But that redoubtable woman's frown was aimed at Melly, not April.

"I, uh, I mean . . . I'm thinking of you, too, Grandma
Beatrice. I mean, what do you want with a teenager around
at your . . ."

Silent too late, the word "age" hung in the air.

"I am neither an ogre who would make the child's life
miserable nor so doddering that I do not recognize the
ramifications of having her live here, Melanie Ardith."

Melly flinched at the use of the full name she hated, but didn't dispute her grandmother. "April needs to have a secure home. A home, not a temporary resting spot. It would be better for all concerned if that home were with her mother, but since you are unwilling to provide that for her, I most certainly will."

Leslie looked from her grandmother's austere profile to her cousin's defensive pout to April's clenched jaw and tear-bright eyes. She wished she could find something to say to ease the tension, to make them remember the love that tied them together instead of the differences that were driving them apart.

"Sure," started Grady, as if there'd been no break in the conversation. "And April can come up and see us in Washington. Maybe we can set up something regular."

"We?" Melly voiced the question they all wanted to ask.

"Uh-huh. Leslie and me. After we get married."

"Married?"

"Married!"

"Indeed?"

Leslie could have rolled Melly's, April's and Grandma Beatrice's responses all in one, but it still wouldn't have covered the range of her feelings. She appreciated his strength, but this bordered on strong-arm tactics.

"Yeah, as soon as we get the details worked out—" Just as she was about to point out that those details included his asking and her answering, Grady cut a look at her that numbed her with its heat. "We'll work out something with Grandma Beatrice. I've found a house in Alexandria and it has a great room I think you'd like, April. You can help us decorate it."

April looked so pleased that Leslie didn't have the heart to object right then.

"Well, we will have to talk about arrangements," Grandma Beatrice announced with a look that disapproved of such surprises, but dispensed forgiveness ... considering.

"But—"

"Of course you will," Grady interrupted smoothly. "But right now we should head back to D.C. Don't you have some things to pack, Leslie?"

"You're right, Grady," Grandma Beatrice said approvingly. "You don't want to get to the city too late."

So Leslie was bundled off upstairs to repack the bag Tris had provided and—between visits from Melly, full of questions, and April, full of excitement—to try to come to grips with Grady and his outrageous announcement. Because nothing had changed ... or had it?

She'd changed. Certainly in the time she'd known Grady, and especially over these past few days, as he'd shown her that what she'd been running from all these years wasn't so scary, after all.

And he'd changed. He risked showing what was beneath that golden surface, at least to a selected few. And he gave from his core of strength. He gave generously.

But was that enough when her circumstances and his dreams remained contradictory?

"Your young man is waiting downstairs."

Grandma Beatrice stood at the doorway, an expectant look on her face.

"Grandma, he's not my young man. At least, I don't know if he really is. He just—"

"Oh, yes, he is your young man." Her grandmother interrupting was amazing. Her grandmother stooping to looking smug was mind-boggling. "Nobody but a fool could miss that in every look he gives you." Then her expression shifted, and Leslie saw the love and the concern.

"Don't be a fool and overlook it, Leslie. You deserve happiness, and I believe the two of you can make each other happy."

Through her own tears she saw Grandma Beatrice was fighting emotion. "Now," she said briskly after a moment. "Are you all finished packing? It's time you two young people were getting on your way. I will inform Grady you are on your way down. And while I think of it, there are a few other things I want to tell your young man."

Smiling despite her doubts, Leslie started to follow, but at the doorway she stopped, slowly pivoting for a final look behind her.

The jewelry box that held her childhood treasures sat alone in the center of the dresser. She opened it without even being aware of crossing the room, and heard the sweet sounds of "Lara's Theme." The music wound down as she unhooked the catch of her bracelet watch and let it slip off her hand until it rested with the other mementoes. The final notes unwound to a halt and she closed the cover, feeling a little sad, and very hopeful.

If she was trying to drive him crazy, she was damned close to succeeding.

Sitting silent and unreadable next to him while a man tried to drive and pray his future wasn't about to unravel at the same time was enough to test anyone's sanity.

Why didn't she say something?

She loved him; he knew she did, even if he'd never truly been loved before. And, God help him, he loved her. But could he make her see that?

At this rate, he'd never find out.

Abruptly he pulled off onto a side road, around a tree-lined curve, then onto the shoulder.

Still she said nothing.

"I know this was pushy." His voice sounded like a cement mixer starting up. He cleared his throat. "This whole weekend, calling your grandmother and getting Tris in on it and everything. I know I don't have any claim on you and I didn't have any right to do this. But I had to take the chance, Leslie. I thought if you could face the past, then maybe you could accept it."

"I can accept it."

"Because if you can't accept the past, then I guess you're right, there isn't any hope of a future for us."

"I said I can accept it."

"You can." He looked at her as he carefully repeated the words, making sure that's really what she'd said.

"Yes. Because," she said deliberately and with more courage than she'd ever shown in her life, "if the past hadn't happened, I never would have met you. And I can't imagine my life without knowing you. I love you, Grady."

He let out a breath in a huff of relief and more. But she wasn't done.

"The question is if *you* can accept it. You have to think very carefully about that."

"I have. For the past two weeks I've done little else. You were right when you said I was used to getting what I wanted, used to making things come out the way I want. At least some things... But you weren't right about some other things. One thing I never could get the way I wanted was my parents." She supposed that trace of sadness would never leave him. "I wish I could, but I've accepted it, and I've found another family in the Monroes." His gaze left a shiver on her skin. "And I hope in you."

When she would have said something, he quieted her with a gentle order. "Listen. First, listen."

Wishing he could express it better, he tried to tell her what he'd gone through these two weeks apart, and the conclusions he'd reached. He told her about talking to Paul and Alicia. He told her about watching the family welcoming its newest member, and the dark-curled girl. He told her he hoped she'd want to adopt, because he wanted a child now to share the love she'd tapped in him, not to prove he could do a better parenting job than his parents had.

"If not...well, I know we'll work it out. Somehow. And I'll wait. But I don't want to wait to get married. I want to marry you as soon as possible. For myself, yes, but also for you, because you need me looking out for you as much as I need you looking out for me."

She'd fought hope for so long that it took her a moment to recognize that the heart-hammering happiness she felt was the fulfillment of a soul-deep hope.

She saw his sincerity and his acceptance. She understood that his rushing her to Charlottesville was meant to show her that she'd healed, that it was time for her to move on. Time to accept his love and to look at a new way of building a family.

Time to love Grady and make her future with him.

She managed to arch one brow with a fair assumption of casualness. "I don't think my grandmother would ever forgive you if we eloped."

He looked at her for less than a second before the light hit his eyes, melting the wariness and worry in them, and melting the last, doubting corner of her heart.

"Then we'll get married as fast as the laws of Virginia allow."

He took her in his arms and demonstrated that the man accustomed to getting everything he wanted definitely wanted her.

## *Epilogue*

Grady Roberts stood by a fireplace that blazed with autumn flowers instead of flames.

Leslie had insisted on a small wedding. Grandma Beatrice had insisted on having it in her home. They'd both insisted he invite his parents, who were too busy to attend.

It didn't matter, not anymore. He had his family.

A smile eased the waiting. He was marrying into a family of insisters. That was okay. Today he was getting what he'd insisted on—Leslie. And in as little time as the law would allow.

With Paul and Michael standing to his left and Bette and Tris on the far side of the minister, he watched April come down the stairway and along the aisle left by the select guests. That was something else he'd insisted on, having April in the wedding. Come to think of it, he hadn't had to do much insisting—Leslie and Grandma Beatrice had thoroughly approved.

April looked nervous, but when she saw his smile, she smiled back. The sullenness wasn't routed entirely, but it was fading. He couldn't begin to explain the satisfaction it gave him that April drew from him the same steadiness he'd gained from exchanging looks with Mr. and Mrs. Monroe and Judi Monroe when he took his place to await his bride.

That's what families did for each other.

*His bride.*

Leslie started down the graceful stairway, and a very basic part of him reacted to her decision to wear a street-length dress. Her legs looked great. And he knew how great they'd feel tonight when he had her all to himself at Tanner's Inn. He hadn't wanted to waste time driving far to start their honeymoon, but he'd made sure they would have the private cabin, not Hank Tanner's old room.

Better not let his thoughts drift too far down that road or he'd embarrass himself on his wedding day.

Then he met her eyes and forgot everything except how much he loved the woman who'd taught him how much he could love.

He saw happiness in her eyes, and love. As she came down the aisle, he also saw a faint, lingering uncertainty. And he did the only thing he could do.

He took a step, then another, and held out his hand.

He was aware of murmurs around him, but heard her softly released breath clearly. The smile reached her eyes.

Never taking her eyes from his, she met his hand.

Side by side they took the final steps.

Side by side they said the words.

Side by side they exchanged the rings; he would always remember her slim hand in his as he slipped the ring on her finger and her touch as she put his ring on.

Side by side they heard the benediction sending them on in life together.

*I now pronounce you husband and wife.*

\*   \*   \*   \*   \*